PLASTIC

MARISA NOELLE

Other Books By Marisa Noelle

The Shadow Keepers

The Unraveling of Luna Forester

The Mermaid Chronicles Series

Secrets of the Deep

Quest for Atlantis

Fight for Freedom

Ghost Pirates

Vendetta

Denizens of Darkness

Vortex Returns

The Mermaid Chronicles Companion Guide

The Unadjusteds Universe

The Unadjusteds Trilogy

The Unadjusteds

The Rise of The Altereds

The Reckoning

The Unadjusteds Companion Novellas

Silver Melody

Matt Lawson

Joe Rucker

Paige Starling

Hal Small

Erica Swiftfield

Kyle Lewis

Jacob Shea

Sawyer Watson

Addison Shields

President Bear

Reviews

⭐⭐⭐⭐⭐ *"A gripping eco-thriller that will haunt you long after the last page." – ARC reader*

⭐⭐⭐⭐⭐ *"An electrifying mix of suspense, horror, and heart—this book is impossible to put down." – GoodReads Review*

⭐⭐⭐⭐⭐ *"Part JAWS, part Erin Brockovich—Sara Monroe is a heroine you won't forget." – Amazon Reader*

⭐⭐⭐⭐⭐ *"This book is what happens when corporate greed meets the monsters we create." – ARC Reader*

⭐⭐⭐⭐⭐ *"Fast-paced and utterly immersive—this book will make you think twice before stepping into the ocean." – Bookbub Review*

⭐⭐⭐⭐⭐ *"A high-stakes thriller with an environmental twist—equal parts terrifying and thought-provoking." – GoodReads Review*

⭐⭐⭐⭐⭐ *"This book devoured me whole. Absolutely unmissable." – Amazon Reader*

⭐⭐⭐⭐⭐ *"A powerful blend of activism, grief, and spine-tingling suspense." – ARC Reader*

⚠ Content Warnings ⚠

This book contains themes and references that some readers may find distressing, including, but not limited to:

- Death of a sibling and grief
- Drowning and near-drowning experiences
- Climate crisis and ecological collapse
- Medical trauma (burns, injuries, concussions)
- Parental injury and hospitalization
- Gaslighting by corporate authorities
- Anxiety, stress, and emotional distress
- Scenes of peril and environmental disaster
- Use of mild strong language (e.g., swearing)
- Implied corporate negligence and corruption
- Insect and marine creature attacks (fictional horror elements)

For Aunt Jeanie,
You lit up every room and laughed the loudest. I made you the villain,
because honestly, no one else could've pulled it off with such flair.

And for Sir David Attenborough,
Your voice, wisdom, and wonder taught me to care—for the ocean, its
creatures, and the planet we call home.

Prologue

THEN

I was given a choice about attending the funeral, and I wrestled with the decision the entire week until the date crept up on me. Funerals were for closure, for saying goodbye, for celebrating someone's life, their journey and all they had achieved.

But Danny died when he was seventeen. What had he really achieved? How could I celebrate such a short life? And how could I say goodbye when I never wanted to let him go?

He shouldn't have gone diving. I should have stopped him. He was fiercely independent, like me, but I could have hung onto his legs or bitten his arm or something. Something to make him stay.

It was my fault he was dead.

How could I live with that?

But what if I came to regret not saying goodbye? What if this was my chance to apologize? To tell him I loved him, to ask him for forgiveness?

I dressed in a plain black skirt with the white blouse I'd worn for my grandparents' fiftieth wedding anniversary and a pair of dark Mary-Janes. Mom's pale fingers wrapped an elastic in my hair. Green. Danny's favorite color. I fiddled with my tights, hitching them up, only to pull them back down, not able to get comfortable in my clothes.

A friend of the family drove us to the funeral. No one spoke in the car. Outside, the winter day was stark and miserable. A perfect day for a funeral.

At the church, I didn't listen to a word the minister said. I knelt with my hands clasped in prayer, even though I'd never prayed before, and begged for forgiveness. I begged for Danny to come home. I averted my gaze from the polished casket near the altar. It wasn't Danny in there. Not my Danny. It couldn't be. He couldn't have left me. Not really. It was all some huge mistake.

After the service, Dad tucked my hand in his and we walked to the cemetery. More words were spoken. Words I didn't understand or care about. Danny's casket was lowered into the ground. Dad was the first person to throw a handful of dirt in after.

I almost yelled at him. He couldn't bury Danny alive. Danny was in there, screaming, waiting for someone to open the lid and let him out. I dashed to the edge of the hole, causing more dirt to cascade onto the coffin, and cried. I begged him to come out. I begged him to get up. I begged him to forgive me until my voice went hoarse and Dad dragged me away.

I don't know whether it was the right decision to go to his funeral. It didn't make anything final for me. It didn't bring closure. How could I possibly go on without him?

Chapter One

Now

I made a wish as a shooting star streaked across the sky, leaving a magical trail of green before disappearing behind a cloud.

"Did you see that?" Dad asked, pulling his eye away from the telescope and taking a swig of his beer.

"Yep. First one of the summer." It was our tradition. Every year, Dad, Danny and I would stay up late on the first night of the summer vacation, but it's just Dad and me now. We hung out on the worn back porch and counted how many shooting stars we could see. There were so many glittering lights in the sky that the wishes usually lasted me until the following summer.

Tonight, I wished for something to take away the aching sadness.

"Name?" Dad asked.

I thought for a moment. We named each one too. "Annabel."

"Like your old doll?"

"I never played with dolls."

"Uh-huh." He attempted to hide his grin behind another swig of beer.

I nudged his ribs. "Whatever."

Dad looked through the telescope again while I listened to the cicadas chirp in the backyard. They were the sound of summer. The time of year when the days were sticky with heat and the evenings brought a cooling ocean breeze; tourists swarmed the beaches, ice creams were eaten, and ocean clean-ups were organized. It was my favorite part of the year.

"Might be a storm coming." Dad's husky voice softened with worry. Danny died in a storm three years ago. Since then, whenever one hit the coastline, he and Mom stayed up the whole night and watched old black and white movies to wait it out.

I turned in a slow circle, listening to the distant waves. Regular and rhythmical, the hypnotizing whisper lulled me into a stupor. There were no signs of a storm, but I'd learned not to question Dad's judgment. "When?"

He pulled his eye away from the scope and rubbed at the stubble on his jaw.

"Dad?"

The cicadas fell silent. The breeze turned non-existent. A shiver coasted across the top of my shoulders.

"Not sure," he finally said. "Could be the Santa Anas coming in. Unusual for this time of year, but not unheard of."

Rubbing goosebumps on my bare legs, I zipped my sweatshirt higher and scanned the amassing clouds. "They look green."

"What do?" Dad put his beer on the table and shoved his hands in his pockets.

"The clouds." I grabbed his battered binoculars from the table. He still had them from his Navy days. I focused in on the distant clouds. Definitely a hint of green. Wicked witch green. "Do you think it could be because of the trash island?"

"I don't think a trash island halfway to Hawaii could be responsible for turning the clouds green," Dad replied.

"Didn't you hear? The Eastern Garbage Patch is no longer halfway to Hawaii. Well, at least part of it isn't. A large chunk broke off and it's moving this way fast. I bet we see it off the coast before the summer is over." My chest tightened. San Diego was home to a wealth of sea life and if the Eastern Garbage Patch arrived, much of it would be in jeopardy.

"God, I hope not." Dad frowned. "If it really is that close... no one's going to want to go sailing near it."

Dad had a sailing business to worry about.

"I'm hoping we'll get some clarity at the press conference tomorrow." I slumped into Dad's favorite deckchair. The bold stripes had long since faded into one murky color and the fabric smelled mildly of beer.

"Press conference or protest?" Dad asked. "I'm not sure how I feel about this activist stuff."

"I'm not an activist! Jeez, just because I care about the environment does not make me some crazy, chain-myself-to-a-tree kind of person."

Danny introduced me to ocean clean-up when we found a seal tangled in trash. I was too young to join the local organization, Green Clean, at the time, much to my annoyance. I waited until my twelfth birthday, signed up that day, and dragged Danny to the beach and made him show me everything. We combed the shore for trash until the sun set. Since his death, my parents were happy for me to honor his memory by doing something practical. Now I couldn't *not* help. Not only did it bring me closer to Danny, but I was fueled by an unquashable desire to rescue as many sea creatures as I could from ocean trash.

"I know, Sara." Dad raised his beer bottle in a toast. "I just want you to be careful."

"The CEO of EnRG will be there. Did you know their cans and bottles make up thirty percent of that trash island? EnRG has a lot to answer for—"

"I think they've answered all they need to," Dad said gently, running his hand along the porch railing. "It's been three years, sweetheart."

"But they can't keep getting away with it." I dug my fingernails into the wood of the armrests to redirect some of the energy from my emotions. "Don't you care about what happened to Danny?"

Dad's lower lip trembled. He reached out, but his hand floated back to his side. "Of course, I care. But putting all my energy into hating EnRG isn't going to bring him back."

I dipped my chin and ignored the solid lump in my throat. "I just... I wish I could... I just miss him."

"Oh, Sara..." His lips twisted into the sympathetic look I hated. The one that made me feel weak and trapped and incapable of moving forward. "There are things you can change and things you can't. You need to accept the things you can't change. For your own sanity, sweetheart."

"How am I supposed to change how I feel?" I spent hours wishing away my misery. "I can't just turn off my emotions, not while EnRG is still out there making their stupid drink and putting their stupid trash in the ocean."

"Sara, honey, Danny's death was an accident. You can't blame EnRG. It's consumers who put the trash in the wrong places."

I glared at him. "An accident which could have been avoided."

It *was* EnRG's fault. It was the bright, orange plastic wrapping they used for packaging and distribution that was to blame. The company was one of the last ones to move on to more biodegradable packaging methods. Some of it collected in the murky depths of Manta Ray Bay. It had tangled with Danny's dive gear and held him down while he was diving until he ran out of air.

EnRG had killed Danny.

The irony was he'd never touched a drop of it. He was dedicated to his fitness and the whole "my body is a temple" routine; he would never have contaminated himself by drinking it.

But it still killed him.

Dad touched my shoulder. All the fight sagged out of me. We had talked about this before, but it never made me feel better. I couldn't get past his death, couldn't get used to him not being here, not here encouraging me, not here teasing me.

"Go for it, Sara," Danny always said, with a swing of his

arm and a triumphant grin. "You can do anything you set your mind to."

I used to take it literally. One time I tried to fly off the roof of the house with a golf umbrella, a dusty old thing I found in the garage with a couple of bent spokes. I broke my wrist. Danny had decorated the cast with cool logos and hashtags like #getbettersoon, #operationbravesara, #projectstupid and #humanscantfly. Now I was old enough to know better. It took more than one person to rid the world of all its ocean trash, to save the turtles and seals and dolphins and all the other marine creatures I loved. I couldn't do it on my own. That's why I joined Green Clean. Although they had sponsorship from local companies and made some money by opening their rescue aquarium to the public, they relied on volunteers like me to help. To help the planet. And maybe myself. For Danny.

Clouds drifted across the sky, sometimes masking the stars, but they moved on quickly. I wondered what it would feel like to wrap myself around a star, to never feel darkness.

"Maybe you should have spent some time with Tyler tonight rather than hanging out with your old man." Dad gave my shoulder a squeeze.

"Yeah, well..." I looked at my bare feet, at the cheap polish already flaking off my toenails. Harper had painted them only two days ago.

Dad took a slow swig of his beer and put the bottle on the table carefully. "What did you do?"

I winced. "Think I might have screwed up a bit."

Dad echoed my wince. "Want to tell your very-cool-and-in-touch-with-teenagers Dad about it? I remember being a teen. I might be able to help."

I clutched the armrests. "I didn't watch him do his first loop-de-loop. He's mad at me."

Dad frowned. "And you didn't go because...?"

"Because I was rescuing a turtle from a six-pack ring and had to take it to Green Clean's recovery site. Then it was too late."

I hoped the dark would hide the flush crawling up my neck. The cicadas came back to life, and a toying breeze returned to tease my hair.

Dad leaned against the wall of the house, his ankles crossed casually. "Sara, you do know you're not the only Green Clean volunteer, right?"

"I know. I do..." Standing, I went to the handrail where a string of fairy lights cast the porch in soothing hues. Their soft colors threw rainbows over the dried grass and my baggy white T-shirt. The lights used to hang over the headboard of my bed, but just before Danny died, I decided I could sleep without a nightlight and relegated them to the backyard.

"But it was hidden in a pile of crap and hard to find. Others might not have noticed. I've got a good eye for these things. I couldn't leave it there..."

"I'm sure Tyler will understand," Dad said. "But, Sara? You don't have to tackle the world on your own."

"I know."

I spotted another shooting star and made a private wish. About hopes and losses and turning back time. I named it Danny 5798.

"Do you?"

I sighed and kicked at some displaced sand on the porch with my bare foot, managing to catch a splinter in my big toe. I winced and gritted my teeth against the pinch of pain.

"I think so," I muttered.

"Oh, Sara." Dad hugged me.

I stood stiff for a moment, worried the level of affection would push my guard down, afraid it would make me feel unprepared for all the things I had to face. Every day I battled against grief. By keeping my shoulders high, my guard up, my jaw clenched, my hands fisted. I stacked up hours at Green Clean in Danny's name. A penance. A duty. A labor of love. Small gestures of affection tended to send my flimsy walls of protection crumbling to the ground. Then I'd have to start building them up again. And that could take hours. Days.

Would I always feel so broken?

"That's better," Dad said.

Stepping away from the hug, I shrugged off the rising emotion. The fragility that hovered a whisper away. The scent of rosemary and mint reached me from Mom's herb planter near the back step, mingled with the salty air rolling in from the ocean. Familiar smells. Comforting smells. Smells I drank in to distract myself.

Dad examined my face. "Sara, you know you could—"

"Can we talk about something else?" I bent and yanked the splinter out of my toe. A pinprick of blood formed on my skin.

"Sure." Dad patted my arm, but I felt him wanting to say something more.

I hid behind the binoculars and watched the sky. It was still green. Even I didn't think a trash island could turn a sky green. Maybe it *was* a storm, but I didn't feel much of a wind and the waves had been pretty calm all day. Although it could all change in an instant. Danny had understood that.

"It's so beautiful out here," Dad said, sweeping his gaze around our small backyard and over the fence to the ocean beyond. "I don't think I could ever get bored of the beach, the ocean, the sky."

"Me neither."

Living two blocks from Manta Ray Marina and a mile from the cliffs overlooking Almond Cove, the air was always filled with the scent of the ocean. The scent of home. I was never entirely happy until part of my body was immersed in the ocean, and I always longed to feel its cold embrace when I was away from it. If Mom and Dad ever wanted to move inland, I would have to stage a protest.

I refocused the binoculars. "Maybe it's cover for the alien mothership observing Earth." I glanced at him long enough to see him smile. "Do you believe in aliens, Dad?"

"Of course."

"Of course?"

Shrugging a shoulder, he leaned back against the table. "It's just a matter of statistics. The universe is infinite. We can't be the only planet with intelligent life."

"Ah, so it's not something you know for sure."

Dad flicked my nose. "How many times do I need to tell you, when I was in the Navy, there was no X-Files department."

Dad left the Navy after Danny died. Mom wasn't willing to risk losing another member of our family, so he bought a boat with Danny's insurance money and now taught rich execs how to sail.

"Ha. That's what you say. You weren't just Navy, you were a SEAL. I bet you know loads of secret stuff." The green in the clouds deepened fractionally, then seemed to extend to the ocean below. With the moon obliterated by the encroaching clouds, it was hard to tell the source of the strange green tinge. Sky, or ocean? I frowned. The cicadas ratcheted up, their noise level causing both Dad and I to glance at the dark backyard.

Dad raised both brows. "Someone's horny."

"Dad!" A laugh burst from my lips, releasing some of my pent-up tension.

"Alien cicadas wanting to get their jiggy on with their three penises? Oh, maybe they have three assholes too—."

"Swear jar!"

As soon as I finished speaking, the cicadas fell quiet once more. Completely quiet. And it had sounded like there were hundreds of them.

"Weird," I said.

"Probably the heatwave."

"But what is that green stuff out there?" I handed him the binoculars.

Dad stared through the binoculars. He scratched his head. Rubbed the back of his neck. The cicadas remained quiet the entire time. After a couple minutes, he lowered the binoculars. "Storm's coming. I hope it passes quickly. We've got a group of new sales recruits coming on the boat next week."

I groaned. "Don't make me cook for a bunch of swanky executives." Probably the same rich execs who worked for EnRG, but I quashed my urge to mention the company again.

"Nah. I need you as my first mate. We'll pack them a champagne picnic and leave it at that."

"Only if I can have a glass."

Dad chuckled. "We'll see."

"Did you order those steel straws I sent you the link for?"

Even though I wasn't looking at his face, my attention was on the faint green light pulsating from beyond the waves, I could sense his silent laughter. "I will."

"Dad!"

"I will, Sara. Don't you worry. I always click on the links you send me."

"Good, you can have a medal *and* a cape."

"As long as the cape is blue. That's my best color." Laughing, he grabbed his beer and drained the last dribble. "We should hit the hay. We've got a busy day on the boat tomorrow."

"Did Mom call?"

Dad slid the back door open, breaking the quiet of the night. A dog barked in the distance. The faint aroma of home wafted out of the open door; old leather and clean carpet mixed with something pleasantly musky and the vegetarian chili we had with our nachos for dinner.

He checked his watch as he stepped into the house. "Earlier. She's having fun with her friends."

"You're joining her the day after tomorrow, right?"

Closing the door behind me, Dad thumbed the lock. The small print of a single rowboat battling a stormy sea wobbled on a loose screw. It was the only painting in the galley kitchen. But the corkboard over the table was filled with family snapshots. The ones of Danny were hidden under more recent photos. No one could bear to take them down, but no one could bear to look at them either, and so they were buried under more recent snaps of the beach and sailing and Green Clean and all the other stuff that filled our lives.

"Yep. At the end of her trip with the girls."

Mom had taken off on a trip around Europe with her three closest friends from high school and had been gone two weeks already. Something she'd been saving up to do for a long time. It was a trip she had put on hold when Danny died.

Dad touched my shoulder. "You'll only be on your own for three days. And Harper is coming to stay, right?"

I nodded. "We're planning on having a three-day rave. Booze, drugs, boys. You know. Might as well go big."

"Ha, ha!" Dad clutched his stomach in fake amusement. "Don't you dare. I'd like the house to be intact when I get back."

"I promise." I showed him my crossed fingers before I stuck them behind my back.

Chuckling, he rolled his eyes. "Well, make sure you tidy up before we get home."

I smirked. "Right at the end. I want to enjoy three days of leaving my clothes on the floor and the dishes in the sink."

"Ha! And don't forget your boat chores."

After we said goodnight, I tiptoed into the small bathroom on the landing and brushed my teeth. Looking out the window, I watched the dark ocean. I searched for the green tinge in the clouds and water. In the distance, I could make out a pulsing green light, so faint it could have been my imagination. No matter how hard I stared, it didn't get stronger or weaker, so I gave up on straining my eyes and finished my nighttime routine.

In my bedroom, I opened my window so the soothing sound of breaking surf could lull me to sleep. I found it impossible to sleep without it. I checked my phone where it lay charging on my bedside table. After scrolling through Instagram and reading about the fires up the coast and liking half a dozen photos of baby seals, I found a new e-mail from Mom. They'd visited the Eiffel Tower, Notre-Dame and l'Arc de Triomphe all in one day. Tomorrow they had booked to go to the catacombs. It sounded creepy. An attachment showed a photo of her in front of the Eiffel Tower with her three girlfriends, all sticking bunny ears behind each other's heads. I sent back a quick email, telling her I missed her.

There weren't any messages from Tyler. My heart sank. I must have really hurt him this time. But there would be plenty of time for me to watch him perform tricks in his two-seater airplane. I hoped he would come around about the turtle.

I got into bed and fussed with the duvet, trying to get comfortable. Grabbing a skimming pebble from my bedside table, I rubbed my thumb over its smooth surface. Danny had given it to me. I remembered the day perfectly.

Danny plucked a pebble from the beach, held it in his hand, then threw it toward the water. I watched it jump. Once, twice... five times, before disappearing under the calm surface.

"Just like that," he said.

I gave him my best scowl. "That's what I've been doing, and I still can't make it jump. And I thought you said it was easier to do it on a lake."

"It is, but the ocean's so calm today it's just like a lake." He sifted through the sand and plucked another pebble from the ground. He offered it to me. "Come on, squirt. You can do it, give it your best shot."

I couldn't see his face with the sun lowering behind his head, but I sensed his smile. It was enough to motivate me. Ignoring the mouth-watering scent of cooking hot dogs from the boardwalk, I snatched the pebble from his hand and squared my shoulders to the water.

Danny placed his hands on my shoulders and whispered into my ear, "One flick of your wrist."

Gritting my teeth, I threw the pebble. It didn't jump once. Just sank through the water with barely a splash. "I'm never going to get this."

"You will, squirt, I promise. We're not going to leave this beach until you've skimmed your first pebble."

"I have to go to bed at eight-thirty," I replied.

"You can stay up later, all night, if it takes that long. Like the first night of the summer vacation when we look for shooting stars."

I grinned but prayed it wouldn't take too much longer. I was already getting tired.

Danny held my wrist, mimicked the throwing motion. We practiced a few times with no pebble, then he found me the "perfect specimen." It was a large, cumbersome shape, and I was sure it would sink straight to the bottom of the ocean.

I took a breath, held it in my lungs, forcing my body and mind to be still. Then I flicked my wrist like Danny had shown me. The pebble flew toward the water, glinting in the sun. It disappeared with a splash and I kicked at the sand, but then it arced out of the water into the air, *across the smooth surface, and bounced three more times. I jumped up and down and roared into the breeze. "Yes! I did it!"*

"I told you, you could."

I hugged him. "You are the best brother ever!"

"Sara Monroe, pebble skipping master. My little sister, ladies and gentlemen. Sara, take a bow."

Beaming, I faced the water and took my bow, throwing in a wobbly curtsey for good measure. Danny picked me up and whirled me around before dumping me in the water. The shock of the cold made my teeth chatter, but after a few seconds, the gentle waves lulled me deeper and I ducked under the surface and swam like a dolphin. Danny joined me, throwing me high, catching me in the air. Waves smashed our legs and salt stung my skin, but I loved every minute of it.

Before we left the beach, Danny found me another perfect skimming pebble. But I didn't throw it; I carried it home and put it on my bedside table. A memento of the day. I could never bring myself to throw it.

Chapter Two

PEOPLE DIED EVERY DAY. Usually when they were supposed to. But sometimes, when they weren't. Like Danny.

I stared at the pebble, the unfairness of it all giving me a headache. The thoughts disturbed my dreams every night. I had become an early riser, unable to ignore the world outside once a shaft of light snuck through my curtains. Although the dawning of a new day often brought the promise of better things to come, it also brought the bracing slap of reality. Before my feet touched the floor, the coat of grief would button itself tight.

Dad burst into my room, disturbing my somber thoughts. He whipped the blanket off my bed and wiggled his bare toes under my nose. Seaweed. His feet smelled like putrid seaweed.

"Dad! You're so gross!" I rolled off the bed and landed on all fours.

"No rest for the wicked." Dad hauled me to my feet. "And I bet you've smelled far worse on your beach clean-ups."

"True. But I don't go around sticking it up my nose."

"By the way, the ocean is still a weird green. I think it's bioluminescence, but you could ask some of your nerdy Ocean Clean friends."

Shaking off my grogginess, I stuck my tongue out at him. "It's *Green Clean*, Dad. You know, not just the ocean? All about the environment?"

"Yeah, yeah, same difference."

After elbowing Dad, I made my way to the window. Bracing against the noisy greeting of some seagulls, I peered at the cloudless day. No sign of the rolling clouds from last night. Maybe the storm had blown away. Lowering my gaze to the ocean, its rippling surface was calm and impatient surfers sat on their boards, waiting for a decent swell. Beyond them was the occasional sailboat taking advantage of the offshore breezes. And further out was that strange hint of green. It was too far to determine the scope, but it stretched toward the horizon. A patch of glowing greenness distinct from the blue all around.

"Bioluminescence?" I frowned. "I thought that only appeared at night?"

Dad hovered over my shoulder and stretched both his arms above his head. "I'm not a biologist. I wouldn't know. But it's been known to happen in these parts. Remember the time I took you to Mission Bay and we collected a jar of the stuff? Plankton, I think."

"That was blue." I remembered clearly. We'd dipped the jar into the waves and come home with it full to the brim of electric blue light. I had set it on my bedside table and fallen asleep staring at it, the blueness ebbing into my dreams. I was so sad when the lights had faded three days later. Permanently. Like a light had gone out in my soul. Danny had cycled me back over there on his handlebars to collect more, but the plankton had moved on. "Simona might know."

"Simona?"

"The Scripps marine biologist who volunteers for Green Clean. She joined a few months back. She's awesome." One of the wings of the impressive not-for-profit Scripps company was the Institute of Oceanography, where Simona worked as a kickass marine biologist. She knew everything about the ocean and was helping Green Clean to devise more creative and cost-effective ways of cleaning up the beach and ocean.

Sometimes I joined her when she practiced Tai Chi on the beach in the mornings or for a dinner of vegan sushi at the pier. She often delivered televised speeches on well-needed information about the climate crisis. And she had the science to back it all up.

"She's an algae expert. She might know something."

"The one you want to intern for?"

"Yep, she's helping me sort it out for a couple weeks later in the summer."

Dad raised an eyebrow. "I'm really impressed by your dedication."

I threw a pillow at him.

"I'm serious."

I blushed. "Thanks, Dad." He threw the pillow back and I managed to catch it before it hit my face. "Anyway, I bet it's because of all the pollution."

"What is?"

"The bioluminescent stuff. It's glowing during the day

because it can't tell up from down. The trash island is getting closer, probably pushing it closer to shore, too." Dropping the pillow, I slipped into a sweatshirt and stumbled into my flip-flops. Dad righted me before I landed flat on my face. "I can't wait to get to the press conference and give Regina Harron a piece of my mind."

"Easy there, tiger. As much as I love your go-to attitude, the sweatshirt and flip-flops don't hide the fact you're in your pajamas. And you need some breakfast first. Pancakes?"

I glanced at my watch. It was still early. The press conference didn't start for a couple of hours. I had some time. "You're on. You cook, I'll get dressed."

"I've got some paperwork to do this morning," Dad said as he stepped through the door. "But I'd like you at the boat this afternoon, after the press conference."

"Okay, okay," I called.

"Unless you want me to come with you? I can move things around—"

"Nah." Although it would be great to have the support of my dad along, I didn't want him there to witness how vocal I could be at these things. Regina Harron, the CEO of EnRG, had a lot to answer for, and I intended to ask some awkward questions. Besides, the non-committal look on his face told me he had a long list of things to do before the next sail.

"I'm going with Harper and Simona. We're all good."

He nodded, then pursed his lips. "Maybe stay at the back?"

I winked. "I'm stubborn and opinionated. That's what

you love about me. It even says it on my report card under 'strengths.'"

"More like stubborn-assed, pig-headed personality traits to be extinguished under the genetic revolution."

"Gee, I wonder where I get it from?"

Dad grinned. "All your mom."

"You tell yourself that," I retorted, pulling clothes from my closet.

Laughing, he double tapped the door frame and backed out of the room.

I traded my PJs for a pair of denim shorts and one of Dad's old Navy T-shirts. Soft and oversized, I tucked the long hem into the waist of my shorts and slipped down the stairs, using my flip-flops as skis. After inhaling a mountain of pancakes, I grabbed a reusable water bottle and flew out the door. The fly screen slammed behind me. Simona, Harper and I were meeting at the beach before the press conference.

"Bye!" Dad called after me.

I managed to cycle the short journey to the beach without getting my flip-flops caught in the wheels. Discarding my bike at a rack along the boardwalk, I jumped down the steps onto the sand. Kicking off my flip-flops by the low beach wall, I scanned the area for members of Green Clean. The small fishing boat they used for their headquarters was anchored offshore, dwarfed by the most enormous and futuristic-looking catamaran I'd ever seen. Both were anchored beyond the swimming and surfing areas as if they had their own private area of the ocean to themselves.

The new vessel, with its sleek lines and a wide deck

entirely solar paneled, seemed like something out of a time travel book. The cockpit sat in the middle of the deck; an insect-like bubble with its singular stretching window made it look like a cyclops of the sea. Smaller motorboats and research vessels circled the catamaran. Maybe Green Clean had found a rich sponsor.

At the beginning of my freshman year, I started an ocean conservation club at school, regaling people with my wealth of knowledge I acquired from Green Clean. Only two people joined. Tyler, and Harper. Everyone else shot stupid jokes at me, like: "There's no need to go off the deep end," or "I'll join *Schooner* or later," or "Sara, why don't you go chill in your *sandtuary*, your hair is *sanding* on end."

I informed the upperclassman my hair was far too wispy to *sand* on end. So there.

The club didn't last long. We had no funding and too much passion. Harper and Tyler joined Green Clean, until Tyler dropped out last summer to pursue his flying lessons. He told me it was his ocean.

In the water, I spotted a plastic cup, a plastic takeout food carton and a couple of other smaller items I couldn't determine. Dumpsters and recycling bins lined the beach wall at regular intervals. It wasn't hard to be a good citizen. Jeez. How lazy could some people be?

Digging my toes into the cool sand, I spied a couple of other volunteers I recognized wearing the green T-shirts with the Green Clean logo across the breast. They used hand extenders to collect trash and debris left over from beachgoers. A pile of beer cans rested in a shallow hole, the byproduct of an illegal nighttime beach party. Behind me, a television van pulled to the curb and a group of people spilled out of the vehicle, carrying cameras and those oversized microphones that look like giant gray cotton candy tufts. They directed the cameras at the catamaran. Maybe someone important was on board.

"Hi!" A pair of arms wrapped around my waist and lifted me off my feet. Giggling, Harper carried me along the beach until we collapsed in the sand. "So, in my dream last night, I got the main part in the school play and we were doing *Wicked*, and I rocked out *Defying Gravity*, but it wasn't about friendship, it was about dolphins and they were all drowning... how weird is that?"

Harper ran on, talking a mile a minute like she usually does. It always brought a smile to my face, unless I was trying to tell her something important, then I was prone to covering her mouth with my hand until she shut up.

"Don't kill the dolphins! Bad Harper!" I mimed slapping her butt.

She giggled. "I can't help what I dream about."

I narrowed my eyes at her playfully. "Are you willing to take a lie detector test?"

Laughing, she flicked sand at me, then made a cross over her heart. "I always tell the truth."

"Apart from the time you stole PJ's car and pushed it into a quarry."

She frowned, but the look in her eyes remained mischievous. "He cheated on me."

"Gah, what would you have done if he'd had a threesome?" I joked, heaping sand over her legs.

Harper sat up, her mess of long dark curls falling over her shoulders. Her light brown eyes were framed by the thickest and most beautiful lashes in existence, and a smattering of freckles decorated the bridge of her button nose.

"Less about cheating exes who don't deserve cars, let alone Mustangs, and more about the press conference. I'm *so* nervous." She shook the sand off her legs. "I've had three black coffees and I wrote out my questions and I gotta go right now, or I'm going to lose my nerve. I am *so* not channeling the Veronica Mars vibe right now."

Veronica Mars was her hero. She could bring every situation back to a Veronica Mars episode. She made me watch all four seasons three times. And the movie. It didn't stop there. She loved movies in general, especially action ones. Marvel, in particular. She quoted them constantly.

"It's no different from the other press conferences we've been to," I said, pulling eco sunblock out of my bag. I couldn't expose my fair skin for more than ten minutes without protection before I burned.

Harper's eyes widened to match her wide mouth. "I know, but it's *Regina Harron*. The *CEO* of EnRG. This is huge!" She cycled her feet in the sand.

I raised both my eyebrows. "It's a big day for the environment."

"It is indeed." Simona approached, dumping a straw shoulder bag at her feet. Her wild hair was twisted into a knot on top of her head and her eyes shone with intelligence. Full lips and high cheekbones indicated a classic beauty, striking even in her work clothes, which consisted of a pair of khaki shorts and a blue polo neck shirt with the name of her lab stenciled on the left side.

After snapping her seaweed chewing gum, she asked, "Are you girls ready to go?"

We got to our feet and trailed Simona to her electric car. The smells of the boardwalk wafted close; fried breakfast, salt and Simona's soap.

"Simona," I said, as I climbed into the passenger seat, "What's with the giant catamaran and fleet in the ocean? And did you see the bioluminescence on the horizon? Do you know what it is?"

After adjusting her rearview mirror, she patted my knee and offered me her amused smile. "One question at a time." I opened my mouth to re-arrange my questions when she carried on. "The catamaran belongs to EnRG." My mouth dropped open. "I believe it's going to be the subject of the press conference."

Both my eyebrows shot high, but I was too stunned to speak.

Harper stuck her head between the front seats. "Maybe they've finally got their act together. Then we won't have to give Regina a hard time, and she'll do the right thing and everyone will be happy and the ocean will be saved and they'll be a big orchestra swell and chests will swoon and—"

"Harper!" Simona flicked her a stern look, popping her gum again. "Enough already."

"Just in time for their deadline to start cleaning up their own mess," I said. "Typical."

"We'll find out soon enough." Simona pulled onto the road to head to downtown San Diego. "Now, what's this about bioluminescence? I haven't seen anything."

I told them both about the green tinge Dad and I had spotted last night and how it was still visible this morning. Both of their gazes turned to the ocean.

"I'll take the boat out later, when we get back," Simona

said. I loved the way she spoke, the way her Spanish accent made her 'r's roll. "I'd hate for the plankton to be distressed."

A half-hour later, after fighting traffic to get downtown, we found a parking spot in front of the impressive Midway, an aircraft carrier named after the famous battle. When I was little, Dad used to take Danny and me to visit the retired battleship every summer. We climbed up and down the decks and he explained what everything was better than any tour guide. He had been stationed on a similar warship when he was a SEAL and could tell us delicious secrets and show us all the nooks and crannies. He always bought us one of the miniature versions from the gift shop. A different version every time. They didn't have a model of the ship Dad was stationed on, so I liked to imagine him on the Midway. I kept the model on my windowsill at home. It always filled me with pride looking at it, knowing Dad had spent many years protecting our country. Danny had his set up on a shelf above his bed, where it remained.

The noise of a small plane drew my attention to the sky. From this distance, I couldn't tell what it was, but maybe it was Tyler up there. He had a few lessons left until he got his license and had promised to take me up. He saw it as a romantic date. I was worried about the pollution.

Turning our backs on the Midway, we crossed the road and walked to the Hyatt, where the press conference was due to take place. Outside there were several press vans unloading their equipment into the hotel.

"No stealing press passes this time." Simona winked at me. I had been known to go the extra mile.

Harper slung an arm around my waist as we marched

through the front doors and found the large auditorium. It was half full already, but we found seats close to the front on the aisle.

An emotional wave hit me, crushing against my chest and making tears sting my eyes. The memories swirled around me. But not just memories, a hard wedge of guilt handed in my throat. All I could think about was Danny. His last day. How he died. How it was all my fault.

Chapter Three

THE ENTICING aroma of hot food drew me down the stairs. In the kitchen, I found a note from Mom propped next to a plate of pancakes and a jug of warm syrup. She and Dad had gone to batten down their small sailboat in the marina before a storm rolled in. The boat was a present they'd bought for themselves when they got married and they treated it like their third child.

Spotting Danny packing a bag by the front door, I grabbed a pancake and chomped on it on my way to the hall. He wore a pair of swim shorts and sneakers.

"Are you going to the beach?" I asked him. "It's freezing outside."

Danny chucked me a smile. "It's all the same when you're underwater."

I looked out the window. Gray clouds rolled onto shore, stirring the palm branches and whisking sand into the air. Even though it was mid-morning, the sky was darkening. The storm would be here soon.

I frowned. Danny had been diving for over two years and I knew he was competent at it. Dad had taught him and constantly warned him to never go diving in a storm. It might seem like the water was calm beneath the warring sky, but it could be just as tempestuous below;

currents could strengthen, temperatures could plummet, lightning strikes could electrify large areas of water, and riptides could form without warning. Marine creatures would often get over-excited during those times, and if he came across any electric eels or lashing stingrays...

Rain sometimes stirred up the mud and sediments, making visibility nonexistent. A diver could get turned around in a matter of seconds and become completely lost. And if they couldn't see their instrument gauge through all the sediment, then they wouldn't be able to tell up from down and could get stuck at the bottom of the ocean... forever. Dad had told us many stories of near misses from his Navy training days. But only when Mom wasn't around. She couldn't bear to hear them.

"You can't go. I'll tell Mom and Dad."

He stared at me, shaking his head. "They're not here."

"I'll come with you. I won't let you go in. Come on, Danny, you know this is stupid."

He crouched and placed both hands on my shoulders. "Look, I don't love the idea of going into the water right now either, but if I don't, a whole cage of lobsters is going to die."

"What are you talking about?" I looked at the amassing clouds, shivered as the wind burst through the open window.

"Will and I found an illegal lobster catcher. He's been leaving crates all over Almond Cove and I want to release them before the storm, before he can bring them ashore and sell them to Sizzler."

I frowned. "They're just going to get caught again, what's the point?"

He shook his head and chucked me under the chin. "Have I taught you nothing? All sea creatures are important. There's bound to be other sea creatures caught in the cage. We can't let them die for nothing. I'm going to release them. In and out. I'll be super quick."

When another gust of wind surged into the room, I shut the window. The door caught on a draft and slammed closed, startling me.

"Why don't you get Dad to go with you? He's an expert diver; he could help you."

"Dad's busy getting the boat ready for the storm. Besides, he likes to eat *lobster.*" He rolled his eyes theatrically, then tickled my ribs. Crossing my arms, I refused to laugh. "Come on, Sara, have a little faith in me. I'm a good diver."

"I know you are, but——"

"Oh my God, you're turning into Mom. Ladies and gentlemen, we have a thirteen-year-old Mom in the house. Stand by for orders."

I stuck out my tongue but couldn't suppress the smile flickering on my lips.

"Besides, I'm going with Will. I'm not entirely stupid." He tapped the side of his head. "It won't take longer than twenty minutes, and if you keep arguing with me, I'm going to get caught in the storm."

"I'm not arguing!"

He hugged me to his side and kissed my cheek. Shouldering his backpack, he charged out the door, throwing me the briefest of waves. I watched him go with a smile on my face. That was the last time I saw him.

When the rain started forty minutes later, and Mom and Dad burst into the house, soaked, I knew I'd made a mistake. I should never have let him go. I should have tried harder to make him stay. It took five minutes for the story to come tumbling out. I was in floods of tears and couldn't swallow down the lump in my throat. Unable to sail through the choppy waters to the bay, we piled into Dad's car and drove the short distance up the hill to the cliff path that led to the dive area. Parking on the clifftop, we hurried down the rocky path to the small beach, ignoring the pelting rain and rumbling thunder. The smell of ozone filled the air and lightning danced in the distance. I slipped several times, gashing my legs on sharp rocks, slipping down the steep path. It took us twenty minutes to reach the strip of sand, and the whole *time I couldn't take my eyes off the ocean. Until I saw Will. He was on his knees, his dive knife in one hand and an armful of orange, plastic sheeting in the other. Tears streamed down his face. By his knees was an empty lobster cage.*

"Where's Danny?" I yelled, already knowing the worst.

"He's still down there." Will stared at the water. His lips were blue and they trembled uncontrollably. "I ran out of air. I couldn't... I couldn't bring him back up... I ran out of air."

I dashed into the water, all the way up to my chest, not thinking about the cold. A rip pulled at my ankles and I screamed Danny's name. The water slapped me, as if punishing me. The salt stung my face and the wind whipped my hair. This wasn't my ocean. This water was strange. This water had taken Danny.

Chapter Four

Blinking back the emotions, I gripped the armrest of my chair to ground myself back in the moment. The press conference was about to start.

"Operation stealth mode." Harper pulled a wide-brimmed straw hat from her bag and pulled it low on her head. A genuine laugh trickled out of me. If anything, the hat made her look more conspicuous.

"And I suppose Veronica Mars used a similar disguise in one of her episodes?"

Harper shook her head and flicked her long curly hair. "Veronica Mars has nothing on my style."

Simona replaced her sunglasses with some reading glasses and took out a notepad and pen from her bag. Harper had her own list of questions. I didn't need a list. I had been asking the same questions for the last few years, usually hurled at the TV, but still, they were etched in my brain.

A few people stood in the back with placards.
Save our Earth!

Stop polluting our waters!

Down with EnRG!

I recognized a couple of fellow volunteers from Green Clean, but they weren't the only eco organization here. The auditorium filled. Paper rustled and people fanned themselves with notepads and menu samples that had been handed out in the street. I frowned at all the plastic bottles placed by people's feet. Then someone tapped the microphone on the stage and Regina Harron appeared.

She was tall and slender, with muted red hair coiffed into a perfect chignon. She wore a navy skirt suit with a pristine silk white blouse. Small studded earrings and a simple gold necklace completed her attire. Authoritative, but approachable. But she'd never answered a single one of my emails. She lived along the coast in La Jolla. I thought she might at least have the decency to reply to a local resident. Especially Danny's sister.

She sat at the table with two other EnRG representatives and the press officer who was tasked with asking the questions. Moving some papers on the table, she ordered them into a neat pile, then addressed the gathering with a huge smile.

"What does she have to smile about?" I muttered to Harper, who shushed me and perched on the edge of her seat.

The press officer gave a brief introduction and then invited Regina to read her statement. She didn't need her cue cards. Bringing the microphone close to her lips, she spoke clearly and emphatically. "It gives me great pleasure to announce some changes in the EnRG corporate structure. Since we were tasked with making our cans and bottles more sustainable, I'm delighted to announce we have found an entirely biodegradable material which is satisfactory for our purposes."

Excited murmurs swept through the gathering.

"Oh... yes!" Harper gripped my knee. "This is fantastic! Now we don't need to give her such a hard time."

I frowned at my nemesis. Danny's death sat like a thorn in my heart, constantly pricking. I couldn't let her get away with it.

"Production will start in the next few months, so even if our cans or bottles or shrink wrap are found in the ocean, they won't harm the sea life," Regina said.

What about people?

A round of applause startled me. How could people be applauding this bullshit? Regina was big corporation. There was something fishy going on here. But even Simona had a smile on her face.

"Although the strict practices at our EnRG factories mean we dispose of our waste in an environmentally friendly way, I am aware the disposal of plastic bottles from all over the world has contributed to the trash island floating off our beautiful coast." She paused to let her statement sink in. A few nodded heads and others murmured agreements. "So, today, I have a surprise for you all."

The press officer perked up and made a face suggesting we all creep to the edge of our seats like we were all children at some ridiculous kiddie theater show.

"I have spent the last two years interviewing and hiring the best experts in ocean clean-up. I have put together a team of ten people at the top of their fields, and we intend to help dispose of the trash problem. We will work with local and global organizations to get the job done, including San Diego's Public Health Agency and the Unified Disaster Council. It is an ambitious project, one I'm sure will be a success. Please welcome Operation Blue Water."

Ten people walked on stage. They all wore khaki trousers and navy-blue polo shirts. There was a logo on each breast of a smiling octopus. They stood beside Regina, their hands laced behind their backs, and gave us their best smiles. Thunderous applause filled the auditorium.

Regina stood and pumped a fist into the air. "Save our oceans."

The audience repeated the mantra.

"Well, this is a turnaround," Simona whispered. "I can't say I'm not relieved."

There was a court case two years ago, after Danny's death. Nothing my parents wanted anything to do with; they didn't want to drag things out. But the town didn't like seeing one of the best Green Clean volunteer's death go unanswered. It was a civil case. EnRG was taken to court. Points were scored on both sides. EnRG was hit with a large fine, which they paid to my family. Hush money. More importantly, they were ordered to find a biodegradable material to make their cans and bottles and packaging. I had expected them to find a few loopholes. A billion-dollar corporation with the most popular drink on the planet wasn't about to start losing money on changing its practices. Even if their packaging was toxic when it started to degrade. Their deadline was up today. And wow, hadn't they surpassed all expectations with the offer to clean up the ocean too?

"Still doesn't help Danny," I muttered, wiping an eye with the back of my hand.

Harper wound an arm over my shoulders. "Oh, hon."

"And it doesn't explain all the reports of EnRG being addictive," I said. "All because of some jacked-up enzyme they put in the ingredients."

"Those are just rumors," she replied.

"Rumors have to start somewhere," I said. "Look at Tyler, he's a walking case study."

He was addicted, not that he would admit it. He refused to believe there could be adverse side effects, even when he acted like he'd stuck his finger in a socket.

"Maybe." Harper shrugged. "This is good news, Sara. Why don't we focus on that? They're finally doing the right thing. Maybe something good is coming out of Danny's death."

"Hmm." I couldn't formulate a coherent reply. Danny should be here. Together we could have made EnRG change its ways. It didn't have to be like this.

Chapter Five

EnRG's promises sounded too good to be true.

I glanced around the auditorium, looking for other suspicious frowns. I couldn't be the only one thinking with a clear head.

There were murmurs of "Save our ocean" among the gathering. A few of the charity reps banged their placards on the ground—all smiles—until the room was called to order. I launched to my feet and waved my hand around until the press officer noticed me. Harper kept tugging on my shorts, but I needed to get my question out.

"I think there might be a few questions in the crowd." The man pointed to me. "Why don't we start with you?"

I took a moment to look at Regina and made sure she met my eyes. Would she recognize me? The room settled and I asked. "How?"

She tilted her head. "How?"

I held the attention of over five hundred people, all of their gazes boring into me. I'd never been afraid of public speaking, but at that moment, my throat went dry. "How are you going to clean up the ocean? The trash island off the coast is twice the size of LA. Bigger. And it's not the only one out there. So, *how*?"

Regina smiled, then tapped the side of her nose. "I don't want to bore you with all the scientific details. That's why I put the project together. Operation Blue Water has the solution." Loud applause rippled through the crowd. Regina raised her hand for silence. "Please, rest assured, everything that can be done is being done. If we can tackle this smaller trash island, then we can take our technology to the Eastern Garbage Patch and deal with that too."

Frowning, I slumped in my seat. That was one of her famous non-answers. A sinking feeling settled in my stomach. What was she up to?

During the next half hour of questions, Regina was peppered for information, but she didn't reveal anything more about the nature of Operation Blue Water. Maybe she didn't understand the science involved, or perhaps she was waiting for another dramatic reveal at some point in the near future. There were rumors of patented technology, so maybe she really couldn't say anything.

As we left the press conference, Simona and Harper chatted excitedly about how Regina's plans were going to revolutionize the eco society. If a company as large as EnRG was publicly supporting the environment, it would go a long way toward securing large funds from other sources.

A nagging feeling shackled my thoughts. Something felt off.

On the way back to the car, we stopped at Simona's favorite vegan ice cream shop. I treated myself to a double scoop of mint chocolate. As I was crunching the last of the cone, I spotted a tacky tourist shop and made a quick detour. They had a multitude of models of the Midway and the other tall ships anchored nearby, but I wasn't looking for a boat. In a dusty corner, I found what I wanted. The wooden plane models were old-fashioned and didn't resemble a Cessna at all, but it was the thought that counted. I hoped Tyler would like it.

In the car, Harper sat in the front and chatted with Simona. I was glad for the backseat and the air conditioning. Exhausted, I closed my eyes and listened to the quiet hum of the car engine. I had been holding myself tense for the last few weeks in anticipation of the press conference. Even though Regina had said all the right things, I didn't believe she would stump up so much money for a non-profit venture without getting something back. I didn't voice my concerns to the other two. They'd frown at me and tell me to relax. So, I allowed myself some time to let my thoughts drift and promised myself I'd get to the bottom of what was going on.

When we got back to Almond Cove, Simona left to take her boat out and investigate the bioluminescence. I was desperate to go with her, but I was expected at Dad's boat soon. Instead, I busied myself on the beach with Harper, helping some of the other Green Clean members pick up trash from the shallows. I kept one eye on the task at hand and one eye on Simona's boat until it disappeared into the faintly green horizon.

"I hope with Regina's announcement that people will start taking the environment more seriously," Harper said as we piled our plastic treasures into a net bag. "I mean, if a company as big as EnRG is seen to be getting in line, then it must have a ripple effect."

"Let's hope so."

Harper was right. Even if Regina was up to something, her creation of Operation Blue Water would have a positive effect. Begrudgingly, I had to acknowledge that.

Out on the water, the decks of the vessels surrounding the EnRG catamaran were hectic with activity. I spotted people dipping scientific equipment into the water. It all looked official, and I reasoned, if the local government was involved, they'd keep Regina in line. The thought eased some of suspicion I'd been unwilling to let go of.

I stepped into the shallows, enjoying the bracing greeting of the frigid Pacific. The coldness always made me catch my breath, even when I'd prepared for it. But it was a coldness I cherished. A coldness that brought clarity and perspective. A coldness that eased worry from my mind and tension from my limbs. A coldness that symbolized everything I loved. The ocean. Its vastness, its power. I never tired of it.

I don't remember when blue became my favorite color, but I loved the entire spectrum of shades, from the lightness of Caribbean seas to the dark storminess of a winter ocean. I never felt comfortable if I was too far from the coast. We'd made a trip inland a few years ago to visit Mom's parents, and I'd twitched and jerked from nervous energy that wouldn't dissipate until we arrived home and I dipped my feet into the cold water once again.

The ocean's touch was both fragile and firm. Both gentle and strong. I never underestimated her. In the last three years, she'd become even more important to me because I knew she protected Danny's soul. I once blamed the ocean for taking him. But over the years, I realized there was no place Danny would rather spend his afterlife.

Harper tied up our net bag. It was full to the brim with six-pack rings, used condoms, tampons, plastic bags, cans of EnRG, and an armful of other indeterminate plastic items. If Danny were here, he'd make a joke about the condoms.

"Are you seeing the T-man today?" Harper asked.

Smiling, I removed the model plane from my pocket. "I'm hoping he'll forgive me for missing his show yesterday. A peace offering."

Harper touched my shoulder. "He will. He loves you. You guys have the kind of love of Iron Man and Pepper Potts."

I chuckled at the image. As soon as Avenger: Endgame had come out on Disney, we watched it six weekends in a row. Now Harper was working on watching all the Marvel movies in chronological order.

"I hope he carries on loving me." A thread of sadness weaved through my chest. I knew I could be high mainte-nance, that my passions often got me into trouble, and that I came across as a bit of a bulldozer. But I couldn't compro-mise my beliefs. Whoever I ended up with in life was going to have to accept that. I hoped it would be Tyler. I couldn't imagine myself with anyone else.

"He will." Harper deepened her touch on my shoulder. "And tell him to hurry up and fix me up with his cousin. I don't want another lonely summer." She jerked her thumb at her chest. "Veronica Mars may like the aloof life, but this girl needs some love."

"I thought Veronica Mars had lots of relationships.

There was the guy with the baby and the other dude who—"

"Yeah, well, none of them successful."

I laughed and pulled on the end of her hair. "Just don't push his car off a cliff, okay?"

She grinned and showed me two crossed fingers. "As long as he's not a cheater. It's a shame I don't have access to Thor's hammer, or Spiderman's webbing, or Aquaman's trident—"

"Shhh already." I covered her mouth with my hand. "Are you working at the movie theater tonight?"

Harper pushed my hand away and raised both eyebrows. "I can get you free popcorn if you want to come?"

"You're on. I love a Jaws revival weekend."

"Will Tyler be working at the fire station with his dad again this summer?"

I nodded. "Yep, I need to make some cash too. Dad promised to pay me for my help on the boat."

"Are you going to restock the kitchen with sustainable foods and throw out the plastic coffee pods again?"

I grinned. "Yep. It's only Dad who drinks the coffee. All those swanky office types prefer expensive champagne."

"Bubbles! I love bubbles!" Harper waggled her eyebrows and threw a hand to her chest. "I think I'd like to be a swanky office type too."

"Not sure you're the office type, hon. But you could go for the famous movie star role. They drink champagne too." I winked at her, then checked my watch, whose mesh strap was reclaimed from retired fishing nets. "I need to move it if

I'm going to make it on time. I've got my first shift on the boat right now."

"Make sure he's got those steel straws and the beeswax food wrappers and—"

"I'm on it." I gave her a thumbs up and backed away, then blew her a kiss, which she caught and stuffed in her pocket. We both laughed as I scaled the beach wall.

On my bike, I pedaled along the boardwalk. Around the corner, I parked in front of the main steps to the marina. Tyler stood on the dock, his back to me, scanning the glistening white boats. His bright blue T-shirt clung in all the right places and flattered the rich color of his skin. He also wore socks and sneakers. I sighed. So inappropriate for living near the beach, but he claimed the socks kept the sand from rubbing between his toes.

I snuck up behind him, wrapped my arms around his waist and kissed the back of his neck. He always smelled of coconut sunblock and oranges. He ate an orange for breakfast every morning, and the combination of scents was surprisingly appealing. "Hey."

He turned in my arms. "Hey, yourself." There was a question mark in his dark eyes. Yesterday, we'd left things on a tense note.

"I got you something." I stepped back and took the plane from my pocket. "I'm sorry for not watching your loop-de-loop thingy. How was it?"

"It was great." His expression was neutral as he turned the plane over in his hand. "But Dad was at work, and Mom is traveling and I could have used the support..."

I chewed on my bottom lip. "I'm sorry. I... I can't... there was a turtle. It was so small."

His piercing gaze made me squirm. "There are other volunteers, Sara."

I looked away. "I know. I'm sorry. I just..." He was right. I could have made a call into Green Clean headquarters and got someone else to rescue the turtle. It wouldn't do any good to let my passions alienate me from him. I'd already lost so many friends since Danny died. I toed the ground, then pushed an apologetic smile onto my lips as I looked at him. "I'm sorry. I know it was important to you. Next time. Next time I'll be there."

He searched my face, as if sensing a lie. But I wasn't lying. I really did want to be there for him, even if I didn't approve of the diesel usage.

"Okay. Let's move on. That better be one special turtle."

"Would it help if I told you I named it? I called it the 'T-man.'"

His mouth curled into a smile. "That's one kickass turtle name." He kissed my cheek, then looked at the plane again.

"Thank you. I love it." His lips moved to mine, and I wrapped my arms around his neck. "Let's not argue ever again."

"Let's not."

"And," Tyler said, "I have something for you too. Two somethings." After putting the plane in his backpack, he removed a paper bag. Delicious smells rose into the air and my stomach grumbled. "I got us one of Moe's vegan hoagies. They're actually not too bad."

Even though he'd been mad at me, he still stopped to get a vegan hoagie. I looked at him. The intense feelings for him I kept guarded close to my heart rushed to the surface.

Staring into his brown eyes, eyes emanating how much he loved me... I needed to try harder.

"Thank you." I snatched the hoagie and took a large bite. "What's the second thing?"

"I convinced my plane instructor to use biofuel." He grinned and performed an imperial bow.

"Now you tell me!" I kissed his cheek, leaving a smear of mayonnaise behind. "Maybe I'll let you take me up there after all."

"My test is in three weeks."

"Are you ready?" I asked as we walked down the steps into the marina. The white boats shone brightly under the strong sun and bobbed gently in the soft currents. Seagulls chattered in the air and on the boardwalk, fighting over the scraps of food spilling out of the trash cans. The marina took up a quarter of Almond Cove. High rocks wrapped around two sides of the marina, a rock climber's fantasy. One part of the cliffs overhung the far side of the bay, while the other revealed a rocky path leading to a narrow beach. Divers often explored the vast underwater cave networks here. But I'd never dived there. Or anywhere else. Just the swimming pool that one time when Danny and Will showed me how.

Danny, Will and I huddled at the shallow end of Almond Cove's public swimming pool. In the summer, it was packed with kids of all ages and families trying to claim a square inch of water. Now, at 7am on a November morning, it was deserted.

My teeth chattered. "I'm freezing."

Danny patted my shoulder. "You're the one who wanted to learn to dive."

Will, with long brown hair and the slightest hint of dimples, threw a cautious look at Danny. "Should we have brought her a wetsuit?"

Danny waved his concern away. "Don't worry about Sara; she's a Monroe. She's tough." He winked at me and my whole world bloomed.

Despite the chattering teeth and the goosebumps lining my skin, I smiled. If Danny said I could do it, I would do it. I lifted my face to the winter sun and pictured myself on a Hawaiian island. Dolphins leaping in the ocean and sunbathing under a hot sun. I shivered again but didn't feel as cold.

"That's it, squirt."

I socked his shoulder. "I'm not a squirt anymore."

Will raised his eyebrows. "Not after today. You master breathing on the regulator and we'll be able to take you out with us before you know it."

I grinned.

"That's right, squirt."

I let that one pass. I'd give anything to go diving with Danny and Will, to understand what secrets the water held beneath its surface, to be with my big brother, sharing in his favorite activity. And let's face it, Will was cute. With his brown eyes and golden brown hair. I didn't mind being around him.

Danny had mentioned a shipwreck and mermaid jewels. I knew it was another one of his stories, the mermaid jewels part, but the ship-wreck was real. When he spoke of his dives to mysterious places, of the colorful fish that swam around him, the dolphins that nosed playfully close, and the hidden secrets beneath the rocky coves, his eyes sparkled with such happiness that I couldn't stand not being able to share it with him. I wanted my eyes to shine like that.

"You ready?" Danny asked.

Nodding, I dropped my arms from where they'd been cradling my waist and reached out for the mouthpiece. Danny helped slide it into my mouth until my lips closed around it. It tasted like rubber and chemicals. Gross.

"Okay, breathe," Danny said. "One step at a time, yeah?"

"I am breathing," I mumbled through the mouthpiece.

Will laughed. "Through your mouth."

Danny pushed my head under the water.

I spluttered and snorted until I remembered to breathe through my mouth. Danny and Will descended with me. Panicky, I tried to draw breath in, but it wasn't enough, it didn't fill my lungs, and I got an immediate headache. With his hands, Danny gestured for me to slow down, to calm down. Refusing to surface, I focused on his face. Those hazel eyes I trusted with my life.

Danny held my hand and laced his fingers through mine. Smiling, Will did the same. I closed my eyes for a moment, concentrating on my breath, knowing I could pop my head above the surface anytime I wanted. Slowly, I got the rhythm of breathing. Dragging the thin air in and out of my lungs was a new experience, one I'd have to get used to.

When I opened my eyes, the three of us were at the bottom of the deep end. Will and Danny were sitting cross-legged, smiling at me. I let the gentle currents in the pool push and pull my body. Releasing their hands, I twirled in a few circles but found it cumbersome with the air canister on my back.

After a few more minutes, Will indicated we should go up. We all popped above the surface at the same time. Danny slipped the tank off my back so it wouldn't keep me under.

"I'm seriously impressed," Danny said. "Took me a couple of times to master the breathing. Look at you go, squirt."

I beamed at him as pride filled me up. "I think this calls for a milkshake at the diner."

Once we dried off and returned the gear to the dive shop, we walked along the boardwalk to our favorite diner. Barefoot, I dragged my feet along the smooth wooden planks of the boardwalk to feel the sand bite into my skin. It always reminded me of home. While Danny constantly complained about sand always finding a way into our house, into the yard, into his schoolbooks, into his food, I loved the feel of it. Sand was a miracle. Made from years of rock erosion. And it gave shelter to so much life. Like the flat-tailed horned lizard we'd discovered in the cavern at Almond Cove.

Danny hovered close, chattering about my first real dive and when I might be able to try the same exercise in the ocean. I smiled up at him. His words were smooth and sonorous, like the sound of the ocean when I put a seashell to my ear.

When we arrived at the diner, we ordered a high stack of pancakes with maple syrup and bacon. I checked my reflection in the window. Although my hair was damp and tangled, and my skin was covered in a fine layer of sand, my eyes were shining, just like Danny's.

"You okay?" Tyler asked, pulling my thoughts back to the marina, to him, to his imminent flying test. "Think I lost you there for a while."

"Sorry. Gah, you know, I get a little lost in thought sometimes. A lot of memories here. What were you saying about your test? You're ready, right?"

"As ready as I'll ever be," Tyler said.

"Won't they teach you how to fly when you join the Air Force?"

We meandered along the finger piers. Dad's boat, *The Cordelia,* whispered into view. It was a Vista 545 sailboat, and even I had to admit it was an impressive-looking boat. All streamlined and sleek angles. The perfect image for those corporate types who came out for their team-building exercises and sailing lessons. And it could cruise around the world too, if you were so inclined. Dad had promised he'd take me after high school if I wanted. I hadn't made up my mind yet. As much as I loved the ocean and everything it contained, there was something lonely about the vastness of it. When you couldn't see a speck of land and all around you was blue, blue, blue.

"They will," Tyler replied, stealing the hoagie out of my hands. "But I want to show my dedication. And if I don't get in, I still want to be able to fly. I could work for my dad and fly one of the fire planes. The fire in Sonora right now is huge. Dad has sent half his crew to help."

"Your dad's crew will get on top of it."

"I hope so."

"And Tyler? You'll get in. There's no doubt." Tyler was one of those types who succeeded in all areas. Sporty, smart, charming. A typical over-achiever. It was sickening. I'd give him a hard time about it if I didn't love him so much. And he didn't flaunt it. He was who he was.

"From your lips to God's ear." He pressed his hands together in a prayer pose, squishing the hoagie. "Oh, and how did the press conference go? Did you kick some EnRG butt? Please tell me you haven't shut them down, I'm not ready to give up yet."

I laughed and told him of Regina's revelations. I didn't mention how uneasy I felt about it. Nor did I reprimand him for drinking EnRG. I knew he'd have one in his backpack. We had an argument yesterday, today was going to be smooth sailing.

As we approached *The Cordelia*, Tyler scanned the water. His gaze turned toward the bay and a frown furrowed the bridge of his nose. He rubbed at the back of his neck, one of his nervous gestures.

"What's up?"

He hesitated, his eyes serious, then spoke. "A diver went missing yesterday. Somewhere in the bay. Thought there'd be more of a Coast Guard presence around. They must have given up."

A wave of shock cascaded over me, and I doubled over, blinking against the sunlight. No one had died diving at Manta Ray Bay since Danny. This couldn't be happening again. Tyler crouched beside me and rubbed my back with reassuring strokes. "I didn't know whether to tell you or not."

"What do you mean, *missing?*" I squeezed my hands together, trying to feel something real, something solid. "Didn't they have a dive buddy?"

"Dive buddy said the dude went off exploring around a corner. Never came back." He screwed up the hoagie wrapper and placed it in the trashcan near the gangplank.

The memories came back to me. Will in the sand. The empty lobster cage. The police arriving at the cove. The flowers. The funeral. The cards. Then silence.

Chapter Six

My world spun.

I put a hand on Tyler to steady myself. He wrapped his arms around me and held me. I leaned into him, into the solidity and strength his body offered and pressed my face into the crook of his neck. Thank God he hated diving. I never had to worry about him in the water.

Slowly, the world stopped spinning and I was able to focus on Tyler's face.

"You okay?" Tyler asked, rubbing my back.

"I think so. I... this is... I can't believe..."

"I know."

"Do you know who it was? The diver?"

Tyler shook his head. "No one we knew."

My stomach knotted and my shoulders throbbed with tension. I shook the shock out of my fingers.

"Maybe we should find your dad."

We walked along the finger pier to *The Cordelia*. My steps were slow and trembly. The sun was so bright, the reflection off the water blinded me. "We can't tell him. I'm not sure how he'll react."

"Got it."

Although it meant I would be late, I walked another loop of the marina to regain my composure. Tyler kept an arm around my waist as I inhaled the settling scent of the ocean. I stopped to kneel on the dock to dip my hand into the water and dab it on the back of my neck. The coolness of the water was refreshing and helped me to refocus. I noted the faintest of green sparkles. A patch of the algae had made it to the marina.

A few minutes later, I was ready to face my dad. Tyler stepped onto the gangplank and offered me a hand.

"Hey, you two." Dad said, coming above deck. "Perfect timing. I've just finished my paperwork."

Tyler removed another hoagie from his bag. This one smelled distinctly of meat. He handed it to Dad, whose eyes lit up. "Thank you!"

"What's the plan?" Tyler asked.

"We've got twelve coming next week for a day cruise, right after I get back from Paris with your mom. Can you two make sure the fridge is stocked with enough water and booze? We need to clean up after the last lot and we'll check the sails and scrub down the decks." Dad offered me a wink, knowing it was a big job. Hopefully, it would distract me from the awful news about the diver. "How was the press conference? Did you give her hell? I didn't get a call from the police, so I assume you behaved."

"Ha, ha." I poked him in the ribs, then told him of EnRG's plans.

"Wow," Dad said, around a mouthful of hoagie. "If she can get rid of the trash island, it will save my business."

Why did no one else see through her façade? My gut told me something was off, but probably best to keep it to myself for now. I didn't want to be accused of going off on another tirade.

"Let's hope," I said and gestured for Tyler to follow me below deck.

Moving through the cockpit, I climbed down the stairs and into the cooler interior of the boat. With the midday sun beating hard above our heads, I was grateful for a bit of shade. A couple of boxes sat on the floor in the kitchen area. One was completely full of champagne, the other a variety of soft drinks and beer. We unloaded both and stacked the various drinks in the fridge. Collapsing the boxes, I piled them in the newly dubbed recycling corner along with a few empty cans Dad had drunk while working down here. Using the new bio-friendly cleaning spray I'd picked up at an eco-fair, I ran a cloth over the surfaces, making sure they gleamed. Sometimes the execs would leave tips, and they were always bigger when the boat was spotless. I quickly checked the cupboard and disposed of the cans of tuna that weren't from sustainable sources. No amount of "someone's going to eat it anyway" or "it's already dead" would ever appease me.

I was about to head back up the stairs when Tyler put a hand on my arm.

"You okay?"

I cocked a shoulder. "Trying not to think about it."

His lips pursed. "Did you ever think about getting therapy?"

I dropped my gaze to my feet. I hated talking about Danny. I thought about him all the time but never spoke about him. That way, I could treasure my memories of him, keep them private and special. "I had therapy for a year. I think I'm stuck halfway between anger and bargaining."

"You could try again... it's been three years."

"So, I should be over it, right?" I snapped.

Tyler rubbed his neck. "No. That's not what I was going to say. What I meant was, it's been three years. Maybe the distance, the perspective will help if you went back to therapy."

I stared at him. I was afraid to blink, afraid to cry, afraid to let the feelings out.

"Think about it, yeah?"

I nodded, then climbed the stairs. Dad had scrubbed the decks with the eco-friendly detergent I'd bought him. Grabbing the hose, I had no qualms about washing it off into the sea. The detergent was made to break down and it could be fed on by microscopic ocean dwellers. Hopefully, it would even do something to the nasty toxins in the water. As I sprayed the hose, Dad lifted his T-shirt and wiped the sweat from his brow. His skin tone had turned a couple shades redder.

"You're burning," I said, and pointed at the biodegradable sunblock. Another little gift I got him last Christmas.

Dad nodded. "It's hot out here today. I think the whole summer is going to be hot."

Wanting to change my somber mood, I turned the hose on him and soaked him from head to foot. Tyler laughed, then ran when I turned the hose in his direction.

"And I'm not even mad," Dad said, shaking the water

out of his hair. He peeled off his soaking T-shirt and wrung it out.

As he turned, I admired the one and only tattoo he'd conceded to on the back of his right shoulder. Probably influenced by Frank, Tyler's dad. It was a classic Navy symbol; an eagle, anchor and trident. Not colorful like the one on Frank's back, but small and understated. I was desperate for my own tattoo. A dolphin, maybe, or a turtle or jellyfish. Definitely a sea animal. Dad said I had to wait until my eighteenth birthday 'at the very least.'

Dad draped his wet T-shirt over a chair and grabbed a soft drink from a cooler. Tyler came out of hiding, holding up his fingers in the shape of a cross, and the two of us left Dad drying out his clothes and headed to the bow. It was my favorite place on the boat. I could lean over, all *Titanic* style, and pretend I was on top of the world. Although, it didn't have quite the same effect when we were still docked in the marina.

I scanned the horizon, pointing out the green glow of algae to Tyler. It had grown considerably since this morning and could now be seen sparkling magically on the water. The massive area stretched from the horizon to the edge of the marina. I hoped Simona would have some answers when she came back, that the algae weren't in any distress.

We climbed onto the bow together and dangled our legs over the edge. Tyler produced a bag of chips for us to devour. With no clouds in the sky, the sun was brutal. I pulled my sunglasses down from my head and added one of Dad's caps. Tyler never minded the sun. It deepened the dark richness of his skin, but I still made him wear sunblock. His mom was Columbian and his dad had Italian and Irish ancestry. Together, they had produced Tyler, who always turned heads wherever we went.

A movement on the horizon caught my attention. An action more jagged than the peaceful drifting of the sailboats. A lone windsurfer performing tricks on the three-foot waves. The triangle of his red sail plowed through the white caps, skirting the edge of the bright green algae.

"Look," I said.

Shielding our eyes from the sun, we watched the windsurfer coast over the waves as if he could command their shape at will. He drew parallel with the EnRG vessel anchored offshore, which was surrounded by a handful of Operation Blue Water boats. The windsurfer edged closer to the glowing algae. With the sun sparkling off the water, the green took on a different bright emerald shade. The color made me think of Mom's favorite ring.

The windsurfer swept up and down the wave, his muscular arms expertly controlling the sail. As one wave crested, I caught sight of several dark shapes within the forming greenroom. My first thought was a pod of seals or dolphins playing alongside the windsurfer. Squinting, I realized the shapes were a handful of giant five-gallon containers lapping at the surfer's heels. Ugh. They must have broken off from the trash island. The windsurfer spotted the gathering mess and aimed his board in the opposite direction. But as he made the switch to change his position, a larger wave, dotted with flecks of the bright green algae, caught him unawares and swept him off his board.

"Total wipeout," I said, feeling bad for the guy. Tyler and I had had countless wipeouts on our boogie boards. That feeling of going under, not knowing up from down—

because you can't open your eyes for all the salt and sand—and then the waves push you down, harder and deeper until your hair becomes a toilet brush for the ocean floor. And just when you think you're going to explode, or have to suck in a lungful of seawater, somehow you right yourself and find the surface. Coughing and spluttering and with a head full of sand, but gloriously alive.

Tyler chuckled. "He'll be getting sand in places he didn't know existed."

"Eww."

Automatically counting the seconds in my head—twenty-five—I waited for the windsurfer to pop back up. His board and sail drifted close to the spot where he'd disappeared. If he'd been tethered to the board, he would have been up by now. Maybe. If it hadn't become caught on something under the surface. That happened. People died because of it. I still couldn't decide which practice was better and tended to copy whatever Tyler did on the day, as if mimicry would assure my safety.

Fifty seconds.

"He's still not up," Tyler said, stepping closer to the tip of the bow and using the pulpit for support.

"Give him a minute." The boat bobbed in the water as a large wave lapped at the hull.

Eighty-five seconds.

"Dad? Can you come out here?" I called.

Dad stepped around the cockpit and made his way toward us. "What's up?"

My stomach churned. "Windsurfer went down. Over a minute ago."

The skin around Dad's eyes tightened. "I'll call John."

He retreated to the cockpit and whipped out the radio handset. I wondered if we should fire up *The Cordelia*, but the Coast Guard would be much faster and didn't have to maneuver through the marina.

The distant beach was crowded. The water even more so. With tourist season in full swing, countless sailboats drifted out there on the sparkling blue, surrounding the EnRG catamaran. Surfers and boogie boarders and swimmers and inflatable dinghies waded in the shallows. The lifeguards might not have spotted the windsurfer go under. I couldn't see the tower from here; I had no idea if they were paying attention. Sometimes they were teenage trainees, more interested in strutting their stuff and preening for the opposite sex than actually rescuing someone.

One hundred seconds.

"Now, I'm worried," I said, watching the emerald patch ebb and flow. The board drifted toward the beach.

Two minutes now. The windsurfer was gone.

Dad yelled into the radio. "Mayday, mayday, windsurfer down."

Two minutes fifteen seconds.

Tyler trained a pair of binoculars on the water. I watched the horizon, trying to determine the invisible tidal patterns and where he might pop up. I hoped he hadn't been tangled up in any of the trash or the propellers of Operation Blue Water's army of boats anchored near the Green Clean catamaran.

Two and a half minutes.

"This is *The Cordelia*. Manta Ray Bay. We've seen a windsurfer go under. Two minutes and counting."

"Copy that," came a short reply. "Sending the Coast Guard's rescue team out now."

A few seconds later, the roar of a powerful engine ripped through the day, scattering gulls to the sky. Dad joined us above deck again and slipped on his semi-dry T-shirt. We watched the red motorboat catapult out of the marina and streak toward the drifting board.

"I can't believe this is happening again," Tyler muttered.

"What's happening again?" Dad asked, taking a turn at the binoculars.

"Diver went missing yesterday."

"A diver?" Dad looked at me. I knew he was checking my reaction. "Unfortunately, summer brings out the accidents."

"Three minutes," I said. No one needed a reminder. He could still be rescued. If he was damn good at holding his breath. Which was entirely possible, if he was as experienced as he looked. And if he was found... like, now.

The boat bobbed again as the wake of the motorboat reached us. Dad rested a hand on my shoulder. One of the coastguardsmen dove off the boat and swam freestyle to the abandoned board. Wearing scuba tanks, three others splashed into the water backward and disappeared.

Four minutes.

"He'll be okay now," Dad said.

"It's over four minutes, Dad."

"He'll be okay. John's crew will rescue him." The grip on my shoulder tightened.

The half-digested hoagie rolled in my stomach and the chips burned back up my throat. Captain John Rogers was the best Coastie Almond Cove had seen for the last twenty years. His rescue record was off the charts. Although he was retired from the physical stuff, he commanded Almond Cove's Coast Guard unit with exceptional skill. But still. Four minutes and change.

I glanced at Dad, too afraid to voice my doubts. Neither of us needed the reminder. I was sure he was thinking of it already, if his grip on my shoulder was anything to go by. He had a familiar pinched look on his face, the one he always wore when he was thinking about Danny.

Five minutes.

Dad's hand became a claw. I wriggled out of his grip.

"Sorry."

Tyler reached for my hand and laced his fingers through mine. He squeezed, hard. A cloud passed over the sun, dipping us in shadow, turning the ocean a menacing shade of blue. The green patch brightened, like a lightbulb under the water had been switched on. Once or twice, I caught sight of a diver at the edge of glowing algae.

Six minutes.

Seven minutes. My stomach clenched.

Eight minutes.

"Shit," Dad said. I didn't bother insisting he put a dollar in the swear jar.

Nine minutes.

Ten minutes.

Even though my watch was digital, I could feel the seconds ticking by on my wrist.

Twenty minutes.

Thirty.

Chapter Seven

I STOPPED COUNTING.

The three of us stood there for a long time. Long after the deserted board had been attached to the lifeboat. Long after the divers ran out of air. Long after the second crew went out, fruitlessly but perhaps with a kernel of hope in their hearts. Dad didn't move, didn't speak. He was barely breathing.

My knees locked together and I didn't have the energy to lower myself to a seat. I stood and watched the horizon, a numbness spreading over my skin.

Thickening clouds scudded across the sky, casting dark shadows on the ocean, highlighting the glowing algae that pulsed with a mysterious myocardial rhythm. The throbbing green light revealed the extent of human debris drifting and bobbing on the waves.

The trash island had arrived.

The size of LA. It ebbed into the ocean, into the bay, into the cove, hovering outside the line of Operation Blue Water boats, as if challenging them to a duel.

The whole thing was ugly. Damn all those companies and consumers dumping all their shit in the water because they couldn't be bothered to haul it out to a landfill. Not that landfills were any better. Green Clean had been doing their best to keep San Diego safe, but this was bigger than them. Regina Harron better be as good as her word. Even from here, I could spot several cans and bottles of EnRG. Their bright orange color was unmistakable.

Revulsion tightened my stomach. Then a wave of anger. The old, three-year anger that never went away.

"They'll never find a body among all the debris," I whispered.

Dad lowered his head to his chest. "I don't think they will. Poor guy."

A few minutes later, Captain John Rogers came to collect our statements. John boarded slowly, an elongated sigh escaping his lips and displacing the corners of a thick mustache.

"Hi, John." Dad stuck out his hand.

John gave a nod of greeting and took the hand. "Noah. Sara. Tyler." He shifted his weight onto the fixed bench and dropped his eyes to a clipboard in his hand.

"We had to call off the search. The trash in the water is coming in too quick. Kept getting our rudders tangled and the divers couldn't see sh—nothing. Excuse my French."

John cleared his throat and scribbled something on his clipboard. "Here's hoping he came up somewhere else and managed to swim to shore."

"Doubtful," Dad said.

"What about the diver from yesterday?" Tyler asked.

"No sign of him either." John pulled on his mustache. "I haven't lost a person in San Diego since..."

Since Danny.

John coughed again and shook his head. "Now two in as many days."

I glanced at the ocean. Manta Ray Bay was a C shape that cut away from the beach and ended in the high cliffs on the other side. There was only one entrance and exit. Anything bobbing within its curve would be spotted easily. The sting of tears prickled my eyes. It wasn't anyone I knew. Thank God. But to see someone disappear in the blink of an eye. There one second, performing fancy artwork on the waves. Then gone the next. Taken. Under. Gone. Forever.

It hurt.

"I shouldn't be trying to sugarcoat it for an experienced mariner like yourself, Noah. Especially considering what happened to... well... you know what I mean." He took off his Coast Guard hat and held it in his hands. "We've been watching the progress of the garbage for some time. I'm surprised more folks haven't gone missing." He shook his head sadly. "EnRG couldn't be here soon enough."

I bristled. No mention of Green Clean and how long they'd been around trying to clean up the ocean.

"And now it's not just animals who are dying," I muttered. "Damn the human race."

"Sara!" Dad reprimanded. "Swear jar."

"I think the circumstances allow."

Dad sighed and scuffed his shoe on the floor. "Perhaps."

John stood. "We've got a meeting with EnRG and Green Clean now. I don't want to have to close the beach and marina, but if this trash keeps rolling in, I'll have to."

"I've got a group coming next week," Dad said.

John held up a placating hand. "I know, Noah, I know. Lots of folks around here depend on the water for their livelihood. I'm doing what I can. We're talking to Operation Blue Water, and I know the local chapter of Homeland Security is involved."

Dad blew out an exaggerated breath. "I know you are, John. It's appreciated."

"Homeland Security?" I asked. "I thought they dealt with, like, terrorism or something. Are you saying the trash island is an act of terrorism?"

John chuckled. "Nothing like that, Sara. Homeland Security gets involved in all sorts of issues. From the environment, to terrorism, to biological contaminants to the distribution of emergency medical supplies."

I hadn't spotted their presence at the beach earlier. Perhaps they were lurkers.

Before he left, John tipped his hat toward us and gave us a few tips about sailing through trash islands. Abstinence was best. Obviously. Repairs to dented rudders were expensive. But abstinence wasn't an option for Dad.

Dad sat on one of the benches and stared at the water.

"Dad?"

He didn't turn but kept watching the horizon. Maybe if he stared hard enough, he could bring back the windsurfer. And my brother too. Then, with a shudder, he turned toward me and plastered one of his 'the world is okay' smiles on his face. It didn't fool me for a minute.

"I'm going to head back for a shower. Frank and I have that thing in LA tonight," Dad said, searching his pockets for the boat keys. He ducked his head and climbed down the stairs leading below. "I'm going to try and not think about this for a little while. I suggest you two do the same. Did you say there was a feature at the movies?"

"Jaws," I replied, which now felt inappropriate.

"Well, whatever you do, stay out of trouble."

Tyler threw him a respectful salute. Dad locked up the cockpit, then ruffled my hair on the way down the gangplank. "Don't wait up. I'll see you in the morning."

"Bye, Dad."

A few minutes after he left, someone called my name. The excited voice was unmistakable and thundered through the air in the marina. Simona skipped down the steps, waving both hands.

Tyler and I left the boat and met her on one of the finger piers.

"Did you find the algae? Is it bioluminescence?" I asked.

She wiped a hand across her brow, causing the silver bracelets on her wrist to jangle. "Got a little hairy out there. Barely made it back before that enormous trash island made an appearance. Ugh. *Madre mía.*"

Tyler searched my face, his eyes watery. He'd been quiet since the windsurfer. We both had.

"And?" I asked. "What did you discover?"

Simona clicked her gum. "It *is* a bioluminescent algae. Largest patch I've ever come across. I took a sample back to my lab and had a look through the microscope. The team is running some more complex tests. The algae's metabolic rate has slowed down, showing signs of distress, but not to levels I'm concerned about. Yet."

"But what's it doing here?" Tyler asked. "It's so big."

"I assume it was displaced by the trash," Simona replied.

"Hopefully, when EnRG fixes the problem, the algae will be back to normal."

"Yeah, well, they still haven't said how they're going to do that," I muttered. But I didn't have any fight left in me. After the press conference and awful drowning, I was thoroughly exhausted and unable to mount any new battles today.

"I guess we'll have to wait and see," Simona said. She touched my hand, a gentle pressure. "Green Clean is talking to them right now. We'll get you some answers."

I brushed my shoulder against hers. "Thanks, Simona."

After Simona left us, Tyler and I hovered at the steps of the marina. My muscles ached from standing stiff and tense for so long. I massaged my shoulders, then fisted and unfisted my hands, trying to work the tension out.

"So, I take it a Jaws triple feature might not be the best entertainment tonight?" Tyler slung an arm around my waist and pulled me in.

"Even with Harper's offer of free popcorn, I'm not sure I can face a creature feature after today." I buried my face in his chest and drew strength from him. "But I don't think I'm ready to go home yet, either."

"So, let's walk." He took my hand and wound me along the marina's main platform.

We didn't say much as we weaved a path along the floating docks. I couldn't stop thinking about the windsurfer and the trash island that had finally made its appearance. Several attempts had already been made to deal with it, and clumps of it had been broken off, but it was too big to solve in any meaningful way. Now it had arrived on the coast, I suspected life at Almond Cove would change for the foreseeable future. A heavy feeling pushed between my ribs and filled my stomach. Not only were the ocean and the sea life in jeopardy, but if Dad couldn't get the boat on the water, he'd struggle to keep a roof over our heads. And more people would be in danger, just like Danny. I couldn't let EnRG off the hook. They had three years to deal with this problem, and only now, at the eleventh hour, had they announced their intervention.

Without consciously agreeing to it, Tyler and I headed to our favorite part of the marina; an area where the lanes narrowed and only dinghies could sail into the tapered channels near where the rocks began. It was quieter here and the cliffs of Almond Cove offered shady patches as the sun arced across the sky. We stopped at a small empty dock and dangled our legs off the decking. At least the trash hadn't infiltrated this area yet and I could pretend, for a moment, that it wasn't out there.

It was late afternoon and the power had drained out of the sun, leaving a pleasing warmth on the back of my neck. I dipped my feet into the water and relished the velvety coolness. I scooped a handful and rinsed my face. I loved how tight the salt made my skin feel. It was Earth's most natural facial. I swished my feet through a couple of patches of bioluminescent algae and was tempted to find a jar to stick them in, but I knew better now. I couldn't do it to them. They deserved the freedom of the ocean. Tyler removed a can of EnRG from his backpack and pressed it against his forehead, the bright orange coloring of the can overwhelming the muted hues of the lowering sun.

He chose to ignore my pointed frown and popped the tab. I gritted my teeth and promised myself I wouldn't comment. I knew for the next hour he'd be all hyped up and deny it had anything to do with EnRG. Although he could be amusing with his incessant banter.

He took a long glug.

"Seriously?" I couldn't help myself.

He shrugged. "They're changing their ways. You said so yourself."

"I'll believe it when I see it." My frown turned to a scowl. "I hate to see you adding your money to their cause."

"But now they have a *good* cause." He grinned. "You can't tell me off for drinking it anymore. Maybe I should pay their warehouse a visit and siphon off one of their trucks." Ceremoniously, he took another long glug. I resisted the urge to give him my spiel about the unwanted side effects.

"They keep their drink in trucks?"

"Yeah, before they take it to the canning site. Then they—"

I raised my palm. "Forget it. I don't want to know."

The knot of tension at the back of my neck came back, a deep ache that had me craving a massage. Then something in the water caught my eye.

A six-pack ring floated by.

"Look. Give me a hand," I said.

Tyler chuckled. "I thought you were done for the day."

"Just be a good boy and do as you're told." Throwing him a wink, I kept my other eye on the floating six-pack ring. "Hand me that jib stick over there, will you?" I waved my hand in the general direction of the beginning of the dock, where an abandoned jib stick stood propped against the wooden rail. I crouched at the edge of the dock and reached toward the water.

Tyler slid the smooth metal into my hand. Still hot from the sun, I pinched it between my thumb and forefinger. Shifting onto my stomach, I leaned out over the dock, tucking my feet behind a couple of wooden posts to anchor my balance. With a quick inhale, I pushed the hook end of the jib stick into the water and hooked the plastic ring. "Yes!"

"How many plastic rings have you rescued from the ocean?"

"I'm going for the Guinness Book of World Records."

Danny had collected them. Rather than take them to a recycling center, he'd built a ton of junk models out of six-pack rings and other trash he'd found in the water. Mom and Dad had eventually thrown them all away as they'd taken up half the garage, but I had insisted we keep a smaller model of a seal. It was my favorite animal, after all.

Tyler pulled out his phone and, pretending to scroll, said, "Think you might be on for a winner. There isn't any record of six-pack ring collecting."

"Ha, ha." Sitting up, I pulled the six-pack ring toward us to find three empty beer cans re-slotted back into their circles. "If they could take the time to do that, why couldn't they put their trash in a trash can?"

The three cans were full of ocean water and covered in slick green seaweed. Bright green, just like the algae. I hated the thought of putting the seaweed in the trash; it provided a home to thousands of tiny, microscopic organisms that would not survive outside their watery home. I'd have to pick it off. And shower, so I didn't smell like a fish market.

Water from the six-pack ring dripped onto my hands with a strange green tinge. Maybe it was some of the algae, broken free from the main pool.

"Because people are lazy," Tyler replied.

"It wasn't that long ago you used to clean up the beach with me, you know."

"That was when I was attempting to impress you." He waggled his eyebrows. "Besides, you do enough for both of us."

"Uh-huh."

"One person isn't going to make a difference."

I opened my mouth to respond, the many arguments of 'it starts with one' and 'setting a good example' and 'helping the Earth recover' lost on my lips as he held up a hand in apology. I threw a tendril of seaweed at him, but he dodged out of the way and it went sailing over his head and plopped into the water below.

"You better drink that while you can." I pointed to his drink with a seaweed-covered finger. "There's a class action coming soon about the side effects."

"They don't have any proof."

"Apparently, one man grew an extra limb. Another a tumor the size of a football. Benign, thankfully."

Tyler looked at the drink, cocked a dark eyebrow, then placed it on the deck between us. "Really?"

I splayed a hand. "Who knows what they put in there?"

Tyler poked the can, then sniffed at it as if it might suddenly come alive.

A laugh died in my throat when the oddest sensation flickered along the fingertips of my right hand. At first, just a feeling something was different, that something atypical was about to occur. Like when I picked up the iron skillet a few weeks ago and forgot the oven gloves. I'd grabbed the handle and almost made it to the countertop before the heat set in. The pain came, fully loaded and unforgiving, making me whimper all the way to the cold tap.

It was like that now. A scurrying sensation flickering down the nerves in my hand, not quite painful but building in intensity. Then a flush of heat as though I'd struck a match. Grabbing my wrist with the other hand, I dropped the six-pack ring and cans and squeezed as an intense pain tore through my fingers. Sudden and fast. I sucked in a breath and held it.

"Ahhhhhh!" I cradled my hand in my lap. It burned. Dark spots flooded my vision.

"Sara?"

Curling into a ball, I shook off the seaweed clinging to my fingers and scraped at the wooden deck, looking for an escape from the pain.

"Sara?" Tyler crouched over me, hands roaming my side, looking for an injury. But I couldn't speak. My jaw clamped tight. I could barely keep it together as the pain raced through my fingers and into my palm. On fire. White hot fire.

"Sara? What's the matter?" A deep frown appeared in his forehead. His eyes darted between my face and body.

"My hand," I spluttered. "It burns."

He pulled me up and pushed me toward the water. Extending my arm in the direction of the cooling surface, I spotted white blisters forming on my hand, and behind them, skin so red and raw, it reminded me of lava. Agonizing. I screamed again. Tyler splashed water up and down my hand, but to no avail.

Rolling backward, I collapsed on the deck. Short, shallow breaths were all I could manage. Blackness ebbed at the corner of my vision. The pain crept onto my wrist. I shook my head from side to side and tried to kick away the pain. Unable to breathe, I squeezed my eyes closed. A dizzy wave made me nauseous.

"Stay with me, Sara!"

And then sweet relief. A fizzy wetness spilled over my burning hand. And then... mercifully... nothing. No pain. No pain. Thank God, no more pain!

"Sara? You okay?"

Crying, I clung to Tyler, the memory of the pain still so vivid. "It hurt so much." I reached out to touch him with a finger and was mildly surprised to see it hadn't dissolved. It was red and irritated and tender blisters were clumped around my wrist and fingers, but the pain had stopped.

"What the hell?" I muttered. "How did you make it stop?"

Tyler prodded his energy drink, now lying empty on its side. "When the water didn't work, I couldn't think of what else to douse you with. As soon as I poured it on you, you calmed down."

I looked from the can, to Tyler, to my hand. Gently I touched the inflamed skin. It was tender, but the agony had faded.

"Looks like a second-degree burn," Tyler said. "We should get you to a hospital."

I shook my head. "It doesn't hurt anymore." I couldn't believe how quickly the pain receded. Maybe I was in shock.

I probably should go to the hospital, but I'd rather dip into the contents of the first aid kit at home than spend hours in the emergency room. I looked at Tyler. "What was in those cans?"

Tyler pulled me onto his lap. He placed a series of gentle kisses on my cheek and then on my hand and fingers. "I don't know. Could it be some kind of toxin from the trash island?"

I shook my head. "It wouldn't have been isolated like that. Most toxins in the ocean get diluted and don't have such an immediate effect." I scanned the docks, my gaze stretching to where I knew the EnRG catamaran sat. Was their method of destroying the trash island responsible for whatever had burned my hand? I narrowed my eyes, suddenly afraid all my instincts were right.

"I've never seen anything like it." Tyler hugged me tighter. I hadn't realized my teeth were chattering. With the sun drooping below the horizon, the heat of the day had released. But it wasn't the evening breeze that had me shivering.

Chapter Eight

Wʜᴀᴛ ᴡᴀѕ ɪɴ ᴛʜᴇ ᴡᴀᴛᴇʀ? What had EnRG done?

My fingers and wrist ached. "I think I want to head home. Will you walk me?"

"Of course." Tyler offered me an arm. "You okay now?"

I nodded, but in truth, I still felt a bit shivery inside.

We skirted a short path through the finger piers until we reached the entrance to the marina. The evening breeze brushed against my arm and stung the irritated skin.

"Holy..." Tyler exclaimed, his eyes roving the ocean.

I followed his gaze. Out on the water, the Green Clean boat was anchored next to the giant EnRG catamaran. A dozen or so smaller vessels bobbed in the water next to them. Except it wasn't really water anymore. The trash spread as far as I could see. From the catamaran to the horizon, Almond Cove in the south to the freeway heading north. A few stray items drifted in the shallows and beached themselves on the sand. Red flags were planted along the beach and families were packing up. The beach was closing. My chest tightened and my eyes stung. All the work I'd done for Green Clean over the last four years, it wasn't enough. Not to stop something like this.

Averting my gaze, I retrieved my bike from the rack and Tyler wheeled it along the boardwalk. "You were right."

"About what?" I asked.

"The trash island."

"What do you mean?"

He blew out a breath, ruffling his spikey fringe. "I mean, I knew it was out there; I saw the pictures, I watch the news. But it felt too big to be true. It was out *there* somewhere." He circled a hand toward the ocean. "It didn't seem like it would affect us here, inland.

"That's half the problem," I said as we turned onto my road. "It's out there, where everyone can ignore it."

"I'm sorry."

I kissed his cheek. "At least now you understand." I shifted my gaze to the ocean. "I wish there was more I could do."

"This is bigger than you. Bigger than Green Clean, I think. I'm not sure what else you *can* do."

We arrived at my house. He kissed my nose and I wrapped my arms around him, discarding my bike to the front lawn. Inside, Tyler led me to the kitchen and sat me down at the kitchen table. He found some antiseptic wipes in the first aid kit and insisted on cleaning my burn. It stung like a bitch. After Googling burn treatment, he apologized for the wipes, spread the cream over my skin and shook out a couple of Advil for me to take. I found a sterile bandage in the kit and Tyler wrapped it around my wrist and fingers. I felt better having it wrapped away so it wouldn't accidentally brush against anything.

I made a quick trip upstairs to check my phone for messages. I could use a hug from my mom about now and I was hoping she'd sent a new email. I wasn't disappointed. But when I downloaded the pictures she'd sent, I shuddered. They were all of her day out in the Paris catacombs. Ten pictures of her and her friends posing in front of skulls and bones mortared to the walls. I smiled, remembering a Halloween before Danny died. He'd dressed as a grim reaper and used white face paint to draw a pattern of a skull on his face. It freaked me out so much I'd refused to go Trick or Treating with him.

I sent Mom a quick message back. *Thanks for the nightmares*, with a laughing emoji.

Downstairs, Tyler and I made popcorn and watched a movie. It was a romantic comedy that had nothing to do with the ocean and ensured Tyler kept his arms around me. He delivered sweet kisses to my lips at all the appropriate times and I felt a longing stir. We had hours before our dads would return.

I looked him up and down, admiring the curvature of his arms and the muscle in his thighs. I ran a finger along his bicep, then kissed the jiggling freckle at the corner of his mouth. The one I could watch for hours when he spoke. The one I kissed with more regularity than his lips.

Tyler turned on the couch and pulled me down next to him. The movie went to credits as we kissed. I blocked everything out; the ticking clock in the kitchen, the odd screech of a motorbike on the street outside, the insects chirping through the open window, and concentrated on him. I let my brain turn to mush as my lips moved along his jawline, down his neck. I tugged off his T-shirt, then pulled off my own.

Tyler's eyes shone in the semi-dark of the living room. I straddled him and felt him wanting me. Could tonight finally be the night? I went for the zipper on his shorts and pulled it down. We'd been here before, countless times, and I mentally checked where I'd hidden the condoms in my room.

Tyler groaned under my touch and pulled me closer.

"My dad won't be back for hours," I whispered in his ear.

Under me, Tyler shifted, and his hand went under my bra. "I know. He's in LA with my dad."

I glanced at the stairs that led away from the living room. "So, we could..."

Tyler smiled and kissed me. "Do what we're doing?"

I kissed his freckle. "Or a bit more?"

Tyler sat up, disentangled himself form me, and swung his feet to the floor.

"What's the matter?" I asked.

His eyes cut a nervous glance. "I know I've kind of avoided talking about this, because, well... this is a bit embarrassing..."

I smiled at him. "Spit it out."

"I don't think I'm ready."

My eyebrows shot up. I thought we'd been waiting for me to be ready. "Okay. Umm, how come?"

He cocked a shoulder and a flush colored his cheeks.

"My Dad always said I shouldn't have sex until I'm prepared to deal with all the potential consequences."

I burst out laughing. That sounded so like Frank. "This is about your dad? Since when do you do everything he tells you to?"

Tyler shifted me next to him and held my hand. "Dad gave me all these horror stories about his cousin getting pregnant when they were growing up. Only fifteen. She ended up having a late miscarriage, but it was awful, for all of them."

"Eeesh. What a nightmare."

He waved away my concern. "My point is, I'm not ready to be a dad, and I'd hate for you to go through the heartache of something like a miscarriage too."

I shivered as my skin cooled and reached for the crochet blanket hanging on the arm of the couch. "You make it sound so serious."

"It is serious."

"But what does it mean? Do we not have sex until we're married and want to have a kid? I mean, I know there are tons of people who live their lives like that, but I'm not sure I can wait so long. I really, really want you, Tyler."

"I don't want to wait that long either. And I want you. I do." He sighed. "Man, look at you, you're beautiful, I'd be a fool to pass it up. But... I'm not ready quite yet."

I touched his freckle with a fingertip. His thoughtfulness and caring made me love him more. Him and his big heart.

"You are adorable." I took his hand with my bandaged one. "And it's perfectly okay. We can carry on doing what we were doing."

Tyler grinned. "You're not mad?"

"Why would I be mad?" I kissed his freckle. "Unsatisfied, but not mad."

He laughed, then took my face in his hands. "I know. I love you. I do. I just need some time."

"Do you happen to know how much time?" I asked.

He touched the bare skin of my waist, circled his thumb over my hips. "I'll let you know."

I put my hand between his legs, partly to tease him, partly to check he still wanted me.

He pulled me down next to him, his hands everywhere, my skin reigniting. I made a mental note to check the expiration date on the condoms. Hopefully, they wouldn't run out before we could use them.

We kissed, and his hands found my bare back. I touched his heated skin, but I didn't go anywhere near his shorts. We would wait. Which was probably a good thing.

We fell asleep on the couch, and in the middle of the night, Tyler woke and told me he better get home before our dads found us. He kissed my cheek and pulled his T-shirt on. Retrieving his backpack from the floor, he shouldered it and headed for the door. "I'll see you tomorrow."

I watched as he eased the door closed behind him, already missing him. Then I plucked my T-shirt from the floor and headed upstairs. Foggy-headed, I changed into my pajamas and stood at the window in my room. The ocean had transformed into a sparkling green abyss. The biolumi-nescence glistened as far as I could see and was entirely intermingled with the trash. It was beautiful, in its own way, like some art deco, avant-garde, new age mash-up piece of art. Except this was real.

My chest tightened as I thought of the windsurfer from earlier. Had he washed up somewhere? Could he, miraculously, still be alive? Gnawing on my lower lip, my hope dwindled. There was no way he could navigate so much trash. Even if it was sparkling with otherworldly beauty.

Chapter Nine

THE GLEAMING debris infiltrated the entire coastline as far as I could see. The algae circled the whole thing, like it even needed highlighting. Harper and I strolled along the sand on clean-up duty. The beach may have been closed to the public but wearing the Green Clean polo shirts gave us access to all areas. While she handed me a bag of popcorn from the movie theater, I told her about the diver and the windsurfer, and the burns on my wrist. She stared at the obviously green water and agreed something seemed weird.

We ambled along the sand with our trash bags and began plucking bits of garbage from the water. Cans—lots of them EnRG—cigarette butts, food wrappers, takeout containers, plastic grocery bags, plastic bottles... The list went on. So much more since the trash island had shown up. We edged closer to the marina where the trash hadn't yet infiltrated and the water was mostly blue.

Next to me, with her cap pulled low and her curls tucked into the loop, Harper wrinkled her nose. "What the hell is that?"

I followed her gaze. Belly-up, a dead fish floated by. I couldn't tell the species from my vantage point, but it was a big one, at least a foot long. Then two more bobbed up next to it. Shortly followed by a further five. Simultaneously, Harper and I took a step back.

"This is all Regina's fault." I glanced toward the ocean, where the EnRG catamaran dwarfed all other vessels. Its solar panels gleamed in the sun and its insectile cockpit appeared ready to pounce. Green waves lapped at the hull and trash bounced off its sides. The sparkling emerald algae rolled up each wave, illuminating the currents. But there were no fish within those waves. Normally, fish and shrimp and other sea creatures would be attracted by such a spoil of algae. So why weren't they feeding on it now?

"Something's in the algae," I said.

Harper's brow puckered as she inspected the ocean. "Simona said it was just bioluminescence."

I elbowed her. "Come on, Veronica Mars, where's your spidey sense?

"I think you're mixing your movies there." She smiled. "But you're right; something doesn't feel quite right. What else did Simona say?"

"That they were running more tests." I dropped my net bag on the dock and shielded my eyes to see better. "Something's wrong. Something killed those fish."

I pointed at the water. The narrow offshoot was filled with floating dead fish. More than I could count. Several silver mackerel, a couple of large salmons, the obvious red scales of a few dozen California sheepheads, several more junior yellowtails and even a three-foot barracuda. They kept on coming, floating by, clogging up the finger piers, their bellies glistening in the noonday sun. Harper covered her nose with a hand. I took shallow breaths through my mouth, but still, I could smell death. "Something is killing the fish."

"Oohh, we can be all Erin Brockovich and class action their ass!" She clapped.

"Hang on there a minute, Marty McFly." I tapped her head. "First, we have to find the evidence of Regina's evil deeds."

Harper deflated. "Oh, yeah, true. I know you want it to be Regina, but you need to be open to the possibility that something else is going on."

I frowned.

"Seriously, Sara, I know her company has been shit to the environment, but she's turned a corner now. And you can't blame her for all the world's ocean trash."

"I don't feel like being sensible and logical right now. I know there are other problems. I know the turtles and polar bears are endangered. The orcas, the sea otters, albatrosses... the list is horribly long. I know trash isn't the only problem. And the ozone has holes and cows fart too much methane. I know. But none of those things killed Danny."

"Oh, hon."

"Something is killing these fish, and I'm going to find out what it is." I marched toward the boardwalk.

"Sara!" Harper ran after me.

I planned to go out in my dinghy. The small sailboat had a shallow rudder and could skirt around the sea of dead fish. I could sail out to the algae and investigate.

"Sara." Harper caught my arm. "Where are you going?

They closed the beach. They're closing the marina tonight. No more boats in or out."

"I can't stand here and watch my ocean, my beach, my town, get destroyed. Regina won't talk about her methods. There's nothing on the news except how amazing Operation Blue Water is. Simona isn't high enough up in Green Clean to throw her weight around. She said the algae was in distress, and she's waiting on more tests. But we don't have time to wait for the results. We need to find out what's going on for ourselves. And expose EnRG once and for all." I ran out of air and my chest seized.

Harper chewed on her lip. "We'll be spotted a mile away."

"Danny would do it. I know he would. I can feel his voice in my head, and he would never back down from something like this. He died saving a cage of lobsters, for God's sake! I can't let him down, Harper. I can't."

"But you can't put yourself in dangerous situations just because—"

"There's something out there, Harper. I can feel it." The memory of the pain in my hand hadn't faded. Those white, burning blisters still visible on my wrist and fingers. The images stayed in the back of my mind. What if there was more out there? What if someone else got hurt? I couldn't let that happen.

"Okay." She fisted her hands on her hips. "Okay. But you're not going out there on your own."

"You want to come with me? You don't have to. Seriously... I get this isn't everyone's fight—"

Her stern frown interrupted me. "I'll have you know I care about the ocean as much as you. Thank you very much. And I think you'll find I loved Danny more than you too. I was the one who was going to marry him."

I smiled. She smiled back.

"Thanks, Harper."

Harper pumped a fist. "You know I'm always up for an adventure, albeit this will be the scariest one I'm willingly signing up to. If I don't become an actress, I'll be a PI, so I need to learn to do the dangerous and daring at some point. We're in this together. Let's Aquaman this ocean's butt."

I giggled, appreciating the levity Harper brought. I didn't know what I'd do without her. In the weeks after Danny died, she was the only one who could make me smile.

Harper flexed her biceps like an overly muscly body-builder or an action hero. "Someone's got to keep you out of trouble."

I grinned and held out my good hand for a high-five. "We're in it together."

"Veronica Mars didn't have a side-kick, but I'm all about teamwork, so we'll call ourselves The Avengers and be done with it."

"Only if I can be Thanos," I said.

She rolled her eyes. "You can't pick the bad guy!"

"Why not? He has all the power."

"Fine, but I'm keeping the glove. And if I get arrested, I'm blaming you."

"We're not going to get arrested. We're performing a civic duty."

She jumped into the boat, rocking it precariously. "You bet we are. A *global* duty."

"On second thought, let's take the sea kayaks." My

dinghy was closely packed in and the sail would be easily spotted, plus the offshore wind was strong enough to prove challenging. The kayaks were lower to the water level and we had a better chance of evading detection. Not to mention the danger of the rudder getting tangled in all the dead fish smacking the hulls and piles. Gurgles and slaps and odd squelchy noises echoed through the finger piers. And the stench. It was like being in the world's biggest fish market. Worse.

Harper stepped out of the dinghy and into one of the kayaks, fastening the helmet strap under her chin. "In and out, right?"

I nodded. "If we can figure out what's going on, we can help my dad. He won't be able to continue the sail next week. Or for the foreseeable future. Not until the trash is cleaned up."

Harper's brown eyes brimmed with sympathy. Waving it off, I climbed into my kayak and pushed off from the dock. We paddled through the silent water. As we rounded the corner of the marina, the waves grew choppier and I fought to keep the kayak facing the break, the oar digging into my tender palm. Only then did I think about what might happen if I capsized. If the algae or trash really was doing something to all those fish, I could be in trouble. The pain in my hand had been bad enough, but what if it burned my whole body?

The disappearance of the windsurfer and diver weighed on my mind. It brought everything back. Tyler was right; there were lots of accidents every summer, but both victims were experienced in the water and I suspected there was more to it. What that something else was, I had no idea, but my instinct lay with Regina. Somehow.

On the water, the glowing green algae glistened. It encased the trash island and spilled into the water in concentric circles, as if its heart beat somewhere in the middle of the debris and soon it would turn the ocean completely green. Mesmerized by the fantastical color, I watched it for a few minutes. Although the individual algae were too small to see without magnification, within the bioluminescence, I got the impression of movement. A unified pulsing, as if it were the heartbeat of some giant organism. Within this light, the trash swirled and collided. So much worse than yesterday. So many cartons, cans, containers. The tide pushing it all together. Ugh. I wondered if mankind continued to treat the planet like this, whether we could live on such islands. We might have to.

Harper knocked her paddle against my kayak. "Let's keep going. Let's get closer."

The freezing spray kept me in the moment, and with waves higher than I'd have liked, all my focus went on managing the currents. I endured a brief moment of panic when something knocked into the kayak and sent me spinning in a haphazard circle. My heart skipped a beat and I yelped. Would I end up on the sea floor like Danny? But then the kayak faced forward and I crested the last wave of the break line.

Harper gave me a thumbs up and we paddled on. I eyed the distance between us and the trash. We were so close, and so far we had evaded detection from the Coast Guard. Although I was sure the huge EnRG catamaran or one of its smaller research vessels must be aware of our presence.

After a couple more strokes with our paddles, we balanced them on our laps and drifted into the huge patch of bioluminescence and trash. The way it illuminated the water several feet into the depths filled me with a sense of dread. And it was so quiet. The jostling trash had been loud before. Was it now preparing to pounce?

"Maybe we should go back." Harper's eyes were streaked with tension. "Suddenly, I'm not feeling so Aquaman."

"One more minute," I said.

Harper let out a shriek as something big knocked into her kayak, sending her plowing into me. I reached for the sides to steady myself. Fearing coming face to face with the windsurfer's dead body, I turned slowly. But it was just a large plastic water canister.

In quick succession, as though it were a magnet, three beer cans, two six-pack rings and a plastic bag stuck to its sides. Then the water canister moved of its own accord, covered in the glowing algae, toward another area of debris. Most of the trash wasn't recognizable from its original form. There was an overall pool of multi-colored muck, lots of netting, and bottles and bags and plastic cups.

A pile of netting and a dinghy-sized clump of seaweed adhered to the water canister mound. And then the new assortment of trash moved toward more of the brown muck, completely ignoring the tide and the waves and the way in which it should be moving. Weird.

"What the hell is going on?" Harper yelled, almost dropping her paddle.

Glancing at the EnRG catamaran, I tried to peer through the dark windows, wondering if there was someone inside watching me. The vessel wasn't far away now, we could be spotted without binoculars. The decks were deserted, but I sensed movement behind the imposing glass.

This entire venture was foolish. What had I been thinking? I glanced at Harper, cursing myself for putting her in danger.

"Let's go back," I said, turning my kayak around. My heart pounded against my ribs and my spine turned to something like a cactus' prickles. "It's not safe out here."

Harper frowned at me, then paddled in a complete circle. "What do you mean, *it's not safe?* I thought that was obvious."

"The algae. Whatever burned me yesterday, I think it comes from the algae."

Her eyes widened and she hightailed it toward the marina.

Balancing against the rocky waves, I paddled after her, but so much trash surrounded me, and I was scared of dripping the contaminated water onto my bare legs.

Quickly, the trash surrounding me became organized. Threaded through with seaweed and all of it glowing bright green, it moved against the current and gathered itself into one large mass. Which was impossible, and yet that's exactly what it was doing.

I jabbed at the trash, trying to get out of the glowing water. Harper was already entering the marina. One of Tyler's EnRG cans rolled along the bottom of the kayak and came to rest against my calf. I picked it up and realized it was unopened.

Prodding the water with a paddle, I nudged the edge of the growing trash pile to push myself away. It shrank away from me, much like a sea anemone would. I poked it again. Harder. Something squelched and a dribble of bioluminescence leaked out of the crevice I'd created. Almost as if it were alive. And bleeding.

Alive?

Impossible.

An absurd giggle burbled out of my throat. Green water dripped from the paddle into the kayak. I tucked my feet closer to my body. The emerald color of the algae pulsed, fading and dimming. An insistent heartbeat.

Spotting a few dozen bottles of Tyler's EnRG drink in the water, I had the urge to collect them and deliver them to the catamaran. But I wasn't about to put my hand in the water.

A louder squelching sound came from the area around the water canister. Like a deep, mechanical sigh. Something breaking, or something powering up? A rubber tire containing an army of Styrofoam cups zoomed out of the depths and entered the ring of light, slapping against the water canisters. A startled bleat escaped my lips and my kayak bobbed on the sudden wake. The trash moved, pulling itself closer together, the squelching sounds increasing in both volume and frequency. And all the while, everything was covered in the glowing green.

Transfixed, I couldn't turn away from the impossible sight. Until a brighter shoot of greenness extended from the water canister. Thick and solid, constantly lengthening, it appeared to be made of sharp plastic shards and netting. The tendril scrabbled, moving pieces of trash out the way, chucking them overhead where they joined the pulsing body of the larger trash mass. Arm-like, the vine thing grew threads that spread across the water toward me. Zeroing in on me, the finger-like appendages glided through the water, advancing. Backpaddling furiously, I moved away from the stretching green arm thing, into the breaking waves.

"Sara!" Harper screamed, paddling back to me.

"Stay away!" I yelled back.

She stopped paddling, sat there on the water, watching me, her face twisted in disbelief.

Between me and the scrabbling vine were the few bottles of EnRG. The thinner tendrils paused when they reached them, then retreated faster than I could follow. Splitting apart and circling around the bottles, they came after the kayak, the claw-like appendages grabbing onto the bow. I hit it with my paddle, but it wouldn't let go.

It tried to steal my paddle, wrenching it harder and harder, like it wanted to play tug-of-war. Afraid I would lose my only tool to get back to the marina, I yanked it away. Desperate, I grabbed the can of EnRG rolling around at my feet, flipped the tab and hurled it at the scrambling trash. Immediately, it slunk away, disappearing beneath the surface as the orange EnRG discolored the green water. I didn't waste the opportunity.

Backpaddling and trying to find a breath, a wave catapulted me forward and I zoomed out of the glowing green and enormous island of trash. I paddled as fast as I could toward the docks, fearing at any moment my kayak would be overturned and I would be gobbled alive by... something horrible and acidic.

Catching up with Harper, we entered the safety of the calmer marina together. Her face was paler than the cresting foam.

"I'm sorry," I said. "We should never have gone out there."

Nodding, she reached for my hand. "You okay?"

"I think so. You?"

She wrapped her arms around her waist, hugging herself. "I don't know yet. But, Sara, I'm scared."

I looked over my shoulder at the glowing green. If Regina knew what was going on within the trash and algae, she had a lot to answer for. No wonder she had evaded my questions. Next time, I wouldn't let her wriggle out of them.

"There's something in that algae," I said, calmer than I felt.

"No shit." Harper shook her head repeatedly, as if trying to shake out the last few minutes. "But I don't think I can believe what I saw. A... a... a... thing with arms, made of trash..." she looked at me. "It can't be real."

"I saw it too," I said quietly. I tied up our kayaks at the dock and helped her onto the pier.

"We need to tell someone. The authorities. The police. FEMA, a government agency. You know, Mulder and Scully. Someone!"

I looked at my best friend. FEMA, the Federal Emergency Management Agency, was a good call, but could they handle something like this? "Homeland Security and the Department of Health are already involved." I scanned the beach, where I saw a few people standing around in official clothing. "Either they're stuck wading through too much red tape, or Regina has been able to disguise what she's up to."

"But how could she do that?" Harper asked.

"You're the Veronica Mars fan. You tell me."

Harper bowed her head. "Money. She's rich. Maybe bribes?"

I smirked. "Contrary to the movies you love, not all government officials are bad. But I do think she's been able to hoodwink them. By creating her special team of experts, she can tell all the other agencies everything is under control, push them back to the sidelines. As it's not costing the state a dime, they'll be happy to let her lead the way."

"So, who can we tell?"

"I don't know, Harps. I'm not sure anyone will believe us."

Chapter Ten

We ran away from the water, the emerald glow of the algae pulsing at our backs. In the shade of our favorite café, we shared a milkshake and whispered about the green thing in the water.

"What was it?" Harper asked. "What kind of trash can morph into shapes and... and... come after people? Why? Why would it do that?"

"I don't know," I said for the millionth time. I had a headache from the milkshake and the sun and now the air conditioning and the experience with the trash. I was sweating and freezing at the same time.

"This is out of Veronica Mars territory. She never had to deal with anything like this." Harper leaned back, one hand tickling her chin in an exaggerated thinking pose. "It needs a name."

"What does?"

"The monster, of course." Her nose wrinkled. "The Great Green." Her eyes widened as she said it and she spread her hands out dramatically, as if signaling a big reveal.

"The Great *what*?"

"That's what I'm calling it. The Great Green. And we're going to be famous for discovering it."

"If we make it out alive," I muttered.

"We *are* alive, and it's not like we're going back in the water, so—"

"I do not want to end up on the front cover of National Enquirer."

"Speaking of, there has to be something on the news..." Harper pulled out her phone and began scrolling through the news channels, which yielded zero results. She turned to TikTok, Threads, and Instagram, where she found a few stories of something weird in the water, but no one had been able to capture anything on film.

I pointed at her phone. "No one knows what's out there yet."

She reached for the milkshake and sucked down the last mouthful. "So, what do we do?"

"I don't know," I said, again. "What would Veronica Mars do?"

"Go back in the water."

"Yeah... *no*." I shook my head. "I don't want to do that." Danny would. But I wasn't as brave as Danny.

"Me neither. We need a daredevil sidekick." She waggled her eyebrows.

"Yeah, well, we don't have one of those. We're going to have to find a way to get some evidence and tell people."

At the bike racks, Harper hugged me goodbye and

promised to call after her shift at the movie theater so we could talk some more. I braced myself to say "I don't know" another million times.

I zigzagged along the road on my bike, barely able to keep my wheels in a straight line as thoughts of what we'd witnessed resurfaced. A gathering on the beach drew my attention. I screeched to a halt on the boardwalk. There were at least twenty people standing on the beach, a safe distance away from the water. One of them stood out. She had red hair. Regina.

Propping my bike on the beach wall, I hopped over it and jogged down to the gathering. As I approached, recognition dawned in Regina's eyes, but I could tell she had trouble placing me.

"Just the person I was looking for," I said, with more authority than I felt. She was surrounded by her Operation Blue Water goons, along with John from the Coast Guard. I hoped he hadn't fallen for her easy promises. Another couple of inappropriately suited guys looked suspiciously like FBI, but their ID badges showed them to be from the local outfit of the Department of Public Health. Disappointing. I would much rather it be the FBI here to investigate Regina's nefarious deeds. Although there were a couple of other men in suits who had no identification on them whatsoever. Curious. And did I spot the bulge of weapons under their baggy suit jackets? Who wears a suit jacket in ninety-degree heat? Somebody with something to hide.

Regina curled her lips into a fake smile. "Ah, a Green Clean volunteer." She stepped around the edge of the crowd and approached.

"I can't thank you enough for all the hard work you've been doing."

I raised both my eyebrows. "It wouldn't be quite so hard if you didn't produce quite so much plastic."

Her smile faltered and she tucked some stray strands of hair back into her chignon. "Yes, well, as you can see, we're doing what we can now. Going to clean up this trash island." She swung an arm, like I was a five-year-old and expected me to repeat after her.

"Hmmm, yes." I crossed my arms. I noticed Simona in the gathering. She caught my gaze, a warning in her eyes, but I ignored her. "And how is it you're going to do that? Exactly?"

"Sara, everything okay here?" John stepped in, pulling his cap off his head and smoothing down his mustache. "This might not be the best place to air your grievances."

I glared at him. "My *grievances?*"

He grimaced and fiddled with the cap in his hands. For all his skill at saving lives, he was crap at people management.

"It's alright, John. Sara is just a caring citizen," Regina said, injecting some pleasantness into her voice.

Anything I said in front of John would go straight back to my dad. Gritting my teeth, I kept my tone cordial and focused on Regina. "So, what's the plan? How exactly are you going to solve the trash problem?"

Regina stepped closer and lowered her voice. "Yes, well, I'm afraid that's classified. Some high-level science going on that's still being tested, registered for patenting, I can't talk about it yet."

Scoffing, I raised my voice. "How does that explain acid

algae that burns like a bitch when it comes into contact with skin?"

A couple of the Operation Blue Water guys swiveled around, surprise in their eyes. Regina blanched, then covered it with a cough.

John stepped close and hissed in my ear. "Sara, it's all under control. I don't think this is the time or place to make a public nuisance of yourself. We appreciated you calling in about the windsurfer yesterday, but... well... this is a whole other matter. One that's best you don't involve yourself in."

"Or what?" I snapped. "You'll tell my dad?"

John scratched at his balding head, obviously trying to figure out how to get me to stand down. I liked John, I really did, but right now he was in my way.

I turned to Regina. "Yesterday, I fished some cans out of the marina. It was covered in the bioluminescent algae. Got some on my hand. Hurt worse than the time I broke my wrist. Acid. It burned like acid." I paused, gauging her reaction. Credit to her, she hid her surprise well.

"We have a lot of representatives from the Department of Health here to make sure everything runs smoothly."

"We sure do," John said.

Simona pushed through the gathering and placed her hands on my shoulders. "I see you've met Sara Monroe," she said to Regina. "One of the more passionate volunteers of Green Clean."

John chuckled. "That's one word for it."

Regina's hand darted to her chest. "As in Danny...?"

I raised an eyebrow. "The very same. Sister to a murdered brother."

"Sara!" John barked.

Simona's grip on my shoulder tightened.

"Yes, well." Regina straightened her shirt. "I think that's a rather exaggerated viewpoint, but I understand why you feel that way."

"I'm so sorry, Ms. Harron," John said, shooting me daggers. "I can't apologize enough for Sara's behavior—"

"Behavior?" I pivoted toward him. "You don't think anyone should be held accountable for Danny's death?"

"It was an accident—"

Ignoring John, I whirled back to Regina. I wasn't going to let her get away. Not this time. "I didn't think you knew who I was, couldn't seem bothered to answer any of my emails. Thought it would be the least you could do, considering."

Her face morphed into an expression of mock horror. "Goodness! I'm so sorry. I know I replied. I'll have to check with my I.T. team. I'm so sorry, Sara, how terribly frustrating for you."

An apology. Is that what I'd been waiting for? But it wasn't about Danny and it was full of bullshit.

I narrowed my eyes at her. "What about the acid? It's coming from the algae, or the trash or the—" I stopped myself from saying 'monster.' "It's dangerous."

A couple of people in the gathering turned to listen to our conversation.

"Sara," John hissed, pulling out his phone, no doubt to call my dad. "Enough!"

"I assure you, if there is an acid problem in the water, it's nothing to do with EnRG." Regina donned a horrified expression and spoke loud enough for the entire gathering to hear. "But please rest assured, Operation Blue Water is here to deal with any and all circumstances regarding the trash island. We've got FEMA representatives and even the local government working with us. Please don't worry, Sara."

She patted my arm. It stung.

"People are going to get hurt."

Regina looked down her nose at me. "The beach and marina are closed. People are perfectly safe."

I pointed at the green water. "I just got back from going out on my kayak. Unless you set up barricades and have a police presence, you are not going to stop people from going in the water."

John hung up his phone. Dad obviously wasn't picking up. "The Coast Guard is on it, Sara. We're not going to let anyone get hurt."

"That's not good enough, John. My dad's livelihood is made on the ocean. And right now, he can't work."

"So is mine," he snapped. "And we are doing everything we can to get the beach and marina back open as soon as we can. We're in high tourist season, Almond Cove needs the money. I'm well aware of the problems."

"We are dealing with the trash problem, Sara. Rest assured, everything that can be done is being done. We'll have your father back on the water in no time." Regina's eyes flashed, but her voice came out light and fluffy. There was press around. It wouldn't be good for her to get caught being flustered by a sixteen-year-old girl.

"Why couldn't you have done that three years ago? Then Danny would still be alive!" I jabbed a finger in the general direction of her head. "He died because he got tangled up in trash! *Your* trash. Your bright orange plastic sheeting held him down until he couldn't breathe. His Scuba tank ran out of air and he couldn't get free."

"Sara!" John half shouted. "I'm so sorry, Ms. Harron. Sara is obviously still grieving... this harassment is inexcusable..."

I whirled on him. "Harassment? *Harassment*? My brother is dead because of her."

Silence struck like lightning. Everyone turned to look at me. I held everyone's attention. But I lost my voice. This wasn't the way Danny would handle it. He would be clever, stealthy, and never let his anger get on top of him. But he hadn't lost a sibling either.

The moment blew by like an offshore fog. Tentatively, Regina patted my hand. It burned where she touched me. An icy burn of cold-heartedness.

"We're doing everything we can."

"But what about the algae?" I asked.

Regina tilted her head. "What *about* the algae?" She swept a hand at the water. "It's beautiful."

"Took a jar of it home last night," John said, a smile back on his face.

My mouth fell open, but I couldn't get the words out. How could she not see the problem? What was she trying to cover up?

"Sara, I appreciate all the help you've given Green Clean and I'm sorry my messages didn't reach you. Let me make it up to you. I'll send you a case of EnRG, on the house, with the new sustainable materials. How does that sound?"

I just stared at her.

John cocked his head. "Well, that's mighty nice of you, Ms. Harron. What do you say, Sara?"

I said nothing.

Regina smiled. "Good. Consider it done."

She returned to her goons and ignored my piercing glare.

My hands fisted, and I kicked at the sand. "What a bunch of bullshit."

John faced me. "What you did was unacceptable. I keep a loose line on you, Sara, because of your dad being on the board of the marina and all the good work he does for Almond Cove. And because of the work you do yourself for Green Clean. But I will not have you harassing Ms. Harron again. Is that clear?"

"Perfectly," I snapped, then stomped off.

Simona caught up with me. She cupped my elbow and dragged me up the beach, back to the boardwalk.

I stared at my hero, wondering if she was complicit. She hadn't come to my defense once during that tense conversation. But I couldn't see her being in league with Regina Harron.

"Simona, do you know what's going on?"

She looked left, then right, her dark hair trailing over her shoulders as she clicked the gum in her mouth. Her bracelets jangled as she raised her hand and pressed a finger to her lips. "I'm trying to find out. The algae sample I picked up is showing signs of unusual activity."

"I knew it." I dipped my head so I could hear her better. "What kind of unusual activity?"

"I don't know yet. But I noticed some unusually fast replication while I was studying it under the microscope."

"Which would explain why there's so much of it," I said, my gaze moving to the water. The green glow shone as far as I could see and was now apparent in the waves lapping at the beach.

"Exactly. But nothing in nature replicates quite this quickly. I've sent it off to the genetic lab at Scripps for analysis."

"It burns, Simona. It's dangerous." I told her about my experience yesterday with Tyler, but I couldn't bring myself to mention the green arm thing that had chased me back to the marina. Now that I was over the shock of it, it seemed so unreal. I didn't know how to explain it and wasn't sure I believed it had even happened.

I unwrapped the bandage on my wrist and showed her my red skin and the blisters. Most of them had popped and were oozing clear liquid. "I think the algae might be producing some kind of acid when it's stressed."

Simona took my wrist in her hands and examined my skin. "You mean like Halimeda?

I looked at her blankly.

"It's a green algae that produces a chemical deterrent when marine creatures try to feed on it."

"Yeah," I said, thinking about other creatures with defensive mechanisms. Squid were known to sever entire limbs to free themselves, and of course, produce their inky black clouds to reduce visibility, giving them a chance to escape from a predator. There were a few species of mollusks that secreted acid through their skin. Redwood ants squirt formic acid into the air. Stumble on a nest and you're up poo creek. Throw a company with nothing to lose into the mix and God knows what Regina could have created. "Like that. But bigger. More intense."

"More intense?"

I glanced over my shoulder at the milling crowd on the beach. "When I did that extra credit project for biology last semester, it led me down a genetics rabbit hole. My understanding is that we're in the infancy of genetic modification; things are being worked on that the public has no idea about. Chemical reactions of natural organisms can be... *increased*, made bigger, modified, altered..."

"You're right." Gently, Simona wound the bandage back around my healing skin. "I think the algae was genetically engineered to dissolve the trash. The scientists modified the algae's DNA, so its defensive chemical secretion was more acidic, more concentrated, and reproduced quicker. Which would be wonderful, if it works."

My stomach clenched. "That's not what it's doing."

"It's only supposed to react with non-living entities. It's not supposed to hurt people."

"Something has gone wrong."

"I'm going to dig a bit deeper." She touched my arm. "I'll let you know what I find out. But Sara, in the meantime, stay out of the water. And away from Regina."

My hand throbbed, a streaking pain flickered down the nerves in my fingers, although I couldn't detect any worsening damage. Or were there unseen side effects still developing inside my hand? I shuddered at the thought.

Retrieving my bike, I said goodbye to Simona and cycled home to find a taxi hovering on the drive. Dad was running around the house in a flap and a suitcase was parked by the front door.

"Oh, Sara, there you are, thank goodness." Dad raced by, pausing to give me a light kiss on the top of my head.

"What's going on?"

"I'm spending a few days with your mom in Paris, remember?"

"Wait, what?"

Dad touched my shoulder and frowned. "We've been through this a thousand times. You didn't want to come because of the internship application you were working on."

"Oh... yeah. I remember now. I forgot it was today." I looked at his suitcase.

My stomach quivered. Dad was an ex-Navy SEAL. I didn't want him to leave me alone right now. Not when his skills might be needed. But I couldn't tell him why I wanted him to stay; he'd never believe me and would put it down to me being "passionate."

"I'll be gone three nights." Dad stuffed a few last-minute things into his suitcase. "Sara, are you okay? Do you need me to stay?"

Here was my opportunity to tell him everything, but I found my lips clamped and my head nodding.

"I'm okay." I'm not going to ruin this for them. My parents hadn't had a getaway together in forever.

"I thought Harper was going to stay with you?"

"She is."

"And Frank said he'd look in on you. I'm sure Tyler will be here... but not overnight." He looked at me sternly.

As if on cue, Tyler walked through the front door carrying a case of EnRG. "This was on your front porch."

Regina worked fast.

Tyler tore off a printed card from the package. "With a

note from Regina Harron herself." He looked at me. "Did you get this for me? I knew there was a reason I loved you."

"Ha, ha," I muttered.

Dad raised his eyebrows at the case of EnRG cans. "Don't drink it all at once. Has weird side-effects, that stuff."

"I don't intend to drink any of it," I said.

As Tyler plonked the case of EnRG on the coffee table, wrestling one free at the same time, Dad swept through the house once more. While he was grabbing last-minute items, I swiped into his phone and deleted the voicemail from John. He didn't need this stress right now. We could deal with it when he got back. Or forget about it completely.

Dad grabbed keys and his wallet and I handed him his cellphone. He planted another kiss on my head. "You sure you'll be okay?"

"What about the boat?" I asked.

Dad looked out the window toward the beach. "It's not like I can go out right now anyway. I had to cancel all the bookings for next week."

Ignoring the last moment to tell him all, I gave him a hug goodbye and then he was out the door and climbing into the waiting taxi. I shut the door, then stood by the window, watching the green ocean, the rolling luminescence, and mountain of gathering trash.

What had happened earlier? With Harper? A weird hallucination. Green algae monsters didn't exist. But something was caught up in there. Something more than plastic and algae. Something had meant to hurt me.

Dad had left the TV on, turned to the local news channel. It showed a scene at Almond Cove, the sparkling algae stretching for miles and the bobbing trash dwarfing the gentle waves. Scientists and curious people flocking to the closed beach. People out on boats taking samples and pictures, ignoring the closed signs. More people were going to get hurt. There was a scene of Regina and all her goons at the beach, a side shot of me approaching her.

"Look! You're on the news," Tyler said.

I didn't reply. A tremendous sense of foreboding filled me and my hands shook.

"What's up?" Tyler asked, hovering behind me.

I turned to face him then crumpled into the couch, the shock of the last few hours catching up with me.

Tyler knelt at my feet. "What's wrong? Sara? You're scaring me. Should I call your dad?"

I shook my head and breathed into cupped hands as the fear shook through my limbs. I told Tyler everything. About the green arm and the conversation with Regina. He sat on the floor cross-legged, staring at me, his gaze darting all over my face.

"I swear I'm telling the truth," I said.

"I believe you," Tyler replied, surprising me.

"You do?"

"It kind of explains the windsurfer and diver."

I'd almost forgotten about them. "You think the green algae is responsible?"

"If Simona thinks the algae is genetically engineered..." he trailed off. "I don't know. I don't know what's possible. But a company as big as EnRG, they have a lot of money they could throw at a project like that." He put down the bottle he'd been holding and rubbed at the back of his neck.

"There's something even weirder." I leaned closer to him so our lips were nearly touching, but I wasn't interested in kissing him. "On the docks, your EnRG stopped the burning on my hand. Earlier today, when the green arm was after me, I found a can of it in the kayak, opened it and threw it at the... *thing*. It retreated immediately."

Tyler whistled. "It's got to be connected."

"But how?"

Chapter Eleven

An eerie green light streamed through the windows, all the way from the ocean and marina, brightening as the night deepened. I couldn't escape it. A low-grade anxiety settled into my limbs as I thought about all the things it could be.

Possibilities cycled through my mind.

What would Danny do?

He'd made it his mission to rescue anything in trouble. No matter how small, or big. He would never turn down an adventure, no matter how dangerous, like rescuing the lobsters. I could never blame him for being so selfless. Not just with animals, but me too.

I rowed after Danny, the waves calm and the paddle solid in my hands. I'd been in the sea kayaks only a handful of times, but Danny was a good teacher and I had mastered the technique already. Even when it got choppy and the water tried to rip the paddle from my hand, I wouldn't let it beat me. It was more fun then, knowing how powerful

the ocean was, even knowing it could turn me upside down in an instant.

"Where are we going, anyway?" I called to him. We were approaching the cliffs of Manta Ray Bay with the small strip of beach at the base of the rocks. There were two ways to the ribbon of white sand, via boat or down the rocky path from the cliffs above. Danny had been diving here for a few months and wanted to show me something. Although the idea was ridiculous, I had a vision of an old pirate jail with an undiscovered treasure chest bursting with jewels. We'd be famous, interviewed by all the national newspapers. And rich. Mom and Dad wouldn't have to work again and we could spend our days cleaning up the ocean and protecting wildlife. Together.

"It's a surprise," he called over his shoulder.

"I've lived in Almond Cove all my life. There aren't any surprises here." I drifted into the shade of the cliffs, glad of the reprieve from the summer sun.

Danny paddled in a circle, a lopsided grin on his face, his shark tooth necklace glinting in reflected light. "Well, if you must know, it just so happens the last time Will and I were here, we found a portal to another world. Several portals. One takes you to a parallel dimension, another sends you back in time, and a third can take you to the North Pole to meet the polar bears."

I rolled my eyes. "Seriously, Danny! We could have gone to the caves and rescued some sea turtles."

"Oh, we'll be able to rescue animals, alright." He faced the front again and didn't listen to any of my further protests.

I grumbled about stupid make-believe portals, and even though I knew every inch of the caves and beach at Almond Cove, I wished we would find some hidden treasure. Plenty of people had been out with metal detectors over the years looking for belongings left behind by the Spanish conquistadors, scouring the sand until it had been combed ten times over. But I held a kernel of hope in my heart that something existed, somewhere. Ever since we'd taken a trip up the coast to Corona Del Mar and visited the old pirate jail there, I'd envisioned romantic fantasies of pirates and ladies clad in huge dresses and cursed treasure. What would it have been like to live in those times?

In the shallows, we jumped out of our kayaks and pulled them ashore. Danny tied them together and wrapped the end of the rope around a rock so they wouldn't drift away with the incoming tide.

"This way, squirt," he said, splashing through the shallows and heading around the rocks.

I scampered after him, following him up and around the rocks, higher than I'd climbed before, but low enough not to feel scared. After a few minutes, I spied a dark opening in the cliff. Danny shot me a cheeky grin. Could there really be a portal of some kind?

Danny disappeared into the dark opening. My knees trembled as I climbed to the edge and peered in. A rope led down to a huge cavern I'd never been in before.

"Danny?" I called.

His head popped above the surface. "Welcome to Portal Place. Please choose your destination wisely."

I laughed and allowed him to help me through the opening and grabbed onto the rope. We slipped down one after the other. It was a good thirty feet to the bottom and I briefly wondered if I'd have enough strength to make it back up. I dismissed the worry. Danny was here. He'd help me if I got stuck.

Inside, the air was cool and still. The reek of rotting seaweed hung around me, only muted by the stronger scent of salt and sun lotion. I turned in a circle as my eyes adjusted to the gloom. The cavern was huge, at least thirty yards across.

"How did you find this place?" I asked.

Danny jumped off the rope next to me. "I inherited Dad's SEAL stealth. Didn't you know?"

I kicked sand at him. "So, where's this magic portal then?"

Danny nudged my shoulder. "Who said anything about magic?"

"Come on, you're not really going to tell me we're going to the North Pole to meet a polar bear?"

"Is that where you would go? Out of all the choices I gave you?"

I nodded. "I'd love to see a polar bear in the wild. Not stuck in a crappy cage like in Sea World."

"Swear jar, Sara Monroe. You are not old enough to say crap."

"I didn't say crap, I said crappy."

Danny laughed and tackled me to the sand.

"What are we really doing here?" I asked.

He lay back and dug his toes into the sand and breathed deep. "Remember when we were looking at Dad's almanac and all the sea creatures we wished we could meet?"

"Um-hmm..."

"Well, I can't take you to see any ugly deep-sea fish or find out what's in the Mariana Trench, but I can show you this..." Danny looked around the cavern, at the rocks, his head swiveling slowly from one side to the other.

I caught furtive movement as I followed his gaze. Crabs. Everywhere. I gulped. I didn't want to be in a cave full of crabs.

"There, there it is." Danny pointed to the ground where it met the rock wall. I followed his finger but couldn't make anything out.

"What is it?"

Danny crept closer, crawling on hands and knees. Suddenly, something scuttled away from him, scampering over the sand, diving into a hole in the rocks.

"There! Did you see it, squirt?"

"*A flat-tailed horned lizard,*" I exclaimed, inching close to the hole it had disappeared into. "*What's it doing here?*"

"*Who knows?*" Danny replied. "*But they're endangered, so I'm glad it's got a safe home like this.*"

"*Don't they prefer drier habitats? Like inland?*"

"*I think he's surviving okay. Plenty of ants and bugs to feed on in here.*"

I smiled at him. This was almost as good as a polar bear. We could tell Green Clean later we'd had a sighting. They would put it on their map and send a rep down to make sure it was okay. Keep an eye on it. Maybe there were more.

"*Right, squirt, we better get back up the rope before high tide comes and washes our kayaks away.*"

I made it halfway up before Danny had to use his shoulder to keep nudging me toward the opening. When my head poked through the hole, I squinted against the dazzling sunlight. A hot breeze blew my hair from my face as I scrambled over the rocks and helped Danny out after me. The noise of the ocean and the shouts from the boardwalk reached me as we climbed back to the kayaks. In the cavern, it had felt so sacred, private, special. Like we'd really been in a portal that had shielded us from the entire world. Just me and Danny.

Mid-morning, Harper and Tyler came over and the three of us packed a backpack with water bottles and a few snacks. The ominous emerald glow hadn't dissipated with the morning sun. The ocean looked entirely green, although I didn't think it was possible for algae to replicate that fast, even if it was genetically engineered. It must be the reflection of the sun. Even the wispy clouds looked green.

While I scrolled through my Instagram account, looking at pictures of sea creatures, I came across a hazy shot of the green ocean taken nearby. Underneath, there was a caption about frothing green water and intelligent vines. But all the comments dismissed the photographer as a crackpot with photoshop skills. We needed real evidence.

I scanned the news for more substantial accounts. I frowned at the screen. I can't be the only one who'd been hurt. There was no mention of the missing diver or drowned windsurfer. I couldn't find anything significant on the internet either. The Instagram post had a few thousand likes, but no one believed a green monster with vines for arms was sitting in the ocean off the coast of Almond Cove. It was too unreal. The picture was blurry and looked like nothing more than angry green waves. There had to be more evidence out there somewhere. Something plausible.

"It's The Great Green," Harper said knowingly.

"Yeah, maybe, but why aren't people saying anything?"

She looked at me. "Why didn't *we* say anything?"

"We didn't think anyone would believe us. I still don't."

"Exactly," she replied. "Besides, Veronica Mars doesn't need help."

Tyler laughed. "You're not Veronica Mars."

Harper turned a thunderous look on him. "Jerk!"

"But seriously," Tyler said, hands high. "If you did see something, maybe you should report it."

Harper waggled her finger. "Confirmation first. Come on."

We walked the couple of blocks to the marina and dashed along the closed boardwalk. Instead of trying to enter the barricaded dock, we skirted around it and began the climb up the steep cliff path to the bluff on top of the bay for a better vantage point.

It took us an hour to climb up the craggy path. The wind tugged at my hair, loosening it from its band, but at least it cooled the sweat on the small of my back. The caves at Manta Ray Bay where Danny had died were beneath us. So many memories were entwined with this place. This is where he taught me to kayak, where we saw a rare flat-tailed horned lizard, and built a dinosaur castle at low tide. We searched for pirate treasure, listened for mermaids' songs, and body surfed in the gentle waves.

Danny was everywhere for me in Manta Ray Bay.

Avoiding the dangerous overhang, Tyler, Harper and I reached the highest point of the cliffs and stood in a line, sipping on our water canisters. Inside my bandage, my skin was slick with sweat from the climb and the material was turning a murky color. I unwrapped it and trickled cool water from my flask onto the red skin to soothe the irritation.

The sun was strong, but the building Santa Ana gusts kept me cool enough. I stared at the ocean. Apart from the EnRG vessels, there wasn't a single boat or sail visible on the ocean. The green trash inched close to the marina and beach and stretched as far as I could see to the north. The algae formed a wider circle around the debris, turning the water in the bay green all the way to the rocks at our feet. To the south, toward Mexico, the water remained blue. I heaved a sigh of relief.

But my relief was short-lived. The green patch of lumines-cence was double the size of yesterday. The trash island, bigger than I could determine the scope of, sat in the middle of it, gleaming with intent. The EnRG catamaran, stuck in the center of all the trash, looked tiny in comparison. I noted the presence of the Coast Guard's largest vessel, an impressive Legend-class cutter, motoring outside the patch of green. Painted bright white with a single red stripe, it commanded the water and its impressive design gave the EnRG catamaran a run for its money. Had John ordered the boat out to protect Almond Cove's residents or support Regina's mysterious deeds?

"That's disgusting," Tyler said, eyes locked on the green trash.

"If that thing is capable of taking on form..." Harper shuddered. "What if it comes ashore?" she whispered, her eyes large.

I hadn't entertained the possibility, but it struck fear deep into my chest.

"We have to tell someone. We'll make them believe," Tyler said. "If what you say is true—"

I glared at him. "True."

He held up his hands. "Already said I believed you. But if the trash develops a sense of... I don't know... *purpose*... then we're up shit creek."

"What do you think it wants?" I asked.

Tyler shrugged. "Whatever EnRG told it to want."

"That's what worries me," I said.

Harper laughed. "You really think the algae is unnatural? That it was born in a lab? That EnRG created it to... to... I don't know... to kill people?"

"We saw what we saw," I said. "And no matter how it was created or how it came into existence, it's become a problem. So, we need to do something about it. We need Simona to—"

"Hey, look!" Harper pointed to the strip of beach at the bottom of the cove. It was a small stretch of sand, but a half-deflated rescue dinghy nosed the narrow beach. "There are people on it!"

I inched close to the edge. Harper was right. Inside the bright red dinghy, which bobbed on the shallow green waves, were four people, all unconscious. I gritted my teeth, hoping they were alive.

"We need to get down there." Shouldering the backpack, Tyler dashed to the rocky path leading down to the cove. The three of us jumped and leaped, grabbed for handholds and sped as fast as we dared until we reached the beach. It was the same path I'd run down with my parents that winter morning three years ago.

My teeth smacked together as I slipped over loose pebbles and I prayed the people in the boat would meet a better fate than Danny.

"Hey!" I called at the people.

"Hey!" Tyler and Harper joined me.

Tyler stepped closer to the lapping green water. A few feet out, trash bobbed in the waves. I grabbed his hand. "Don't."

"How do we get to them?" Harper asked.

Scanning the rocks, I spotted a fallen branch I thought would be long enough. Helping me to anchor it, Tyler took the weight at one end while I guided the tip toward the deflating dinghy. On the third try, I managed to snag the handhold on the side of the boat and drag it closer. Someone in the boat groaned. Thank God.

"Hello?" Tyler called, as we pulled them onto the narrow beach.

Another groan.

Avoiding the green water, Tyler and I grabbed one of the canvas handholds and yanked the raft further onto the sand so it wouldn't disappear with the outgoing tide.

Four people lay in the dinghy, limbs spread haphazardly, chests rising shallowly. Their skin looked a painful, sunburned red and I wondered how many days of exposure they'd endured. Blisters formed around their mouths, and they'd tried to use a corner of loose tarpaulin as a shade. Empty water bottles lay next to blackened feet. The stench of urine rose from the raft.

Harper grimaced. "How long do you think they've been out?"

"Eesh," Tyler said, crawling into the dinghy. "I've never seen a sunburn so bad." He crouched and pressed two fingers to a lady's neck. Her eyes fluttered and she groaned.

Without warning, she sat bolt upright, her eyes snapping open, and screamed. Tyler stumbled out of the boat, landing on his butt in the sand.

"It's okay!" Harper rushed forward. "You're okay. You're safe."

The scream cut off. The lady looked around, her eyes wild and vacant, until they settled on us.

"Water," she croaked.

I dove into Tyler's backpack, unscrewed a flask of water and handed it to her. Her brown hair was bleached blonde. She swallowed, coughed. It took effort for her to part her lips and a thin line of blood appeared between them. She gulped at the water, most of it dribbling down her chin. But she didn't stop glugging. She gripped the flask in her hands, her cracked fingernails marking the metal canister.

"Too bright," she murmured. "Too bright."

"How long have you been out here?" I asked.

The lady pushed her scraggly hair off her face and managed to kneel. "What day is it?"

"June 18th."

The lady spluttered, then snorted water out her nose. "Feels like we've been out here for days."

Tyler crawled across the sand closer to the lady. "It *looks* like you've been out here for days."

"We left Baja this morning. We've been down there for a week's holiday, thought we could sail around the trash to get home to Oceanside." In the boat, one of the men began to rouse. All together, they were two women and two men. "Celebrating twenty years of friendship. Thank God we left the kids at home. But Rachel and Dan." She shook her head. "Rachel and Dan. They didn't make it."

"They didn't make it?" Tyler mouthed at me, rubbing gooseflesh on his arms.

"Let's get you out of the dinghy," I said.

The three of us managed to rouse the other passengers and get them to solid ground. They collapsed on the sand, in the shade of the cliff, drinking all the water we'd brought with us. Tyler took out his cellphone and held it high, trying to get a signal.

Harper sat with them, crossing her legs, the skin around her eyes tight. "What happened?" she asked. "Are you okay to talk?"

"It doesn't hurt anymore." One of the men nodded. Bald, his head was redder than a fire hydrant. How could it not hurt? "Our yacht was attacked." He looked toward the horizon. "Out there. Out on the deep green sea."

A prickle of fear itched at the back of my neck.

"Attacked? By what?" Tyler asked, scrabbling up the rocks to get a signal and shooting me wary looks. I'd left my own phone at home. After losing it twice during clean-up duties, Dad had insisted I only took it with me if I went out at night.

The four of them looked at each other. The woman who hadn't spoken yet shook her head. With her blonde hair pulled in a bedraggled ponytail, the ends swept against her sunburned shoulders. She shivered as a tear leaked down her cheek. She patted it away, taking care over her raw skin.

"It felt like something grabbed onto the boat and winched it down," the bald man said.

Startling us all, the first woman laughed. The laugh turned into something wild and hysterical, sending a shiver racing down my spine. Tyler came down from the rocks to look at her and Harper gave me a high eyebrow, her lips thin. The woman wore a crazed look in her eyes. She slammed a palm on the sand. "A monster! It was a monster!"

The air around us stilled until all I could hear were green waves lapping gently at the sand. But they weren't benign. Somewhere in the glinting green was a deadly algae.

A gust of wind blew through the cove, lifting my hair and chilling the back of my neck. Harper reached for my hand. I held on to it to find she was freezing. The waves whisked higher, coming closer even though the tide was supposed to be going out. Random pockets of white foam raced toward us like galloping horses. The woman mentioned a monster. I wondered if it had green arms.

Tyler directed a question at the man who hadn't yet spoken and who still, miraculously, wore a pair of glasses. His rugged beard made him look professorial.

"With all due respect, you guys say you went out this morning, but you look like you've been sitting in your raft for over a week. No offense."

"I can't explain it. I can only tell you what I saw. And Marianne is right. There was a green... *something*."

Marianne carried on giggling, a hysterical noise she couldn't control. She held onto her sides and rolled sideways into the sand.

The bald man hitched a thumb toward shore. "I saw a creature. A bright green creature, probably covered in that algae. But it was an impossible creature."

"I'm not a novice on the water," the second man said, pushing his glasses further up his nose, then wincing when they pressed into his burned skin. "But I've never seen anything like this before..." He looked at the other members of his group but couldn't quite bring himself to finish the sentence.

"Marianne is right," the woman with the ponytail said. She spoke so quietly, so seriously, that the icy rod in my spine ballooned to my ribs. "It was a monster. It had a face, and huge glaring eyes. And those arms. So many arms, like thick vines. And they all ended in sharp points. Stabbing, always grabbing and stabbing..."

The other three nodded.

"Got it!" Tyler said, pressing his phone to his ear, then spitting a rapid-fire message to the emergency services.

The woman took a breath and pressed a thumb and forefinger to the bridge of her nose. "I'm an accountant. I deal in facts and figures. Please believe me when I say I'm not crazy. It was made of trash. And green slime. A trash monster covered in bioluminescent algae. So big. So, so big. It was like King Kong. Or Godzilla, or... or... no, it was so much bigger than that."

"And no one spotted it?" Tyler asked.

The lady shook her head. "We were alone on the water... and... and it happened so quickly, *I* almost couldn't believe it."

They confirmed what I already knew. The algae wasn't merely algae anymore. It had combined with the trash and become something else entirely. Something evil. Something dangerous.

"We believe you," Harper said. "We've seen it too."

A shocked silence fell over the group. They stared at us, relief in their eyes.

"You have?" The blonde lady asked.

I nodded. "We've had our own up close and personal with... *The Great Green.*"

The bald man cleared his throat. "It crawled onto our boat and took her under. It shed plastic cups like a dog sheds hair. And after we were all bobbing about in the water, trying to get into the raft, that's when it burned. Man, it *burned.*"

Marianne winced and rubbed at her arms. I detected a few small white blisters the length of both arms and across her chest. The same white blisters that had crawled across my fingers. "I thought I was in hell. Burning alive in hell. I passed out. When I woke up, we were in the raft. And the pain was bearable. But no one knew where Rachel and Dan were. It took them. It killed them. It was so, so big. Too big. Impossibly big."

"The trash island is the size of downtown LA," I said.

All four of them looked at me, shock and resignation on their faces. Then the man with the glasses spoke. "How the hell can we kill a thing like that?"

No one answered. There was no appropriate reply. Sirens sounded in the distance, blaring louder and quieter as an ambulance weaved up the cliff road.

No one spoke. We sat there together, listening to the sound of the waves slapping against the dinghy and the gulls flying overhead. The atmosphere took on the eerie sense of being around a campfire in a vast wood and telling ghost stories. Except, this was so much more than a fabricated story. I knew that. We all knew it.

My brother's voice mingled with the breeze, fierce and urgent, whispering warnings. Almond Cove had become a bad place.

Chapter Twelve

THE INJURED GROUP refused to get into the Coast Guard's boat, they refused to go back in the water. It took three ambulances and six emergency responders to get the four survivors from the dinghy up the cliff path and into the vehicles. The entire process took most of the morning, putting them on stretchers and carrying them up the cliff. We made sure they were hydrated while they waited, and then the three of us spent another hour answering questions from the police. No one mentioned a giant green trash monster. It was on the tip of my tongue the entire time, but I wasn't prepared to face their skeptical looks and a trip to the psych ward.

"Did you see their skin?" Harper asked after the ambulance had driven away.

"Second and third-degree burns," Tyler said. "The third-degree burns probably hurt less. Their black feet? Happens when the nerve endings die."

I remembered the pain of my own second-degree burn. That was bad enough and I didn't want a repeat experience.

Gusting winds flapped my clothes. The Santa Anas had been building for the last couple of days, and their fierceness stung my burns. I could only imagine what the winds were doing to the fire in Sonora right now.

"Will they be okay?" Harper asked, her voice shaky.

Tyler crossed his fingers. "Third-degree burns can cause permanent damage."

I grabbed Tyler's phone and scrolled through it. The only news reports I could find were about how good of a job EnRG was doing. There were a ton of press shots of Regina on the beach, on her catamaran with all her Operation Blue Water staff and a smattering of FEMA employees. Nothing about acid. Nothing about a monster. How was she able to keep this quiet?

If I went to the press, or the police, or FEMA, how would I make them listen to me? John was annoyed at me. I had no hope of convincing him.

When we were free to go, one of the cops dropped us off at my house. I didn't go inside but turned to Tyler and Harper.

"We need to figure out what the hell is going on. And how to stop it."

Harper slipped into the porch swing and folded her legs. "Suggestions?"

"We go find Simona." I turned to Tyler. "Will you drive us?"

Five minutes later, we were on the freeway and heading to Scripps, where Simona worked. I chewed on my lip and tapped the window as Tyler drove. The green algae stretched further up the coast than I liked. And the trash. So much trash. As if the entire garbage patch had decided to unfurl along the California coast.

Tyler's cellphone rang, and when he saw it was my dad calling, put it on speaker.

"Hi, Dad," I said.

"Oh great! I'm glad I reached you." The sound of European honking horns blasted in the background. "I wanted to let you know I landed. I'm here, about to go meet your mom."

"Okay," I replied noncommittedly.

"You okay?" he asked. I could hear the frown in his voice. "I saw about the trash island on the news. It's so big. I'm not sure even EnRG can cope with it."

I bristled. Not only was my ocean, my home, being invaded by the world's trash, but there was a monster too. A presence nobody seemed to know about.

"We're doing what we can. Green Clean. Simona. Even Tyler is helping." I chucked him a smile.

There was a pause on the other end of the phone and a motorbike screeched by in the background. "Sara, maybe this is bigger than you. I think you should stay away from the beach for a while, yeah? At least until I get back."

My pause was equally as long. "Sure, Dad." I hated lying to him, and I was usually bad at it. But this time, he couldn't see my face.

A few minutes later, we arrived at the Scripps Institute of Oceanography. We parked and went on foot in search of Simona's building.

When we entered the foyer, we couldn't get past the imposing security guard stationed by the front desk. He was friendly, at least, and told us she hadn't been in the office all day.

Frowning, I looked at my watch. She said she was waiting on more tests. Wouldn't she be here? I was disappointed I couldn't remember any of her colleagues' names who I could call down to talk to us. But they might not share the information anyway.

"I know where she lives," I said as we got back in Tyler's car. The air conditioning conked out and we rolled our windows down, feeling the wind in our hair. It brought with it the scent of the ocean and something faintly putrid. Probably the trash.

On the way, I tried to remember Simona's cellphone number, but I never bothered memorizing numbers once I entered them in my phone, which I'd left at home. I sighed, punching random numbers into Tyler's phone, getting a couple of strangers on the end of the line before giving up.

We drove a few minutes to the Institute's living areas. Simona rented a small apartment on the third floor with a view of the ocean. The attractive building was Spanish in style, like most of the housing in the area, with curved roof tiles and white walls. Pink roses grew in the beds outside the main entrance and a paved walkway led toward the beach. There were stencils of iguanas on all the doors. It reminded me of the flat-tailed horned lizard I saw with Danny all those years ago.

I pressed the buzzer, my impatience stinging my pores, the blustery winds rankling my mood.

"What do we do if she's not here?" Harper asked.

"She has to be here," I replied.

Tyler chuckled. "She could be out shopping, getting her

hair cut, retrieving more samples..." he trailed off when he caught my scowl.

"I need her to be here," I said as I pressed the buzzer again.

I pressed it five more times, then leaned on it for five minutes straight. Raking my fingers through my hair, I let out a string of swear words and kicked the low brick wall surrounding the roses.

A minute later, a grad student wearing a Scripps T-shirt sauntered up to the door and held it open for us. I smiled at him as we all rushed inside. I took the stairs two at a time as I hurried to the third floor, then stopped short outside Simona's door. It was wide open and hung askew from its sheared hinges.

"What the...?" Tyler looked back and forth along the deserted hallway.

I inched closer to the broken door, trepidation flowing through me. So many people had been hurt during the last couple of days. The diver. The windsurfer. The group on the yacht this morning. And Danny. Always Danny. I couldn't bear it if something had happened to Simona too.

"Not a good idea," Harper said, while Tyler blocked my progress with his hand.

I looked at them both. "What if she's in there? Hurt? And needs our help."

Tyler took his cellphone out of his pocket. "Should I call 911?"

"Give it a minute," I said as I pushed past them and stepped around the broken door.

Inside, the wood-floored hallway led straight to the kitchen and open living area. The balcony doors were wide open, one of them sporting a spiderweb of broken glass, and a deckchair lay upside down on the small balcony. A sea breeze ruffled a stack of paperwork on the kitchen breakfast bar. The glass coffee table between two comfortable purple couches, where I'd spent many a night discussing the fate of the ocean, was shattered. A coconut lay off to the side, as if it had fallen out of a fruit bowl. A picture of a dolphin on the wall hung askew. They were the only signs of a struggle.

Tyler checked the bedroom and I peered into the bathroom. Both empty. Moisture hovered in the air of the bathroom and a fan whirred. Someone had been in here recently. When Tyler and I re-joined Harper in the kitchen, she held Simona's cellphone in one hand and her handbag in another. "Who leaves without taking their phone or wallet?"

I considered her question. I regularly left the house without either. I'd lost too many cellphones to the ocean and saturated too many dollar bills beyond recognition. But Simona was different. She was a responsible adult.

"Is it time to call 911?" Tyler asked.

I narrowed my gaze at the scene. Simona hadn't left willingly. Someone had taken her. "This is Regina Harron."

They both stared at me.

"She did this. She took Simona because she was asking too many questions." My voice rose as I became more convinced by my theory. "Simona is part of the joint initiative. I know she was asking awkward questions, for all of us. And she was running those tests. I bet she found something and confronted Regina."

Tyler walked over to me as he dialed 911. "I think that's

a stretch. Regina isn't some nefarious villain from a Marvel movie. EnRG doesn't kidnap people."

"How do you know?" I asked. I appreciated what I was suggesting was far-fetched. But bad people existed. Bad people with tons of money had a lot of influence and could make other people go away. Especially nosy young marine biologists with renowned reputations who might be able to smear the EnRG name.

It took thirty minutes for the cops to show up and they suggested we wait outside for them to arrive. "Just in case."

It was the same cop from this morning at Almond Cove. He gave us all a questioning eyebrow and remarked at the coincidence of us being at two scenes of interest on the same day. I merely smiled and spread my hands. "I'm lucky that way."

"Civic duty is our motto!" Harper pumped a fist.

When we were finally released, we headed back to Tyler's car and piled in. He drove at a moderate pace back down the freeway, his hand tapping the steering wheel, his lips twisted in thought.

On the way, I used his phone to call the local hospitals, demanding to know if a Simona De La Cruz had been booked in. No one was able to give me the answer I was hoping for.

"It doesn't mean anything," Tyler said, when I thrust his phone in the well between our seats. "It might be she's not booked in yet. The bathroom was still warm. She might still be on her way in an ambulance."

"Regina has her." I gritted my teeth.

Tyler squeezed my knee. "Simona is probably in triage.

Which is good. It means it's not too serious if they haven't rushed her through and booked her straight in."

"Or it's really serious and they haven't had time to book her before tending to her," Harper said, looking over her shoulder through the back window.

I glared at her. "Not helping."

She raised her palms. "Sorry."

"Give it some time," Tyler said. "We'll call around again later."

"Guys." Harper tapped my shoulder. "I think we're being followed."

Tyler's gaze flicked to the rearview mirror, and I turned around in my seat. A black SUV was behind us.

"There's loads of black SUVs in the world," Tyler said.

"I didn't say which car was following us," Harper replied. "And yet you zeroed in on the exact one which is."

"Try switching lanes," I said, watching the traffic behind me.

Tyler switched lanes. The black SUV switched lanes. Tyler moved across two lanes. The SUV did the same.

"Shit," he muttered.

"I bet they've got Simona. I bet they did something to her," I whispered.

"It's not like they can do anything to us, right?" Harper asked, her gaze darting between us. "I mean, they can't run us off the road or anything. There're too many witnesses."

Tyler shifted in his seat, gripping the wheel with both hands. "Witnesses can be fed lines. And gotten rid of. The stories my dad tells..." He shook his head. "Never mind, you don't want to know."

I knew the stories well. My dad had the same. They'd worked together for twenty years.

"I think you were right," Harper said to me, her eyes catching mine in the mirror. "EnRG is behind this whole thing. Why else would we be followed?"

A tendril of fear coiled in my stomach. There was no doubt in my mind something bad had happened to Simona. That something bad might happen to us. EnRG, Regina Harron and The Great Green, they were all connected.

"I bet you it's those FBI types from the beach," I said. "They seemed a bit out of place at the time. I reckon they're some kind of crack security team. Hand-picked by Regina to do her evil deeds."

"What do we do?" Harper asked, her voice squeaking.

"I'm calling my dad," Tyler said, pressing Frank's number.

"Code Red," Tyler said to his dad when he picked up. "Sara's house."

"Be right there," I heard Frank reply.

"Code Red?" I asked as Tyler left the freeway. "What's a Code Red?"

He glanced at me. "You don't have one? With your dad?"

I shook my head.

"I guess my dad's more paranoid." A ghost of a smile played on his lips. "He always said if I was ever in trouble and needed him, he'd come. To say 'Code Red.' No explanations, and he'd come."

Tyler's hand rested on the central console. I put mine over his and squeezed.

The SUV followed us off the freeway. Although I was

scared shitless at their intentions, I was relieved Frank was on his way. No one messed with Frank Williams. He was built like a Mack truck and didn't take no for an answer. He used to terrify me when I was younger.

A couple minutes later, Tyler pulled into my driveway. I was half hoping the SUV would sail on by. But it pulled to the curb and parked. I couldn't see through the tinted windows. How many people were in there? Would they have guns? Would they fire at us?

My throat dried out as I pictured all the possible scenarios of how this could go. None of them good. I should have gone to the press. I should have blown the whistle already.

We sat there. Tyler's engine ticked over. I couldn't stand the tension any longer and put my hand on the door handle.

"Maybe we shouldn't get out," Harper said.

"They can't shoot us in the street," I snapped, throwing the door open. But that's exactly what I was afraid of.

I staggered out of the car. On the way to the front door, I waved at the SUV, pretending to be confident and unafraid. Tyler and Harper scuttled to my side.

All the doors of the SUV opened. Four men, dressed identically in black suits and mirrored sunglasses, spilled out of the car. They crossed the yard like lava gushes over rocks; with destructive purpose, and formed a loose but threatening line between us and the driveway.

"Sara Monroe?" One of the men stood on the first step leading up to the porch. He didn't remove his sunglasses, and I didn't confirm or deny.

I scanned the street, looking for Frank's car, but it was

deserted. Palm trees broke up the sidewalk and a kid on a scooter rolled by, his mom trailing behind. The sun burned in the cloudless sky and a bead of sweat dripped down my spine.

The man pulled out a small notepad from an inside jacket pocket and flicked it open. He tapped on one of the pages with a pen. *Tap-tap-tap.* The rhythm matched the rapid beat of my heart. "Harper Jackson and Tyler Williams?"

Harper reached for my hand, her pinky finger wrapping around mine.

"Don't know them," I said. Tyler shot me a warning look. "What did they do? Rob a bank?"

Tap-tap-tap.

The man's lips pursed, considering. The other three remained mute. I couldn't see through their mirrored glasses, didn't know what they were thinking.

"Nothing like that." The man smiled, his thin lips stretching into an intimidating grin. He gestured to the door. "We should go inside."

All my instincts urged me to run and scream. But judging by the bulging biceps on all four men, I didn't think we'd get far, and I had little faith we could all pile into Tyler's old car and get out of the driveway before they blocked our exit. *Hurry up, Frank.*

I frowned at the questioner. "What did you do to Simona?"

He glanced at his notepad, as if it contained the FBI's most wanted list. "Simona...?"

I glared at him.

Tap-tap-tap.

"We could go inside. If you invite us in, I can tell you what's going on."

"What, like a vampire?" Harper said, gripping tighter to my hand.

The man laughed, his perfectly gelled hair moving like a helmet as his brows rose. He looked at the other three and they laughed too. I didn't like the feeling in the air one bit. Tense and heavy and full of loaded anticipation. I reckoned my chances were better facing off against The Great Green.

Tap-tap-tap. The sound grated my nerves, pulling at my thinly held together composure.

The other three men stepped closer until Tyler, Harper and I found ourselves cornered at the door. Then, a car screeched around the corner. My shoulders sagged with relief as Frank's red corvette came into view and pulled to an abrupt stop behind Tyler's car. He stormed out of the vehicle, pulling his shirt wide so the suited men caught sight of the black handgun nestled in the waistband of his trousers.

"What's going on here?" He stomped up the porch, giving evil eyes to each of the men, one at a time. "And take those damn glasses off so I know who I'm talking to."

In his fireman's lieutenant uniform, Frank commanded immediate respect. His military hairstyle and bull neck added to the authoritative and powerful air. I bet he could take all four of them. My calves quivered as some of the tension leaked out of me. All four men took their sunglasses off. Suddenly they didn't look so scary.

The man with the notepad held out a hand. "Ryan

Phillips. Pleased to meet you. EnRG security team." He said it like we should hold up pom-poms and start cheering.

Frank didn't shake, but moved in front of us like a human-sized shield. "Why does EnRG need a security team?"

"They're a multi-billion-dollar company," the man replied. "The CEO is often concerned for her personal safety."

I bit back on a retort. It was *us* who needed protection from *them*.

Frank eyed him seriously. "I don't see what that's got to do with these three."

Phillips cleared his throat. "We need a word with these kids." He lowered his voice. "We're afraid they've been privy to some classified information which could make them a target."

"Target?" Harper yelped, her hand going to her mouth. "Did he say *target*?"

"It's all right," Frank said to her. "I'm here to sort it all out. No one is after you."

The sun beat down on my back and my stomach clenched tight. I glanced at Tyler. He kept his face neutral, but I knew he'd caught the threat too.

Frank spent an extended moment scanning the street, looking at each of the men and then glancing at us kids. "Okay, so shoot," he said to the man. "Why are you throwing around such weighty words and terrifying a bunch of sixteen-year-olds? Have you no tact? And with no parent present, no less. You do realize you're violating their civil rights?"

Phillips made a similar performance, taking in the palm trees waving in the breeze, watching the kid on the scooter turn the corner, looking through the dark windows of my house. "Shall we go inside? It's a little more private."

Frank's hand moved to the waist of his trousers where his gun rested. Although I couldn't see any weapons on the four EnRG reps, they must have had them concealed somewhere. I didn't like where this was going.

"In that case, I think it's best I have my lawyer here." Frank moved his hand slowly to the front pocket of his trousers. He removed his cellphone.

The other man raised a hand and plastered a placating smile on his face. His bright blue eyes were filled with coldness. "I don't think that's necessary. We just need the kids to sign some NDAs."

I looked at Tyler. He shrugged. What the hell was an NDA?

Phillips clicked his fingers and one of the other men produced a stack of papers.

Frank stood with his feet planted, his finger poised to dial on his phone. He let out a low whistle. "Non-disclosure agreements? Why the hell would a bunch of sixteen-year-olds need to sign something like that? What is it you're afraid they've seen?"

The rep swallowed. *Tap-tap-tap*. "It's a matter of public safety." He scanned the street again. I followed his gaze to the green ocean. But it wasn't an ocean anymore, it was a scrapyard of trash. Green trash. The new playground for The Great Green. "And *personal* safety. We don't want the kids getting hurt. I'm a lawyer too. One little squiggle and this will all be sorted out."

I blanched. Harper gripped my arm with both hands. Frank raised a burly eyebrow. "Are you threatening them? You're a grown man, threatening three sixteen-year-old kids."

Phillips held up both hands this time. "No, no. Nothing like that." Frowning, he paused as if trying to figure out his next tactic. "I wouldn't want anything to happen to them. The ocean... the trash... the algae—"

"What about the algae?" I asked, stepping around Frank.

The four reps looked at each other, helplessly. Then Phillips said, "We can't talk about it unless you sign these." He pointed to the NDAs.

Frank glowered at them. "I'm confused. Why don't you spell it out for me? If there is a genuine safety concern, then it should be one of San Diego's Public Safety agencies here to talk to the kids, not you."

Phillips held Frank's gaze. "As I said, we represent EnRG's interests, not the local government. Operation Blue Water is liaising with the local governmental agencies. It's our job to chase down security leaks."

"What if we don't sign?" Tyler asked.

Phillips stared at him, his expression unchanging, his face an unreadable mask. "That would be unfortunate."

"We could go to the press," Frank said, letting the statement dangle. I liked that idea. That's what they did in all of the thriller movies Harper loved. Always leave evidence with the media in case things go bad. I gulped. I didn't want to have to be in that kind of situation. But here we were.

The rep smiled, as if he'd caught us in a trap. "And who would believe you?"

Frank cocked his head. "I guess that depends on what we say. I think the media will be extremely interested in a story about some EnRG goons threatening a bunch of sixteen-year-olds and the chief of Almond Cove's fire department."

Phillips shifted his weight. "I'm not sure you'd be able to prove it."

They stared at each other.

"Kids today," Frank said. "Kids and their smartphones. They're always recording stuff when you least expect it."

I wished I was recording this, but my phone was inside, probably out of battery, next to my bed.

One of the other agents piped up. He was older, with wispy graying hair and a sunburned scalp. "This doesn't need to get ugly. EnRG doesn't want—"

"Why doesn't Regina Harron come down here and talk to us herself? Let her explain what's going on," I said.

All the reps looked at me. The older guy spoke again. "That's not possible. Ms. Harron is tied up with... well... confidential things..."

Phillips picked up the chat. "We represent EnRG's endeavors to clean up the ocean. They are using new... technology that isn't known to the public. We're worried the kids might have seen it, and that could be a problem. That's all. We don't want to get anyone ruffled."

"New technology?" I goggled at the man. Did new tech include a freaky-ass green trash monster? "How about you tell us what you think we've seen, and I'll tell you if we have?" No way I was putting myself out there first.

A pained smile crossed the man's lips. "No can do, I'm afraid."

I crossed my arms. "Ditto."

"Which is it?" Frank asked, his neck thickening. "Are they in danger? Or did they see something they shouldn't?"

"Well," Phillips replied, drawing out the word. "I guess it depends on the way—"

A car drove by the house. A normal car with a mom behind the steering wheel and two small kids strapped in the back seats. Nevertheless, Phillips whipped his head around and removed a gun from its holster.

I stepped back. Now I knew they were armed, my sassy confidence drained out of me. When I turned back, Frank had his gun out too.

"I think it's time you all left." Frank gestured to the SUV with his gun. "I'm not sure why a bunch of pumped-up security guards are handling this situation. Next time, come back with a warrant."

"I'm a lawyer—"

"I don't want to hear it," Frank snapped.

There was another stare-off. Eventually, the four reps backstepped down the drive.

"Stay away from the water," Phillips said. The expression in his cold blue eyes changed. This time there was concern. "It's not safe out there."

"No shit," Frank said. I resisted the urge to call him out to the swear jar. "There's a trash island the size of LA. No one's going in the water."

Phillips nodded, then the four of them got in their car. They sat there and they didn't drive away. Frank ushered us all inside. We shut all the blinds, and with the house dim, I went around turning on lights. It made me feel better, like we were in a bright cocoon shielded from the impossible happenings out in the ocean. If I couldn't see it, maybe I could forget it had ever happened. But I knew I couldn't wallow in denial forever. If EnRG was coming after me and my friends, how would we defend ourselves against such a large organization?

Chapter Thirteen

Simona, Simona, Simona. *Where are you?*

Before I could process the encounter with the scary EnRG security team, I dashed upstairs to grab my phone. Mercifully, I'd left it charging and it had a full battery. I found the numbers for the local hospitals and started calling. The first one didn't pick up. The second one rang twenty times before a person connected.

"I'm looking for Simona De La Cruz. Has she been checked in?"

"I'm sorry, I don't know. We've been inundated all day. A nasty acid attack and everything is in chaos. Can you call back in a bit?" The person hung up.

Tyler called me from the kitchen. On my way downstairs, I spotted a new email from Mom. I scanned it briefly, wishing she was here. I noted the snapshots of her and Dad in The Louvre—including a picture of the Mona Lisa—and several of them eating snails and frogs' legs near the Sacre Coeur. What I wouldn't give to be there with them, across the ocean, far away from a real-life monster. The end of her email warned me to stay out of the water. She didn't like the reports she'd been hearing and her Instagram account was flooded with wacky stories of an ocean monster. I sensed the panic in her words.

How I missed my parents. They were so far away. But at least we had Frank on our side.

Pushing her warnings aside, I opened Instagram and hunted down the stories. More blurry images and videos. A frothing green ocean, lots of trash, but nothing concrete. There'd probably been a lot of phones lost to the water trying to get footage. The comments below were condescending and derogatory. No one believed the stories. We needed evidence, proper evidence, before we could go to the press.

"Sara?" Tyler called again.

"Coming!"

I dashed down the rest of the stairs and through the living room, ignoring the collection of scenic ocean paintings. Passing the mantle, where the swear jar sat squat and half-full with dollar bills, I made a mental note to add a couple of dollars. It was crowded by several ships in bottles Dad had built. But the biggest in the fleet rested as a centerpiece on the dusty coffee table, knocked askew from when Tyler dumped the case of EnRG Regina had delivered.

While punching another hospital number into my phone, I joined the others in the kitchen. Unwashed dishes sat on the kitchen counter with my half-drunk cup of green tea from this morning. Needing something to do, I poured out a bag of chips into the wooden salad bowl, but no one touched them.

"Okay, what the hell is going on?" Frank demanded.

"On top of the wildfires my station has had to deal with, we're getting phone calls from distressed residents and boat owners. I've treated more acid burns than I can remember. Worse than any acid attack I saw in my SEAL days. People are talking about... *monsters*." He chuckled, but it was a hollow sound. "I know the trash is a problem, but it's just trash. Right?"

"Wrong," I said as my phone rang out. I put it down and focused on Frank.

"I think you better sit down, Dad," Tyler said.

Frank narrowed his eyes at his son, but nodded. "Let me get a glass of water first."

The three of us watched him get a glass from the cupboard, move to the sink and turn the tap on. Water filled the glass, but it wasn't see-through like water usually is. It was green.

"Frank!" I called a warning. But it was too late.

The green liquid slopped out of the cup, covering Frank's hands. He screamed, dropping the glass on the floor, where it smashed. Tyler and I rushed to his side, being careful to step over the sharp shards.

"Guys, step away. Slowly." Harper's voice was cold and serious.

Frank cradled his hand, groaning, and dropped to a crouch. Tyler cupped his elbow so he didn't collapse in the broken glass.

"It burns!" Frank yelled, his eyes wild and unfocused.

I stared at the rushing green water splashing all over the sink. It didn't circle down the drain like water is supposed to do but ran up the sides of the basin. Thin green tendrils explored the steel sink, spreading out like a subway system, searching in all directions. The metal sink clanked and groaned and sloshed. Like there was an animal inside. Green light pulsed from the drain. Green water poured from the tap. No, it wasn't water. It was thicker and darker and almost solid. But it made watery sounds. The green monster wasn't confined to the ocean. It was in the water system now too.

Holding onto his dad, Tyler looked up at me and whispered, "Can you reach the tap, Sara?"

I stared, transfixed by the gleaming water as it filled the sink, snaked across the lip and threaded across the counter. Over the dishes, down the cupboard doors. Exploring faster than a flame seeks an oil trail. Some of the tendrils drifted into the air, as if sniffing for something. Harper backed up until a chair took out the back of her knees and she abruptly sat down. "Do something!"

So much for Veronica Mars.

Green finger-like feelers emerged from the sink. They glinted in the dim kitchen lighting, and the deep glistening green within cast eerie shadows on the walls. The family snapshots pinned to the corkboard shone unnervingly under the strange new light. Beneath a photo of Dad and I at the beach last summer, I caught a triangle of Danny's face. A photo of him with his best friend Will. Danny's smile, a slice of his nose and part of his right cheek were all green. The rowboat painting rattled on its lone screw.

"Oh, shit!" Tyler muttered, ducking away from the searching tendrils and trying to drag his dad out of the danger zone. Blisters bubbled along Frank's neck and hands, hissing green steam.

The fingers multiplied rapidly, until I lost count after

twenty or so. They stretched higher, hands following them, spreading across the counter and down the cupboards to the floor. Picking up the glass shards of the cup Frank had dropped, the fingers grew nails. No. Not nails. *Talons*. Curled and wickedly sharp, they clawed at empty air, using the glass fragments to give itself substance. Another gathered my teacup, a third stole the silverware stacked at the side of the sink. Five others broke the dirty dishes into sharp porcelain shards and ingested it all. The green tendrils consisted of more than water, using my kitchen utensils and crockery to morph themselves into something far deadlier.

I inched forward, reaching out for the tap, my entire body quaking with the anticipation of being burned. The hands tried to block my way. A six-inch kitchen knife, held aloft by a thickening green arm, hovered over my head. I held my breath and tried again. I remembered the pain, how much it hurt, the same pain Frank was now experiencing. I wasn't up for a repeat.

With a quick inhale, I darted forward and snapped the tap off. The hiss of rushing water cut off and we were left in a whirring silence, apart from Frank's plaintive yelps. His eyes rolled wildly and he gritted his teeth. Some of the water gurgled down the drain. Most of it remained. Grasping green claws found the edge of my shorts and held on, burning holes in the denim and irritating my skin.

Tyler yanked the gun out of Frank's waistband and fired. The boom reverberated in my ears. A wisp of smoke trailed to the ceiling. The hand stopped, letting go of my shorts, and the bullet passed through its palm and wedged into the wall beyond.

"Double shit!" Tyler said.

Frank screamed again as one of the tendrils crawled up his neck, nicking him with the sharp glass talons. The kitchen knife dropped, taking a slice out of my calf muscle.

I screamed along with Frank.

"What do we do?" Tyler yelled, his frantic eyes searching my face.

In the sink, some of the green threads started to slip back down the drain, but there was so much of it, crawling on the counters and slithering on the floor, carrying sharp shards of glass and metal and porcelain.

"EnRG," I gasped. "We need EnRG. There's the case in the living room."

Tyler batted a green tendril off Frank's neck.

Inches from the sink and surrounded by deadly green vines, I was afraid to move. Slowly, I turned my head to look at Harper. "Can you go?"

Nodding, she pushed herself off her chair and fled the room. She was back a few seconds later with two bottles of EnRG. I unscrewed the cap on one and poured it over Frank's hand and head. The blisters on his hands stopped hissing and his eyes cleared.

I opened the second bottle and poured it in the sink, sprayed it along the counter and floor, anywhere I could see a hint of green or broken glass or metal fingers or anything out of place. Harper brought me more bottles and I went through half the case, saturating the kitchen with bright orange fizz. The remaining green water hissed and burbled, creating a cloudy steam. It dropped the silverware and chunks of porcelain, then effervesced back down the drain. The sink shook, like all of its nuts and bolts were coming loose. A great metallic groan burped up from the drain.

Then a horrendous sucking sound stole all the noise from the room, including my own panicked heartbeat. The Great Green drained away, leaving the sink clean and shiny. No hint of a green glint.

Exhausted, I slumped into a chair. The dangerous shards of glass lay at my feet and glistened on the countertop. Glass. Just Glass. No wonder there wasn't much verified evidence online. Taking photos during the last few minutes had been the farthest thing from my mind.

With Tyler's help, Frank got to his feet, flexing his fingers and examining his skin. Red and lined with blisters, but it looked like he got away without any third-degree burns. Tyler sat him at the table and inspected his skin. Frank bathed his wounds first in EnRG, then bottled water, while Harper swept up the remnants of glass. Then she pressed a wad of paper towels against the cut on my leg, mopping at the blood running down my calf.

"How bad is it?" I asked through spread fingers.

"It's not too deep. You're going to be fine." She finished cleaning up the wound and wrapped a bandage around my leg.

"We should get you both checked out at the hospital," Tyler said.

Looking up from a bowl of bottled water and dabbing his face with a paper towel, Frank said, "Will someone please explain to me what the hell is going on?"

Chapter Fourteen

FRANK STORMED out of the house, his footsteps pounding the sidewalk, his fists pumping. He hadn't even let us bandage his burns. "No one is going to take over my beach. No one is going to tell me I can't protect my ocean. No ridiculous comic book monster is going to hurt my kid... And as if I don't have enough to deal with, with all the wildfires! Worst fires for decades."

The four EnRG reps slunk out of the car, their dark suits like black shadows. Phillips stood by the car, his hand on the door, watching.

We ran after Frank all the way to the marina, yelling at him to stop. The reps followed at a cautious distance. Their mirrored sunglasses were pulled down and I couldn't read their expressions. Could they kidnap us in the middle of the day?

With dread filling my limbs, I noticed the path to the beach was completely deserted. No one sat on the beach, or walked the boardwalk, or browsed the tourist shops and restaurants. Everything was closed. It reminded me of when there'd been a bomb threat in one of the beachside restaurants a couple years ago.

A few official types walked near the lapping green water. Some had "Operation Blue Water" stenciled on their backs, others had the bright yellow lettering of FEMA. Relief took some of the sting out of my worry when I spotted the FEMA reps. They were a national organization. Regina couldn't possibly control them too. But did they have any idea what was out there?

"Dad, it's too dangerous." Tyler tugged on his arm.

"Seriously, Frank." I jogged beside him, wincing against the sting in my leg. "Tyler is right, you saw what it did in the kitchen."

"Those reps are following us too," Harper said, casting nervous glances at our backs.

Frank whirled around, eyeballing us all and jutted a finger at the ocean and the EnRG catamaran. "If that ridiculous boat and its entire fleet of vessels can float around in the middle of all that trash, then I'm damn well going to take my boat out too. Then we'll see what's what."

I stopped arguing. Frank was going to do what I wanted all along. What I'd tried to do until The Great Green had attacked my kayak. Frank needed to see it for himself. Maybe with a grown-up on board, things would be different. I didn't pretend to understand how the monster worked, how it chose its targets or when it decided to release its acid, but I wanted to learn. Understanding its behavior was crucial to neutralizing it. Despite the presence of Operation Blue Water and FEMA on the beach, I had a feeling EnRG had tied their hands.

What the hell had Regina created. And why?

When the marina came into view, I noted two Coasties manning the entrance. Although we wouldn't be able to get past them, at least they would be witnesses to any action the four reps might take.

The marina itself remained trash free, but the water was entirely green. Like the Emerald City in *The Wizard of Oz*. But this water wasn't a sanctuary, it glistened with menace. It lapped at the berthed vessels, a lulling whisper on its breath. My stomach sank as I couldn't spot a single fish in the shallows. Did that mean the algae had marked its territory? Danny's face filled my mind, and he yelled at me to turn around. But I couldn't. He had died because of ocean trash. I couldn't let anyone else die such a horrible and unnecessary death.

"I'm coming with you." I elbowed past Tyler.

He shot me two raised eyebrows. "I don't want either of you going out there." He turned to his dad. "This isn't something you can kill with a gun."

"Worked pretty well for you in Sara's kitchen," Frank snapped, and started storming toward the two security guards.

"I merely startled it——"

"Son," Frank whirled around again, "No big corporation, no shady security agency is going to tell me what I can and can't do when it comes to protecting my kid, my beach, my ocean, or the responsibility I have to my residents. Okay?"

Tyler nodded and remained silent. This was the side of Frank that had always terrified me. When we'd been caught out late one night at the beach after curfew, he'd found us, marched me back home with fury rippling off his bulging neck muscles, sat us on the couch and gave us a murderous eye. He didn't need to say anything. I received his message loud and clear, and Tyler and I never broke curfew again.

Now I'm glad he was on our side. With his Navy SEAL background and current career as a chief in the fire department, he was going to kick some green trash monster ass.

Behind us, the four reps in black suits followed, keeping a safe distance but letting us know they were there. At the end of the boardwalk, we approached the marina entrance. It was blocked with temporary barricades. John and another Coastie were the ones who flanked the wooden steps.

John held out a hand, the thick commendation ribbon on his breast pocket shining in the sun. "Can't let you go in there, Frank."

"Aye, John," Frank nodded. "I understand. But I've had word my boat's been vandalized. I need a quick check to make sure she's all right."

He lied seamlessly. Maybe it's what you needed when you were involved in stealth operations. Like now.

John swept a scrutinizing gaze over us, his suspicious eyes settling on me. I gave him my best, innocent smile. "Why don't you give me her berth number and I'll run down and check."

Frank dipped his head. "You might not notice anything. I had some valuables…"

John shook his head. "You know you shouldn't keep valuables on the boat, Frank."

Frank's lips twisted in a parody of *gee shucks*. "I know. I know. Wife's told me enough times. But I need to check. I'll be super quick. I can leave the kids here as collateral." He laughed, a great barrel of a laugh that startled a nearby gull.

I laughed along with him, but there was no way I was getting left behind. I shot a glance over my shoulder and noted the security reps hovering in the shadows, watching.

"I wasn't born yesterday," John said, staring at me again. "I don't know why you're here, or what the hell you think you're doing trying to get near this goddamn awful trash, but I know you're not here to check on valuables."

I pointed a finger at him. "If those valuables aren't here when the marina is open again, it will be your fault."

"Leave it, Sara," Frank muttered. "John is right. He's not stupid."

"We go back a long way," John said to Frank. "Our departments work closely together. Let's not put a strain on that."

I refused to let it go. "Do you even know what's going on in the ocean? The trash isn't just trash."

"You're right, it's not just trash." John took off his garrison cap and rubbed his balding head. "It's part of the Eastern Garbage Patch. It's a catastrophe, sent to test us all. Thank the Lord for EnRG."

I goggled at him. "No mention of Green Clean and how hard we've been working for years and years."

"Green Clean is a fantastic organization, but let's face it, they don't have the money for a clean-up this size." John chewed on his lip and fiddled with the brim of his cap. "We appreciate your work, Sara.

"Didn't feel like that yesterday."

"You can't go around harassing CEOs who are cleaning up our ocean. Regina is our best chance of getting the ocean back to normal before the July Fourth celebrations start. Our town makes a lot of money from that one weekend."

I threw my hands in the air. "What, so you trust her blindly?"

"There are a lot of organizations here, Sara. Not just Operation Blue Water. Working together. Perhaps if you had more of a team spirit, you'd see that."

"Team spirit? This isn't about *team spirit*. Gah!" Anger steamed from my pores. "Have you even been in the ocean recently?"

"The ocean is closed." John hardened his gaze. "I haven't heard back from your father. You tell him I still want to talk to him."

"He's in Europe," I muttered.

Frank stepped in front of me. "Sara is under my care while her parents are in Europe. So, anything you want to say to Noah, you say to me."

John touched Frank's shoulder. "You should get on your way, Frank. I know you've got your hands full with all those wildfires. Climate change has made the Santa Anas spring up at unusual times, spreading flames everywhere inland. I don't know how your crew is managing without you..."

Frank's ears turned pink. "Goodbye, John."

Without another word, Frank ushered us around the corner to the small path that snaked around the back of the marina and led to the cliffs above Almond Cove.

"I can't believe John is playing the clueless act. His cutter has to be out there for a reason." I pointed to the ocean and the distant white vessel.

"Aye," Frank said. "Something's not right here."

"What now?" Tyler asked.

"We go in through the back door," Frank said, weaving a determined path along the winding trail.

Hoping to keep the EnRG reps from noticing where we were going, we broke into a jog. But it wasn't long before I heard the clip-clop of dress shoes running behind us. I shot a look over my shoulder to see the reps gaining on us.

"Stop!" Phillips yelled, his sunglasses hanging askew. "You can't go in the water."

We ran faster. When the main entrance was out of view, Frank crouched, parted a chain fence, and dropped ten feet to one of the finger piers below. The impact of his landing made the pier wobble and a ripple of green water spread across the narrow channel. A puff of green steam rose from the water, as if The Great Green was waking up. Maybe this wasn't such a good idea.

"Come on," he urged, offering us each a hand, "before those reps catch up to us."

One by one, we dropped down to the dock. Tyler helped take the impact away from my injured leg. The EnRG guys arrived and leaned over the railing.

"Step away from the water," Phillips called.

Frank whirled around, his burned neck flushed with fury. "Tell us what's really out there—what EnRG's done—and maybe then I'll talk to you."

The lead rep shook his head. "Sign the NDAs, then we'll tell you anything you want to know."

Frank mirrored the rep's action and shook his own head. "No can do."

He began walking backward along the dock. The rest of us followed. I threw a glance over my shoulder. The four reps stood in a line, watching us. Phillips rested a hand on the butt of his gun, but he didn't pull it out of its holster. His brow was deeply furrowed, his foot tapping the ground. He put a hand on the chain as if to follow us, but remained on the path, not looking at us but at the green water.

"They're not going to follow us," Harper whispered. "They're afraid of The Great Green."

A shiver ran through me and my bandaged wrist ached. I didn't know how Frank could stand the ocean breezes brushing against his burned skin.

I narrowed my eyes at the shrinking suits. "Which confirms EnRG knows exactly what's going on."

"Then why aren't they doing anything about it?" Tyler asked, walking next to me.

"Maybe they can't," I replied. "I mean, look at John's reaction. He's acting completely clueless, but anyone who goes on the water must know what's going on. Regina must have something over him."

"Probably offered to finance his next year of bonuses," Harper muttered.

Frank pulled at his jaw. "I don't think so. John's always been an upstanding member of the community. You'd find his name in the dictionary next to integrity. I think it's good old-fashioned denial. He's worried about the town and sees trusting Regina as the easiest way out of this mess."

"I'm disappointed in him," I said.

"Aye, me too," Frank replied.

"Can FEMA help?" Tyler asked.

I shook my head. "FEMA won't be able to stop EnRG. They don't have experience with this kind of thing. We need one of those secret governmental agencies who can handle people like Regina Harron."

Harper nudged me, a small smile on her lips. "Like Mulder and Scully."

We reached Frank's motorboat. It was small but powerful, and I was sure it could outrace a trash monster.

I recalled the four shipwrecked survivors, how blistered their skin was, how raw their scalps were. I shuddered. But we would be prepared. If The Great Green came for us, we knew what to expect. It was a small comfort.

Frank made us all put on life jackets. I wasn't sure they'd help if we got swallowed up by several thousand tons of trash, but fastened it anyway. He flicked the engine on, and we shot out of the marina like a speeding bullet.

I waved at the four reps as we streaked by, their mouths gawping.

Frank looked at us as he steered, heading straight for the trash. "So where is this motherfucker?"

Instead of answering his question, I said, "Maybe go around the trash, not into it. The rudder will never survive."

Frank had never been one for subtleties. When he and Dad worked together in the Navy, Dad was always the brains behind the operation, Frank the brute force. The one who would 'interview' the prisoners under the cone of a dome-shaped light.

I watched the ocean, looking for signs of an attack. The EnRG catamaran sat unaffected on the pile of trash, like the king of the dump. Was Regina in there, watching us? Was she holding Simona prisoner behind those dark windows? As soon as I got back to the house, I would call the hospitals again.

Blue gas cans dotted the largely green mass of trash. Torn Styrofoam rested on splintered planks of plastic. Six-pack rings entwined themselves around various scraps of translucent plastic. Plastic everywhere. Plastic wrap, plastic food containers, plastic straws, plastic milk bottles. Milk bottle lids and tin cans and stuff no longer recognizable from its original purpose. And a ladder. A full-size wooden ladder right in the middle of it all. I'd seen pictures of trash islands before, but the reality was a hundred times worse. And it was all so green. A green so bright, so brilliant, it was hard to look at. Like staring at snow on a ski slope. The green radiated out of every niche and crevice within the trash. It seeped out of the water and discolored the air five feet above the surface with its jade-green light.

The Coast Guard cutter loomed on the horizon on the far side of the trash. I was sure John had seen us jetting away from the marina and was now probably calling for backup.

"Let's go talk to those EnRG people." Frank yanked the wheel and we made straight for the insectile catamaran.

We cut a path through the trash, our wake spreading out bottles, water canisters, old netting and takeout containers, plastic bags and a multitude of straws. Toothbrushes, cigarette butts, children's toys, bottle caps, water coolers, even an entire kiddie playhouse. Styrofoam cups bobbed on the surface, tangled up with six-pack rings and a multitude of plastic sheeting. Everything was green. Sparkling, eerie, alien green. And there were no fish. I couldn't blame them. If my home had been invaded, I would have emigrated too.

From one of the smaller vessels, someone spoke over a foghorn. "You are entering unsafe waters. Please turn around. You are entering unsafe waters. Please turn around and go home."

Before we could respond or even attempt to turn around or carry on to the EnRG vessel, the trash surrounded us. It moved against the current, circling our small boat and slowing our speed. I couldn't spot any green appendages, but I knew they wouldn't be far away. Within the murky trash, darting movement caught my attention. But it wasn't fish. Dark shadows flickered between the trash. Different sizes, winking and zipping so fast I could barely keep track of them. I had the impression of eyes. Lots of blinking eyes following our progress. Dread froze the back of my neck. When it had been burning green vines, the monster had appeared rudimentary. But eyes led to a soul, led to a brain. And I had no idea what that implied.

"What do we do?" I asked, tightening my life jacket. The boat slowed as a wall of trash grew around us.

Harper wrinkled her nose and Tyler retched, doubling over the side of the boat. A terrible stench rolled toward us.

I scanned the water. There were dead fish... everywhere. And other large animals; dolphins, seals, and juvenile shark carcasses intermingled with the trash. Some of them floating belly up, their silver stomachs turned green. But mostly, they were scraps of flesh and bone. Tyler pulled the neck of his T-shirt over his nose. I took short, shallow breaths through my mouth, but it didn't stop my stomach from rolling or my tongue from tasting the vileness of rotting flesh.

The foghorn blasted again. "You are entering unsafe waters. Please turn around. You are entering unsafe waters. Please turn around and go home."

"I'm not sure we *can* turn around anymore," I muttered.

Frank continued in his single-minded trajectory, pushing

the throttle to the max. The boat whined and skipped over the trash, shuddering violently. The EnRG catamaran wasn't far away. It was surrounded by the smaller Operation Blue Water vessels, like a chain of defense. Off to the side, the smaller boat belonging to Green Clean bobbed in the water forlornly.

The stench of decay mingled with something else. The faintest trace of salt, but also something heavier, something more putrid I couldn't define.

"Holy mother f—" Tyler's eyes went wide and his brown skin paled.

"Tyler! There's no need for... holy shit!" Frank yelled, releasing his gun. In the water, a whirring noise came from the middle of the trash.

The boat sputtered to a halt—rudder jammed. Dead in the water.

The wake of the motorboat rippled away from us and we bobbed on the currents, knocking into the green, sludgy trash.

"I want to go home," Harper said, her eyes filling with tears. "I don't want to be a private detective anymore."

"I think we're pretty stuck," I said, plonking down in a seat. The entire scenario played out in my mind. EnRG would send one of their boats over here, take us on board their evil catamaran, and we'd never be heard from again. Just like Simona. We couldn't go anywhere. And there was no way I was going to make a swim for it. I was ninety percent sure we'd all drown or be burned alive. Is this how Danny had felt when he knew he wasn't going to make it?

I missed my mom. I missed my dad. I missed Danny too. So, so much.

And I hated Regina Harron. The emotion burned through me. This was all her fault.

Frank bent over the rudder, hoisting it out of the water to find it entangled in putrid, shining netting. "Tyler, hand me my knife."

Tyler scrummaged under the seating and came up with a ten-inch hunting knife. Frank started hacking away at the netting. One of the EnRG vessels started up, making a path toward us.

The trash around us grew, like it was building an enclosing wall. Would it offer us up to the EnRG vessel? Or take us down into the depths where we'd all be dissolved by a violent green acid?

"Hurry!" I said.

Frank sawed the knife back and forth, but there was so much netting, and the boat was getting closer. The ocean started burbling and those awful winking eyes appeared all around. Winking and blinky. Green slits in circles of black, following us, watching us, staring at us. If it had a mouth, I was sure it would speak. No, not speak, roar.

"Sara." Tyler grabbed my arm. Green waves lapped at the boat. But they weren't just waves. Within each small crest, the glowing green produced something else. Tendrils. Attached to thicker arm-like branches. Scrabbling at the hull. Each attempt reaching higher. First, a couple of inches. Then half a foot. Then a foot. Then higher. We shrank back.

"Get me out of here!" Harper curled into a ball and threw her arms around her head.

A skittering sensation flashed down my limbs, making

them weak and trembly. My mind went into freefall. I couldn't think straight, could only stare.

The tendrils were longer than my arm. Made of scraps of plastic, the searching shoots scratched at the hull. Their joints consisted of glowing green sponge, riddled with strands of putrid seaweed. It thickened and grew, new appendages shooting off in every direction from each of the original branches. The tendrils became vines and weaved through the trash, adding more to its mass, constantly growing. It gathered straws and cups and containers and scraps of plastic and chunks of Styrofoam, all the time adding to its bulk until it became this great hulking mass sprouting from the ocean. Multiplying. Always multiplying, until the vines snaking through the trash were too many to count. Each limb glowed with the eerie green bioluminescence.

"Hurry!" I yelled at Frank.

"Dad! Look!" Tyler yelled.

"I can't look! I've got to free the goddamn rudder!"

When one green arm, made from an assortment of plastic bottles, torn sponge and food containers, came stretching up to the rim of the hull, I screamed. The limbs bent at unnatural angles, twisting with wet squelches and guttural sucking noises, shedding drops of alien green. One more effort and it would enter the boat. My hand burned in anticipation.

Curse words flew from Frank's mouth as he yanked the rudder free and went for the starter button. Tyler, Harper and I huddled as low as we could get in the ancient speedboat, hoping it wouldn't quit on us.

The boat sped in a wild circle, churning trash and green water into the air. The vines waved above our heads. Each appendage ended in a sharp point. Eyes blinked open along their lengths, watching. Harper covered her ears and screamed. Finally, the motorboat gained traction and we shot off in the direction of the marina.

As Frank steered, the rest of us hung onto the handrails. Tyler put an arm around my body and anchored me tighter, whispering in my ear words I couldn't hear over the whine of the engine and the slap of the waves and Harper screaming. But his tone was reassuring, and I tried to focus on the feel of his body touching mine. His smell. His everything.

"Faster, Dad! Faster!" Tyler yelled.

But his words were a curse. For the boat slowed, almost to a stop. We hadn't made it out of the trash and dead animals rocked against us, their stench overwhelming. The arms made noises. The glowing trash arms skittered and searched like a mischief of angry rodents trapped behind a wall. Both starboard and port side. Both stern and bow. The skittering. And clunking and bashing and thumping sounds.

The boat stopped. The skittering noise overwhelmed everything else. Frank yelled that the rudder was fine. Then, with breakneck speed, like a rollercoaster, the boat was yanked backward. I held my breath. Tyler yelled in my ear. He let go of the grabrail and we both tumbled into the cockpit.

"Shit!" Tyler yelled as splashes of green liquid—much thicker than water—crawled up his arm. The drops, oddly resistant to gravity, scurried all over him on unseen legs. "It burns!"

So quickly. Sometimes it seemed the burning was delayed; other times, it was immediate. Maybe it depended on how threatened The Great Green felt, what kind of mood it was in.

The vines waved above our heads, blocking out the sun, sprinkling green water over all of us, pricking us with splash burns. They grew claws of sharpened plastic and descended. The green claws wrapped around Tyler's wrist. With the boat rocking wildly, I struggled to his side. Clasping my hands around his arm, I prepared for a deadly game of tug of war.

One by one, Tyler picked off the talons. But as soon as one came loose, another tightened around his wrist. "Double shit!"

I bent down and tried to help, clawing at the fingers with my nails, but like barnacles on a whale, they were welded fast to his skin and my own fingers began to burn. The green talons tightened their grip. And shook. Shook his hand again and again until the violence juddered off my hold on him. Tyler screamed as blisters formed on his wrist and steam rose from his skin.

A head emerged from the water. Compact and solid, as if the trash had turned to flesh, muscle and bone. A skull, looking like it had been made in a scrap yard. So big, so putrid, it peered at us with huge, green eyes and hovered above us, balancing on its trash torso. Dripping with tendrils of rotting flesh, grinning at us manically, it opened its slash of a mouth as if to speak. It held its burning vines high in the air and smiled, showcasing all of its parts and the long sharp teeth in its plastic mouth.

Harper crawled to us, using her long fingernails to dig at the green tendrils around Tyler's wrist.

One green hand rested on the lip of the boat. Followed

by a second. The boat heaved, tipping dangerously. Harper and I freed Tyler, the acid-like substance searing our fingertips.

Screaming, clutching his wrist, Tyler collapsed to the floor. Writhing in pain, he held his wrist to his chest. His eyes rolled and he kicked out, managing a solid connection with one of the monster's appendages. The green skull turned toward Tyler. Expanding, bigger than a grocery trolley until it reached the size of a small car, then the skull laughed through its broken mouth. The horrible sound drilled into my core. Like metal sparking against metal, it sent vibrations through my chest.

Wrestling with the tiller, Frank pushed it one way, then the other. With Tyler on the floor and the boat tipping wildly and two long green arms dripping toxic goo all over the bottom of the boat, I didn't know what to do. I had a moment. Maybe my life flashing before my eyes. The sadness of my parents. The weight of their disappointment in my poor decision-making process. The imminent reunion with Danny. I dreamed of seeing him again. But not like this.

I refused to go out like that.

Gathering my courage and chomping down on the scream in my throat, I gave the monster my best death stare. It seemed to consider me for a moment. Tyler thrashed and screamed. Steam rose from his wrist. White blisters burbled and hissed. Scurrying through the lockers in the boat with trembling hands, I found what I was looking for and sent a silent prayer that Tyler was so predictable. The six-pack of EnRG gleamed brighter than a beacon. I released a can, shook it as hard as I could, then popped the tab. Aiming at the hovering monster, I sprayed it in the face. It shrieked, its face melting and steaming back into the ocean, but its tendrils didn't let go of the boat. Grabbing the side of the boat for balance, I kicked out with my right foot, connecting with the monster's ugly mouth. I kicked again and again and Harper hit it with a wrench. It shuddered, fell backward, and lost its grip on the boat.

The hull slammed back to the water. Frank swore and pushed the throttle, which whined in protest. Harper huddled on the floor.

Frank leaned against the throttle with his whole body, and finally, the boat catapulted forward, up and out of the sea of trash and decay, like a rocket taking off. Speeding away from the trash, I afforded a glance at the EnRG catamaran. Regina stood on the deck, her hair flapping in the wind, a pair of binoculars trained on us.

Popping the tabs of the rest of the EnRG, I poured it over Tyler's wounds. His screams dimmed to a muted whimpering. He gasped as the liquid doused his burns and turned his hands over, looking at the extent of the damage. Both his hands were red and one wrist sported an ugly bracelet of blisters. Harper and I both had raw, red fingertips. But there was something in the EnRG drink which neutralized the acid and made the pain go away. Silver linings and all that.

Once we tied up the boat, we all remained on board, not speaking, unable to put into words what we'd been through.

Frank took out a bottle of whiskey from the same locker I'd found the EnRG, unscrewed the cap, took a long pull, and offered us all a sip. "Fuck me."

"Swear jar!"

Chapter Fifteen

WE CLIMBED out of Frank's boat, keeping our heads low. I scanned the docks for the EnRG goons but couldn't spot them anywhere. Maybe they'd hoped one of the EnRG boats had picked us up.

"That was..." Frank's fear-filled blue eyes glinted in the sun. I'd never seen him afraid before. Not Frank. "That was... I don't know what that was." He looked at me. "You said the trash island was the size of LA. Does that mean the monster is too?"

Harper gulped.

"I guess," I replied, relieved the trash still hadn't made it into the finger piers. But that didn't mean the algae couldn't combine with something else and attack us here. "I don't know. The head thing, the arms... it was only a section of it."

It felt weird talking about it out loud, as if giving voice to it made it real.

Tyler rubbed at his wrists where The Great Green had restrained him, the resulting blisters red and oozing. "It doesn't need to be the size of the whole trash island to take us out. It only used a fraction of its size. We're insignificant."

"But we got away," Harper said, wrapping her hair around a fist. "We got away. So maybe it can't use its entire mass."

I shook my head. "The entire trash island is green. All of it covered in the algae. I reckon it can use all its mass, but it hasn't figured us out yet, how much of a threat we are, or how to take us all down. But it will." I looked at each of them, the surety of my words sinking through my sun-flushed skin. "It will."

"Not on my watch," Frank said. "We need to get there first. And I don't care if it's the size of a large city, we're going to take it down."

"Hard agree," I replied.

Frank crouched over the boat. Inside, there was a puddle of water in the corner. Not just water, but tinged a faint shade of green. A milk bottle cap floated in the middle of it. A distorted one that looked more oval than circular. It continued to change. The edges became rough, as if sprouting antennae and searching for something. The main body? It must have fallen loose from the trash monster. Could it grow and morph away from its parent?

"Doesn't look so dangerous now," Frank muttered.

"We need to get out of here," Harper said. "And come up with a plan."

"Any plan needs to involve FEMA and people who know how to fight this thing," Tyler said.

Frank stared at the water, his expression hard enough to cut diamonds. "I'm not sure they can handle it."

"We have no idea what this thing is capable of." I brushed my arm against Tyler's. "What if it takes over the ocean? Spreads around the world? It already got into the water system. What if it spreads... everywhere? And people start drinking it?"

Tyler grimaced. "Burning from the inside out."

Harper's eyes whirred with fear. "Everywhere?" she whispered.

Frank pulled at his jaw. "I don't know how it got into the water system. Ocean water doesn't infiltrate the drinking water system. It's not possible."

"Unless it wanted to," I said. "And it found a way in."

"Like it was targeting us," Harper said, speaking so quietly it was hard to hear her. "But how would it do that?"

"That's one of the things we need to find out."

"But, Sara," Tyler grabbed my hand. "What do you think you can do about it? Isn't Operation Blue Water dealing with it?"

I narrowed my eyes, not at him, but at the bobbing catamaran. "I don't know what they're here to do. All I know is everything was fine before they turned up. So no, I don't trust Operation Blue Water as far as I can throw them."

Frank stood up and propped his fists on his hips. "We need your friend Simona."

My lips tightened. "She's still missing. I need to call the hospitals again. But she must have colleagues who know what's going on. She had a sample undergoing further testing. Someone must have results somewhere."

"Okay," Tyler said. "Maybe there is something we can do. We take them another sample."

"And where do we get a sample from?" Harper asked.

For the first time in hours, my mood lifted. Finally, this was a tangible plan, something practical we could do that didn't involve sitting around waiting for someone else to help or avoiding menacing men in black suits.

"The boat," I replied.

I crouched by the boat and reached for a Tupperware container in one of the seat lockers. I poured out the packets of crackers and energy bars and held it above the calm green water.

"Careful, Sara," Tyler warned. I could hear the memory of the pain in his voice, and my own hand and fingers ached in sympathy. No way did I want to experience those kinds of burns again.

I scooped up some of the green water, along with the milk lid and some of the murky smudge. In the boat, the water remained calm. In the container, the water whirled in a circle, like it spinning into a whirlpool, like it might burst free of the container any second. I snapped the lid on and swallowed hard.

On our way out of the marina, John accosted us.

"Of all the asinine, senselessly moronic things to do!" His neck bulged as thick as Frank's and his face turned bright red.

Frank whirled on him. "Leave it alone, John. We won't be going back in the water. Your job is done."

"Why don't you do something?" I asked him. "Haven't you seen?"

He cut a nervous glance to the water but didn't reply. We left him standing there, hands on his hips, staring after us.

We snuck along the back streets. People strained at the

barricades on the closed boardwalk while police told them to keep back. A few snapped pictures of the trash. Would any of them have real evidence? The afternoon sun beat on the back of my neck and slickened my palms, making it hard to hold the Tupperware container. I gripped tighter. No way did I want to drop this thing.

Tyler cradled his wrist as we walked. An array of new signs were posted at regular intervals on the desolate beach.

Toxins in the water.

Closed for the foreseeable future.

It was written in bold red lettering. No one could miss it.

Chucking a glance at the ocean, I stared at the glinting green water. The trash island was the size of LA.

The size of LA.

The thought drilled into my skull. That was over four hundred square miles of plastic muck. If the algae had combined with all that trash... how could anyone defeat something so big?

We snuck away, down a series of side streets, moving away from the beach. Away from the stench of decay, the cleaner scents of cotton candy and barbequing hot dogs wafted in the air. My stomach rumbled. Feeling eyes on me, I looked up and down the street, expecting to see a bunch of men in black suits with scary guns. But there was no one there.

The milk lid floated in the shallow pool of the container, moving from one side to the other with more force and speed than an inanimate object should be capable of. I picked up my pace, wanting to be rid of it as soon as possible.

When we reached my house, I went inside and set the

container on the kitchen table. Somehow, it slid across the table and butted into the corkscrew board with all our family snapshots, then remained still.

Frank went through the whole tube of burn cream treating all our injuries. With my wrist re-bandaged, I felt mildly better. The burns didn't sting anymore, but the skin felt tender whenever it came into contact with another material.

Harper checked the Almond Cove News Network on her phone. There were breaking news reports about the local area. The four of us hovered around the small screen to listen to the breathless reporter. The image was of the Coast Guard boat approaching the coast. No sight of the monster in the video clip.

The reporter's tone was mocking as she spoke of stories of people coming into contact with a green monster in the ocean. There was speculation something had been awakened from a part of the undiscovered ocean and was making itself known. It was hard for her to keep the smile from twitching on her lips. The vague and blurry shots gathered from Instagram and other social media outlets were dismissed as hoaxes. No one believed a green monster with vines for arms and the ability to secrete an agonizing toxin could exist.

EnRG. They'd skewed all the evidence and made the people of Almond Cove sound like a bunch of raving madmen. On TV, Regina Harron spoke to the camera, saying there were toxins in the water emitted by the trash island and capable of causing intense hallucinations as well as second-degree burns, or worse. John stood right alongside her. They advised everyone to keep out of the water and they were confident Operation Blue Water would make the ocean safe once again.

"What a bunch of bullshit!" Harper yelled at the screen.

I scrolled through my own Instagram account, then went on Google, looking at the few captured images of The Great Green. It was clear to me, but then I'd seen it up close and personal. In the comments below each picture, there were reams of sarcastic remarks by the cynical public. The people responsible for uploading the photos and videos sounded more and more crazy as they tried to defend what they'd seen.

"They've handled everything," I said, the pit in my stomach growing deeper. "They've managed the press, FEMA, the Coast Guard. How the hell did they manage it?"

Harper's hand covered mine. "We're on our own."

"Just how Veronica Mars likes it." I smiled at my friend. "What would Veronica Mars do now?"

"She'd solve this puzzle and blow the whole thing wide open." Harper's knee hammered up and down, but there was a determined glint in her eyes.

Frank pulled at the stubble on his jaw. "We have the sample. We get it to Scripps, and we'll prove to everyone what's really going on—"

Frank's cellphone rang and his face dropped as he listened to the person on the other end. When he hung up, he gathered us around.

"There's been an accident at La Jolla beach. Major... collision of several boats. Or that's what they're calling it, anyway. My department is needed. I want to be here for you guys, but these people need me more."

"Can we help?" Tyler asked.

Frank shook his head. "I want you guys to stay here. Don't answer the door to anyone. And call Scripps. I'll be back as soon as I can."

He dashed down the steps toward his bright red Corvette, which was still parked in the drive behind Tyler's car, gleaming in the fading sun.

The three of us hovered on the porch as Frank revved his engine. I scanned the street for black SUVs but couldn't spot anything suspicious. Maybe they'd decided to leave us alone.

Frank drove away. The rest of us went back inside the house, locked the doors, pulled the drapes and huddled around the kitchen table. We picked at the stale bowl of chips I'd poured out earlier and rang Scripps. The line was busy. I wasn't surprised. So I switched my focus and rang the hospitals again. The first two didn't pick up. The next three were swamped with patients—acid burns, obviously—and couldn't spare a second to talk. Scripps again. Still busy. We spent the afternoon eating chips and calling hospitals. And Scripps.

"We need to find Simona," I muttered as I shot her emails and messages on my phone, hoping wherever she was, she might be able to log in to something.

"Maybe when we take the sample to Scripps, someone there will know what's happened to her," Tyler said.

"I'm hoping they'll come collect the sample," I said. "No way do I want to touch that thing again."

"One hundred percent," Harper said.

The next five hospitals didn't have any record of Simona. If she was in the hospital, she had to be in one of the ones who weren't picking up or weren't talking. The next time I called Scripps, someone picked up, put me on hold, and never came back to the line.

I rubbed my face, trying to massage the worry away. "I don't know what to do."

"Veronica Mars wouldn't sit around here waiting," Harper said around a mouthful of chips.

Tyler flattened a chip under his finger, breaking it into tiny pieces. "What do you suggest?"

"She'd kick this Giganto's ass right back into the sea," Harper replied.

"Giganto?" I questioned.

Harper sighed and rolled her eyes at me. Flicking her phone into life she shoved a picture of a comic-book monster under my nose. "You know, big Atlantean sea monster used as a Doomsday weapon until The Thing from *Fantastic Four* nuked its ass."

She looked at us as if she expected us to know all the monsters and villains from her Marvel obsession.

She waved a hand at us. "You guys are no fun."

"Seriously though," Tyler said, looking at the picture again. "I think The Great Green might be worse."

"It's definitely bigger," I said, dropping my head into my hands.

Tyler's phone rang. A discordant jangle of notes that would get the attention of a bull shark in a tank. While answering, he stood and listened to the other person on his phone. His face leached of color.

"What is it?" I whispered.

He waved me away and stepped out the back door.

"I don't like this," Harper said.

Between us, the Tupperware sloshed again. It wobbled on the table, then settled back down with an abrasive clang.

"We should keep that outside," I said. Wary, I picked it up as carefully as I could. As I lifted it, a brilliant green light shone out of the container, turning the dust motes green, casting the curtains and ceiling in a sparkling emerald. I glanced down and almost dropped the container. Harper came to my side. Together, squinting, we peered inside. The milk lid wasn't a milk lid anymore. No longer round, it pulsed with a glinting green energy. An irregular shape constantly moving, tiny feelers reaching for the sides of the container.

I shoved the whole thing on the back porch as Tyler came back inside, phone back in his pocket.

"What's the matter?" I asked.

"It's my dad. He's been hurt."

My stomach dropped. "How?"

"Broken ribs. Concussion. He's in the hospital. I have to go."

"Go," I said, holding his hand as I walked him to the front door. We cracked it open, cautiously peering outside. The street was quiet, but I knew people were watching. "Do you need me to come with you?"

Tyler shook his head. "You need to find Simona. And get that sample to Scripps."

He wrapped his arms around me and I gave him a tight squeeze. Then he dashed to his car. I followed, keeping my eyes on the street. Once inside, he rolled down the window. "I'll call you later."

Harper and I watched his car disappear down the street,

then returned to the house and slammed the door closed. I bolted it for good measure.

"We should have gone with him," Harper said, glancing over her shoulder at the ominous kitchen sink.

"You're right," I said. "I am such a bad girlfriend." I reached for the door again, but Harper put a hand on my arm.

"But neither of us have a car and it's too late now."

Chapter Sixteen

HARPER AND I WERE ALONE.

I spent another hour calling hospitals but still couldn't track Simona down. She had to be somewhere. But the longer it went without finding her at a hospital, the more convinced I was Regina had her. A hospital I could visit. But Regina? She was a whole other thing.

As I paced the living room, I drank water from a plastic bottle for the first time in years. No way was I going near the tap.

Near midnight, Tyler messaged to say Frank was doing okay, but they were keeping him in the hospital for observation.

We took refuge in my room as the Santa Ana winds ravaged the house. I sat on my pillow with my knees curled beneath my chin next to a sleeping Harper. Her long hair trailed across the pillow and her eyelids fluttered as she dreamed.

The wind knocked against the house. I remember trying to fly during the Santa Ana winds when I was little.

Spreading my arms, leaping into the air and letting them carry me a few feet. For something without substance, they were incredibly strong. Maybe they'd be a worthy adversary for The Great Green. I grabbed the skimming pebble Danny had found for me and held it close to my chest, rubbing my thumb over the smooth surface, praying to him for strength.

What would he do if he was here now? Probably something dangerous. I couldn't fault his kind heart; after all, it was the quality I most admired in him. He taught me all about the ocean, how to protect it. Now it was as much a part of me as it had been for him. A memory surfaced.

Danny threw the front door open and a shaft of sunlight turned the threshold into a magical portal. He was going on an adventure, and there was no way I was going to let him have all the fun. He threw a glance back at me, a cheeky grin balanced on his lips, donned his sunglasses and slipped out the door.

I ran after him. "Wait!"

On the porch, he turned to face me, his hands on his knees. "What's up, squirt?"

"Stop calling me that! I've grown two inches this year already." I held my hand high above my head to indicate how tall I was. I almost came up to his armpit.

He flicked my nose. "I'll have to start calling you Titan instead."

I grinned, liking the sound of it, then noted he was wearing his Green Clean T-shirt. "Can't I come with you? Please?"

"It's going to be a couple of hours. You can't get bored and wander off."

"I won't. I promise. I want to help with the trash."

"It's stinky," he warned.

"Not as stinky as your armpits," I giggled.

He kicked my feet out from under me and caught me before I fell, then tickled my ribs until I dissolved into a heap on the floor.

"Come on, I'll help you beat your trash collecting record," I said, gaining my feet. I threw myself at him, trying to kick his feet out, but he held my head with an outstretched hand and I couldn't get anywhere near him.

Laughing, he waited until I ran out of steam. "No trying to tackle me."

I crossed my arms. "Fine." I'd get him back, one day. One day I'd be as strong as him.

He glanced down the block at the rolling surf, then back at me. After checking his pocket for his cellphone, he nodded and hustled me down the porch. "Come on then."

Danny kicked the stand of his bike and hoisted me onto the handlebars. "Hold on tight."

I giggled as he set off, enjoying the wind in my hair and feeling like I was flying. Danny's breath beat on the back of my neck, but I didn't mind, it was worth being with him.

When we arrived at the beach, Danny locked up his bike and pointed the way to the rocky cliffs. We wound our way down the narrow path, releasing loose gravel and startling the odd seagull. The morning sun was strong but pleasant and I sniffed deep to fill my lungs with the scent of the ocean. It was the most comforting smell.

"Found any mermaids yet?" Danny asked as we reached the beach.

I laughed. "There's no such thing! I might be eight, but I do know what's make-believe."

He whirled around to face me, both his eyebrows high. "How can you say such a thing? You'll hurt their feelings."

Laughing, I plucked a pebble from the sand and skimmed it across the water.

"Why, just the other day Seraphina was here, asking how plentiful the fish would be this summer and promising not to sing any more sailors to their deaths."

Enjoying the story, I searched for another flat pebble.

"I had to give her a strong talking to. The windsurfer who broke his leg last summer took months to recover. He only recently got back in the water."

Hiding my smile, I asked. "Did she say sorry?"

Danny nodded. "She said she'd try really hard not to distract anyone else with her songs."

I stepped close to him, my gaze scanning the horizon, taking in the small white triangles of sailboats far offshore. I wanted to believe in the magic he cast. Maybe there were mermaids out there. Or had once been.

Suddenly, Danny jogged away from me, concern twisting a frown onto his face. "Sara, don't look." He dashed to the water line and hunched over something. It looked like a large boulder had been washed on shore, but then it moved.

Not a boulder, a seal.

I took a step forward.

"Stay back! I don't want you to see this, Sara."

But seals were my favorite animals and I wouldn't pass an opportunity to get close to one. Sailing past them in the marina where they gathered on the buoys and often knocked each other off with angry barks was funny and all, but I'd never been this close before. I wanted to touch it before it slipped away.

I dashed down the beach to Danny, then came to an abrupt stop. Tears immediately filled my eyes. The seal was lying on the sand, listless, a plastic bag strangling its neck. A thick line of red trailed from the bag down its body.

My hand flew to my mouth. I wanted to look away, but I could only stand rooted and watch.

Danny removed the penknife he got last Christmas from his pocket and, with expert precision, wiggled the blade under the tightening leash of plastic and cut the seal free.

I sank to my knees as Danny cupped water in his hands and poured it over the seal's neck, washing the blood away.

"It's not too deep," Danny said. "It'll be okay."

"Who would do such a thing?" I asked, my fingers creeping toward the edge of its flipper. The seal lay there panting, its whiskers twitching with every exhale, its eyes roving between Danny and me.

Danny shook his head as he continued to clean the wound. "We need better solutions for our trash. So much of it gets dumped in the ocean."

I touched the flipper. It felt different from how I expected. Not smooth, but rubbery. Like Mom's handbag, but slimy.

It barked at me and I skittered backward, covering myself in sand.

Danny laughed and stepped away from the animal. "I think it's ready to go back in the water."

The seal wiggled its body and humped down the beach, where it slipped into the water and disappeared with one flick of its tail.

"What about the other seals? The other trash?" I asked, pulling on his hand.

Danny hugged me to his side, flicked my nose. "Don't you worry about it, squirt, your big brother is on it."

And that was enough. Danny was my big brother by four years. If he said he would solve the problem, then he would.

Chapter Seventeen

I STAYED up most of the night listening to the wind and thinking about Danny. When I got scared by the Santa Anas when I was a kid, he'd let me crawl into his double bed and snuggle next to his warmth. He kept a reading light on, claiming he was going to read late, but I knew he did it for me so I would feel safe.

I wished he was here now as the wind shrieked and protested, tunneling by in powerful gusts, whisking sand from the beach into the air. It brought the smell of salt into the room, even though the window was closed. Ghostly moans grew in volume. Whirring and scuttling noises slammed against the house. A loose screw in the bottom of the fly screen scraped against the frame. Every single hair on my body stood at ninety degrees.

I glanced at the shadows in the room. Any one of them could be a person, crouched in the dark, waiting to pounce. Would those EnRG reps dare enter the house? I knew "security" was a euphemism for other things and doubted a bolted front door and a few locked windows would keep Ryan Phillips out if he wanted in.

The night passed and the morning brought a new level of exhaustion, both mental and physical. Downstairs, I kept all the blinds and curtains closed and made a strong pot of coffee with bottled water. Although I hadn't eaten much in the last twenty-four hours, I wasn't hungry. While I nibbled at the leftover scraps from the bowl of chips, Harper ate a bagel with smooth peanut butter. I left the sticky mess of EnRG on the floor and counter, in case The Great Green made a repeat appearance.

"So, what do we do?" she said, fingering the last crumbs into her mouth.

"I always thought it was you who had the plan."

She shrugged. "I'm getting tired of thinking about Veronica Mars. I think we need our own name." She tilted her head and pursed her lips.

"Something like Monroe & Jackson Associates?"

She flicked her hand at me. "Waaaay too boring. And it would be Jackson & Monroe, anyway. Let's go for something like The Green Killers."

I laughed. "That makes us sound anti-environment."

"Jackson & Monroe, monster hunters of doom." She winked and made finger guns, blasting invisible baddies around the kitchen. "We're going to head to Scripps, right?"

"Yep, as soon as I finish this coffee."

She turned her plate in a circle, again and again. "What if they don't let us in? Or they don't believe us?"

"They have to." I dropped my head into my hands. "I really hope... They have to... I don't know..."

Harper squeezed my hand. "I'm scared too."

"I want my mom. And my dad. Does that sound ridiculous? And my skin still hurts."

"Mine too. And no, it doesn't sound ridiculous," Harper said, pouring us both more coffee. "I wish mine hadn't traveled to visit my sister in New York. I could use some grown-up involvement too."

"Let's check the news first." I rose and walked into the living room.

We sat on the couch together and flicked to the news channel.

"Holy..." Harper muttered.

The picture showed the ocean, right here at Almond Cove. I recognized the catamaran and the Coast Guard ship stationed close to the horizon. A breathless reporter covered the story.

I clutched Harper's hand. "What do you think has happened?"

She didn't answer, but turned up the volume.

Devastating events unfolded. The Coast Guard cutter stood tall in the early morning light. A mellow patch of glowing green ocean ebbed toward it. As soon as the bioluminescence touched the edge of the ship, all hell broke loose. Huge green waves made of nothing but trash formed where there had been none a second before, slapping at the hull. Crashing against it again and again until visible holes appeared on the port side. The ocean churned. The trash swirled. The bow of the ship dropped a couple of yards. Then, a whirlpool emerged, encompassing the length of the vessel and dragging it under the surface. The last sliver of the stern disappeared. The green trash bubbled for a moment, then turned calm once more.

I bolted forward. "Holy crap..." I muttered, ignoring the presence of the swear jar on the mantle. "It took down an entire Coast Guard cutter!"

"And did nothing to the EnRG catamaran."

"John has to get involved now."

I frowned at the TV as the footage played again. The news was going global and no one knew what to make of it. Breathless journalists spoke into cameras, stirring the public, but none of their stories were anywhere near the truth. They claimed there was no evidence of a green monster. All the reporters spoke of how the toxins in the trash island were manipulating the water into acting strangely. Everyone was buying it. Even the FEMA spokespeople.

One brave reporter highlighted some of the crazy stories from social media, presented the vague images and blurry videos. The news reporter read through some of the comments. He said the public was starting to question if there might be something else in the water. There were snippets of a stressed-looking Regina attempting to laugh off the accusations of a monster, saying Operation Blue Water was still in control.

I shook my head at her words. They weren't in control. They'd lost it completely. Whatever they had created, however much good they thought they could do, it had all gone to hell.

A creeping sense of alarm tingled my spine. "I'm going to check on the container. We need to get it to Scripps."

I inched open the sliding door that led to the back porch. After checking the garden was empty, I edged out, intending to grab the Tupperware from where I'd left it near the telescope. Seeing the telescope reminded me of Dad.

And Danny. It was only a few nights ago we'd spent the evening out here, when we first noticed the green tinge.

I scanned the back porch, but the container wasn't there. Frowning, I dashed down the three wooden steps. It wasn't under the porch and it wasn't anywhere in the small garden. Not even in the bushes.

My heart thudded in my throat. Where the hell had it gone?

I dashed inside and slid the door closed, locking it firmly.

"The sample's gone," I said.

Harper arched an eyebrow. "Gone? What do you mean, *gone*?"

"It's not on the back porch anymore. The entire container is gone."

She glanced at the ceiling, at the walls, as if expecting to see green tendrils snaking toward us. I half expected to see them too.

"So, what do we do now?"

I looked at my best friend. My parents were in Paris. My boyfriend was in the hospital with his injured dad. The only other adult I trusted was missing. The fear was real. I'd never felt at such a loss. "I don't know."

Avoiding the sticky patch of leftover EnRG on the kitchen tiles, I poured us some more coffee and brought it back into the living room. We watched the Coast Guard ship sink again and again and swallowed some painkillers for our burns.

Dad called to check in.

"It feels like you've been gone forever," I told him.

"Sara, is everything okay?"

I wanted to tell him everything, but what could he do from seven thousand miles away? "Everything is fine."

"Here, talk to your mom."

I heard him pass the phone to her, then Mom's voice came on the line. "Sara? Honey? How are you? Everything okay?"

I looked at Harper, who shrugged at Mom's audible words.

"Everything is fine," I said.

A pause. "You don't sound fine."

It was a Mom statement. She expected me to fill in the subsequent silence.

"It's... you know, the beach is a mess. The ocean... Frank's in the hospital—"

"Why is Frank in the hospital? Did something happen? What's going on?" Mom's voice went on and on, peppering questions at me faster than a shark could snag its prey. "I saw the Coast Guard ship sink. You're staying away from the water, right?"

"Frank had an accident at work. He's fine. He's going to be fine. We're all fine. Apart from the Coast Guard cutter. I don't know what's going on there."

Another pause. "I don't like the word *fine*. Sara, honey, I've been hearing strange reports of something in the water at Almond Cove—"

"Mom, it's just—"

"Sara, is there something in the water at Almond Cove?"

Telling her the truth would do nothing to provide them with an earlier flight. It wouldn't get them home any faster. I couldn't bear to think of them both so far away, worrying about me and The Great Green.

"Sara?"

"Everything is okay. I had another argument with Tyler, that's all. I'm okay. The water is fine. Almond Cove is giving shelter to a section of the Eastern Garbage Patch. It's toxic, it sank the cutter. That's all."

Harper laced her arm through mine and gave me a sideways hug.

"You're sure?" Mom asked.

"I'm sure."

Mom blew out a gust of breath. "Okay, if you're sure. We'll see you in a couple days, sweetheart."

"Bye, Mom." I hung up.

"You did the right thing," Harper said. "There's no point worrying them unnecessarily."

I smiled at her gratefully. I was keeping them safe from getting caught up in it all, but man, I wished they'd get home soon. I'd have to get through another two days without them. I didn't know if the monster would give us another night off.

I didn't have any more time to think about it. A piercing scream came from outside and forced every hair on my body into high alert.

Chapter Eighteen

I LAUNCHED TO MY FEET, dashing for the door, Harper on my heels.

Ignoring the returned SUV, hunched like a fat spider in a web, I tripped down the porch steps and stumbled to the front yard. The scream continued from the house next door, punctuated by short gasps and wails. Mentally, I went through all the scenarios that could cause a scream like that. Since the birth of The Great Green, I've been able to add a multitude of impossible situations.

I arrived at the front door seconds before Harper. I jabbed at the doorbell and shouldered the solid wood, but the front door was shut.

"Help!"

"Let's check the back," Harper said, already heading for the gate.

"Mrs. Larson?" I called as I slid open the glass door on the back porch.

Harper tripped over a planter and stumbled inside.

"Help!"

The plea for help came from upstairs.

"Come on," I said to Harper as we made a beeline for the staircase.

I took the steps two at a time and found Mrs. Larson on the second-floor landing, completely naked, dripping with green water and gripping her arms. There were pressure marks on her limbs.

The Great Green.

Mrs. Larson's wide eyes fixed on me. "Help me." Her voice became a husky whisper, as if her throat had been clawed out. Blisters completely covered her face and clustered over her skin, down the length of her arms and legs, across her chest.

"Shit!" Harper whimpered.

I flew back down the stairs, calling over my shoulder. "Get her a towel. Something! I'm going for the EnRG."

Inside my house, I found a couple bottles of EnRG from the case Regina had sent and snatched it up as well as my cellphone. I ran back over, calling 911 on my way, but I couldn't get through.

When I got back upstairs, Harper was attempting to pat away the burns with a towel. Mrs. Larson had crumpled to the floor, her eyes rolling. I knelt by her side, pouring the EnRG over her blisters and reddening skin.

"This is bad," Harper said.

As gently as I could, I rubbed the EnRG into Mrs. Larson's skin. The reddening skin calmed, and the blisters stopped growing. "I think it's working."

Mrs. Larson groaned. I covered her with a towel and dripped a few droplets of the orange drink between her lips.

I handed Harper my phone. "Try calling 911 again."

Harper took the phone and got to her feet, walking to the top of the landing as she spoke into the phone. I sat next to Mrs. Larson as she groaned and whimpered and passed in and out of consciousness.

"It burns!" she muttered.

"It's okay now," I said in my best reassuring voice. But it was a lie. The Great Green was in the water system. Not just at my house, but everywhere.

While we waited for the ambulance, I kept my hand on Mrs. Larson's wrist, measuring her pulse, terrified she'd slip away for good. When the paramedics arrived, I let them in the front door and led them to the bathroom where we'd been waiting with Mrs. Larson.

One of them, a guy in his twenties, sighed deeply when he took in the blisters on her skin.

"This is the worst one I've seen yet."

"What happened?" the other asked, a woman around my mother's age.

I opened my mouth to reply, then hesitated. Would they believe the truth?

"We don't know," Harper said. "Sara here lives next door. We heard screaming and came around. I think she was in the shower and somehow got all these burns and blisters."

The man shook his head. "What the hell is going on around here? First the ocean and now the water system. I can't make any sense of it."

"You know about The Great Green?" I asked.

He looked at me. "You mean the huge trash island out there that's covered in algae? Yeah, everyone knows about it."

"It's not just trash."

"Not you, too," the younger man said. "The toxins in the water cause hallucinations. Operation Blue Water and FEMA have explained all that. There isn't some monster eating our coast." He added a laugh, but no one returned his smile.

"You can't believe everything fed to you from a news report," I said, then turned to the lady. "The water isn't safe. People need to know."

She put a hand on mine. "They do. I've never seen so many *acid attacks* in the three decades I've been a paramedic. I know something is going on here. But I'm not sure I'm ready to believe in a monster either."

"You have to say something," I said.

The lady gave me a curt nod. "I will when I can. This isn't the first acid attack we've gotten a call-out for today. And it won't be the last. The hospitals are overrun and I don't have time to file reports. I help the people I can and hope it's enough."

"How bad is it out there?" Harper asked.

The paramedics lifted Mrs. Larson onto a stretcher.

"Bad," the lady replied. They carried Mrs. Larson down the stairs.

As they loaded her into the ambulance, I put a hand on the lady's arm. "EnRG. The energy drink, it calms down the burns. It's the only thing I've seen work. If I were you, I'd buy a few cans and keep them in your ambulance."

She gave me a quizzical look. "EnRG?"

"It's a long story," I said.

We watched the ambulance drive away. I kept my ears strained for more screams from the neighborhood, but everything was eerily silent. The SUV was parked opposite my house. They were in there, watching me. Watching Mrs. Larson. Why hadn't they helped?

"Come on." Harper grabbed my arm and led me back to the house.

Exhausted, I hunted through the garage for Mom's case of sparkling water. Glass bottles. A recycling effort I could get behind. I poured it into a pan and heated it, then washed up as best I could. Even though I knew the water from the bottle was safe, I still tensed up when I brought the washcloth to my face.

I didn't turn on a tap. I didn't flush the toilet. We drank Mom's sparkling water and filled the coffee pot with it twice. The coffee tasted weird.

My phone bleeped and I found an email from Simona. It contained one word.

Okay.

"What the hell does that mean?" I showed Harper.

"That she's okay?"

I sighed. "This doesn't prove anything. Regina could have sent the message on her behalf, trying to get me to stop prying. And if she really was okay, she'd give me more information."

"Maybe she can't right now," Harper said.

"That's what I'm worried about."

I looked outside and examined the area for anything strange. But everything was strange. The sky looked green. The ocean sparkled that awful green and the trash towered. Yet, the catamaran sat there, undisturbed, untouched.

I wished I had a clear picture of The Great Green in action. I'd upload it to every social media platform I had on my phone. I'd make people believe.

I replied to Simona's message, insisted she give me more information and asked her a question only she would know the answer to. As I ate dry Cheerios and paced the living room, Harper threw out impossible plans.

"Why don't we go to the cops?"

"What are they going to do?" I flopped on the couch and hugged a cushion. It was an embroidery my mom had completed. A picture of a huge water lily. "They're not going to have the equipment to deal with a monster that size. *Any* monster. And that's assuming they even believe in The Great Green. Everyone is happy to accept the toxic hallucination theory."

"Fair point. The FBI?"

"Same answer as above."

Harper grasped her knees. "There must be some government agency who deals with this kind of thing."

The ghost of a smile played on my lips as I thought about the conversation I had with Dad about a possible Navy *X-Files* department.

"Yeah, I think they drive around in a black SUV, wear black suits and mirrored sunglasses and are owned by EnRG."

"They're not government, they're private security," she said.

I raised my eyebrows. "Even worse."

"Regina has a lot to answer for."

I hugged the cushion tighter as a plan began to form. "Yes, she does."

Harper tilted her head, her eyes narrowing in my direction. "What are you thinking? I know when you're plotting something. Let me in on it. Jackson & Monroe, monster hunters at large, are about to get a job, aren't they?"

I looked at my friend, trying to ignore the new coil of nerves snaking through my stomach. "I'm not sure I should get you involved."

"Sara, tell me. I'm not going to let you do this on your own."

I chewed the inside of my cheek. "Are you feeling brave?"

"That depends. Does it involve going out on the water again?"

"Nope."

"Okay, hit me with it."

"We can't wait here for something to happen. The hospitals are overrun. I can't find Simona. Everything is falling apart and no one is doing anything about it. It's up to us."

Harper smiled. "Totally agree."

"So, we're going to pay Regina Harron a visit." In my bones, I knew it was the right decision. "Regina is the only person who knows what the hell is going on. She created that thing, she can tell us how to uncreate it."

"If Regina knew how to stop it, don't you think she would have done it by now?"

"I don't know, I can't see into Regina's head. She's big corporation, do they ever do anything for the greater good?"

"But surely she wouldn't want to destroy the entire ocean?"

I shrugged. "Who knows. But unless we go to her, we'll never find out."

Harper's shoulders slumped. "I keep waiting for the

world to wake up and realize what's happening. But she's got everyone under her spell, doesn't she?"

We glanced at the muted TV. There were breaking news reports left, right and center. Acid attacks. Toxins in the water. Nothing about a monster. Maybe no one was brave enough to be the first to say it. Godzilla and Jurassic Park were for the movies, not real life. But when something impossible happened? Denial became the name of the game.

I wasn't hallucinating.

I shook my head. Frank, Tyler, Harper and I couldn't have all had the same hallucination. And those people we rescued in the dinghy. They had a similar story. The Great Green was real.

It was much easier to believe in toxins and hallucinations. They could be dealt with, there would be science involved. The CDC, FEMA and all the other governmental agencies were highly experienced with crises. But no one had experience with a monster.

"We need to show people her true face. Everyone knows the Coast Guard cutter sank. They have no idea why. There were no green arms or grinning heads or blinking eyes. It just... *dissolved*. The stories are out there, but no one is believing them."

I punched a fist into the opposite palm. "We can't wait for everyone to play catch up. We need to act. Now."

She nodded along with my words, a smile stretching on her lips.

"You don't have to come with me," I said, realizing I didn't want to put her in danger. "But I'm going. I'm going to pay Regina Harron a little visit and see if I can find out anything useful. Something that might help."

She stood. "Of course I'm coming, you idiot. Jackson & Monroe is not a one-woman outfit, I'll have you know." She wagged her finger at me.

I hugged her. Fighting The Great Green was so much better with Harper.

She squeezed me back until the tension drained out of my limbs. Well, most of it, anyway.

"So, when do we go?" Harper asked.

"As soon as it's dark," I replied.

"Seriously?"

"We need to wait for her to get home."

"What do we do? Walk right up to her and ask?" she said. Twilight pressed against the windows. A faint green hue leaked in with it. I sipped from my cold coffee mug.

"Yep."

"She kidnapped Simona." Harper threw a hand in the air.

"Maybe we'll find her, too."

"That's not what I meant."

"I know what you meant."

"There'll be those security reps everywhere."

"We can do it," I told my friend, but in truth, although I knew where Regina lived, I had no idea how to get inside her oceanside mansion.

"Hopefully those security goons will be too busy staking out your house?" Harper raised both thumbs in a parody of jolly optimism.

"I hope so, because I don't think we have the time to wait

for Frank to get out of the hospital or my parents to get back." I pointed at the window, at the green light pulsing around the edges of the blinds. "We have no idea if that thing can come on land. And if it can, I hate to think what might happen. Nowhere will be safe." I shuddered, imagining those stretching green limbs crawling up my stairs, over the creaky one, into my bedroom, filling my nostrils. "We need to know how to stop it."

"We might end up in jail," Harper said.

"I'll be there right along with you." I smiled at her. "There's no one I'd rather be in jail with."

Night pressed in. Harper peeked around the blinds and quickly shut them again. "Everything is so green."

"A month ago, I would have said that's a good thing, considering the water shortages."

She sat down beside me and lowered her voice as if she were afraid there were bugs all over the place. Her eyes roamed the ceiling, the light fixtures, the smoke alarms. "That SUV is still out there. How are we going to get out of here?"

"I've got it all worked out," I said, knowing we wouldn't be able to get anywhere near the front of the house without being followed. "We're going to go garden hopping, then we'll catch the bus."

Harper grinned and offered me a high five. "Operation 'Torture Regina' is a go."

Chapter Nineteen

WE WAITED until it was dark, then we waited an hour longer. Even though it was nighttime, an eerie green tinge seeped through the windows. Alien green. Jungle green. Acid green. Spooky green. My hand ached as I fingered the healing burns. I did *not* want to get up close and personal with The Great Green again.

Not bothering to check the front windows, I led Harper to the back door and quietly slid it open. Still no sign of the missing container.

"You seriously expect me to scale a hedge that big? I mean, it's got thorns, I've got shorts on—"

I pressed my finger to her lips. "Shhh."

I watched the small garden for signs of movement. Apart from the telescope on the back porch nestled next to Dad's favorite sagging deck chair, there were only the table and chairs on the patio to break up the murky gloom. Crickets chirped in the scrub grass and the tail of the Santa Ana winds rustled the hedges. The green glow of the ocean rolled toward us, filling my stomach with nausea. What was the monster up to right now?

I waved Harper down the steps. We tiptoed across the dry grass toward the far hedge. She winced as I gestured for her to crawl through.

"There's a gap," I whispered, showing her the way.

We pushed through the thick hedge. Small branches scraped against my cheeks and tangled in my hair while the smell of dry earth and leaves rushed up my nose. Harper had more trouble with her thick, long hair getting caught on barbed twigs. We made it out the other side and stood in the large garden of the house behind us. The sprinklers were going and water splashed my shins. I gritted my teeth, expecting it to burn. But it was just water.

Hoping the whirring sound of the sprinklers would mask any noise we made, we inched along the hedge.

"Now what?" Harper said, scanning the dark for a way out. The other two sides of the garden were lined with five-foot wooden fences.

"Now we climb and jump."

Her eyes widened, but she didn't comment. She approached the fence to our left and I boosted her up. When her head popped over the edge, a security light from the house came on, illuminating her shape. She froze, until I hissed at her to keep moving.

A dog started barking. Harper swiveled over the top of the fence. As the back door of the house swung open, I leaped up, grabbed the top of the fence, and hoisted myself over.

"Hey!" A voice called after me.

I landed on both feet, bending my knees to reduce the

impact, but the scrape on my calf reopened. I didn't have time to deal with it now. Then we ran. There weren't any more fences and we ran through gardens, leaping over small hedges until we reached an alley.

A stray cat strolled by and a couple of boxes shifted in the wind. Blood dripped down my calf.

"Where now?" Harper panted.

The dog was still barking, but the crickets had shut up for once.

I nodded in the direction of a streetlight. "Main road is that way. We can catch the bus."

Forcing myself to walk at an inconspicuous pace, we reached the end of the alley and emerged into bright lights. This part of Almond Cove bustled with activity; couples and families pouring in and out of diners, the surf shops lit up and displaying their wares on the street—not that anyone would be surfing right now.

People walked up and down the sidewalk, chatting and going in and out of the shops. Many of them were tourist traps selling postcards and magnets and cheap bikinis that fell apart after one use. The smell of greasy burgers and barbecued hotdogs made my stomach rumble. I wished I'd eaten something more filling than dry Cheerios, but I hadn't had the stomach for anything more substantial. A kid gripped a powdered doughnut in a thick fist, licking at the sugar. The powdered ones had been Danny's favorite. I really wanted a doughnut. And my dad, Mom, Tyler, Frank. Everyone. But I had to do this on my own. Or, at least, with Harper.

Shivering, Harper stepped close to a patio heater outside one of the restaurants. It wasn't even that cold, but I felt the chill in my bones too. We were both dressed in a pair of denim shorts. But at least we had dark sweatshirts to keep us warm and sneakers to help us run fast. Usually, I hated sneakers. Living so close to the ocean, sand was always in the air and had a sneaky way of winding its way into my shoes and clothes. But flip-flops weren't great for covert operations.

Harper pointed down the street. The La Jolla bus was turning the corner. Relief sang through my limbs. We'd made it out of the house, and soon we'd be at Regina's property, where we'd uncover what we needed to know.

As I stepped toward the approaching bus, irregular movement on my left caught my eye. A dark shape materialized from the alley we'd recently left. One of the men in black suits, his mirrored sunglasses still pulled down, reflecting the lights on the street.

Beside me, Harper cowered. "What do we do?"

"Where do you think you're going?" The man spoke. It was the older EnRG rep with the sparse gray hair. His polished shoes shone under the streetlamp and his hair ruffled in the breeze. He glanced at my leg. "You're hurt. We should take care of that."

I yanked Harper toward the approaching bus. He followed, his footsteps tapping against the sidewalk. Strong fingers circled my wrist. I wondered if I could signal to someone for help. A couple of yards away, a mother scolded a young child who'd left his sweater in a shop. A couple of teenagers huddled close, but they only had eyes for each other. No one glanced our way, too busy looking in shop windows and licking ice cream cones.

"Sara." The voice was right next to my ear. A voice so

close I could feel the heat of breath and smell the whiff of stale coffee.

"Leave me alone," I pushed the words through gritted teeth.

Unrelenting fingers circled my arm. A vice-like grip I couldn't pull myself out of. Harper froze. The bus came to a stop, its tires screeching. The door opened, and the driver looked at us questioningly.

"How about we go back home?" The man asked, pulling on my arm. He was stronger than he looked. "Get that wound seen to. Then have ourselves a little conversation."

I held fast to Harper's hand. She edged forward, slowly raising a hand to signal the bus driver to wait. The grip around my arm hardened and I winced. What if he had a gun? What if that was the next object he would thrust against my body? My thoughts spiraled as my throat dried out.

Fear raced along my spine.

I think I peed my pants a little bit. Harper didn't move, her mouth wide open.

Then, a fierce rage swallowed the fear swimming in my stomach. "I have no interest in a conversation with you."

The bus driver moved his hand to the button to close the doors. My chest tightened. Yanking my arm away from its tight hold, I pivoted toward the man. All of my anger erupted. "How dare you! How dare you threaten me when all I'm trying to do is save the ocean."

People turned to stare. The bus engine ticked over.

I pointed a finger at the suited EnRG rep and narrowed my eyes. "You know what's out there. You know Regina created a monster that's hurting people." I pointed at the red skin on my wrist. Someone behind me muttered the word "monster". I couldn't tell if it was sarcastic or not. A woman raised a phone and hit record. "And yet you do nothing. You are helping an evil woman. People are going to get hurt because of you."

He lowered his hands and a flicker of emotion crossed his face. "If you'd sign the NDAs—"

"This isn't about a stupid NDA!" I hurled the words at him, my breath coming in angry gasps. "This is about a threat to our town, potentially the whole coastline. You need to let me stop it."

He shook his head slowly. "You can't stop it." His voice was low and his eyes skirted over the bunched people, centering on the woman recording the whole exchange. Good. "You're just a girl. And it's... it's... huge."

"Well, I'm damn well going to try."

Slowly, I backed toward the bus. People stared at me, muttering under their breath. I didn't care. They needed to know what was in the water.

"Don't go near the water. Don't turn on the taps in your house. Drink bottled water. From glass bottles, not plastic. *Please*."

I stumbled onto the bus behind Harper and the driver gave me an appraising look.

The doors slammed closed behind me and I doubled over, resting my hands on my thighs. As the bus lurched away, I turned to look at the people outside the window. The rep stood on the sidewalk staring at us, his face pinched with guilt. But would he do anything?

The bus driver leaned over. "What did you say about a...

monster?" He whispered the word. I couldn't tell if he was playing with me or not.

"Don't go in the water," I said.

The man nodded and his eyes glistened. "My son died out there windsurfing recently. I wondered... never mind."

The windsurfer Tyler, Dad and I had watched drown. He was this man's son. I didn't know what to say. No words helped that kind of grief.

"I'm sorry for your loss," Harper said, dragging me to a seat.

I sagged into a chair and tried not to cry. I knew Regina had to be stopped. The Great Green had to be stopped. But after having been accosted so physically, I felt so small. The rep had said I was just a girl. He was right. I *was* just a girl. How could I stop something as big as The Great Green and an evil corporation?

One step at a time.

Don't think about the big picture.

Just one step at a time.

Danny's voice spoke in my head. That's what he always said when I got frustrated learning something new.

"One step at a time," I whispered.

Harper wound her arm through mine, then pulled a rumpled tissue out of her pocket and handed it to me. "It's clean."

I took it and mopped at the drying blood on my leg. It started bleeding again. Neither of us had a Band-Aid so I used the tissue to apply pressure until the bleeding stopped.

At least we were safe. For now. I didn't know who the rep had been calling as the bus pulled away, but he had no idea where we were going. Harper curled herself into me. We hugged, holding onto each other tightly. I was so tired of being afraid.

Harper nudged my arm. "Move over, Veronica Mars. Sara Monroe is on the case."

I smiled weakly at her. "Thanks for coming with me."

She nodded. "Shit just got real."

"Are you still up for it?"

"Abso-freakin-lutely!" She cocked a shoulder. "With great power comes great responsibility."

I smiled at the familiar quote, then said, "Not sure I'm feeling particularly powerful right now."

She tapped the side of her head. "Knowledge is our power."

The bus took the long route to La Jolla, along the coastal road, where the green of the ocean shone at us mockingly, as if daring us to come and fight.

The bus ride gave us a chance to catch our breath and get over the shock of almost being kidnapped. Every few minutes, my legs would quiver as the adrenaline leaked away. Harper held my hand. Behind us, people chatted quietly about the ocean, the trash, putting all their hopes in EnRG. I heard a couple mutterings of toxic burns, but no one had a clue what the problem really was, that EnRG was behind it. There was one guy in his twenties who stared at the others as they spoke about hallucinations and hoaxes. Without warning, he launched to his feet, swaying danger-ously as the bus lurched around a corner.

He pointed at me. "Those girls are right. There's some-thing in the water. I've seen it."

"There's something in the water all right," an old man piped up. "A whole bunch of toxic trash. That's what you've seen. Was going to take my granddaughter out on the cata-maran. The summer is ruined." He shook his head.

The younger guy scoffed. "Not trash. Not *just* trash. An... animal. It burned my legs." He hiked up his shorts to reveal angry blisters wrapping around both thighs.

"It's the toxins all the trash brought," an elderly lady said from the front of the bus, her handbag perched on her knees. "It causes blisters... and hallucinations. You shouldn't have been in the water."

The young guy stared at her, at everyone. "Why does no one believe?"

I looked at him. "They don't want to. They don't want to believe something truly dangerous is in the water." I scanned the mute group. Some muttered, some looked away. "That something so big and horrible could be created by an evil organization and that Operation Blue Water has lost control. EnRG plastic killed my brother three years ago, and now they're killing our ocean."

The old man snorted. "We are not living in a comic book."

"Then how do you explain all the sightings? The shaky, fearful video clips? The stories on social media the press refuse to substantiate? A Coast Guard ship sinking in frothing green water? A crew of six people attacked by a... by a... by a monster and ending up with third-degree burns? How do you explain what's happening?"

The old man shook his head and looked away.

"You young people," the old lady muttered.

Others stared at me, but no one offered a reply.

"I've seen it," I said. "Just like him." I pointed at the younger guy. "I've got the same blisters. So do my friends."

"Prove it, then!" someone called. "Show us this green monster."

"I'm on my way to do that right now."

Silence descended on the bus. Exhausted, I slumped back in my seat. Outside the window, I spotted press vans heading to Almond Cove. I hoped no one was stupid enough to go in the ocean. Luminescent green waves swept onto the beach parallel to the road. Even in the dark, the vibrancy of the color was obvious.

"She better know how to stop this," I hissed under my breath. "There isn't a damn fish in the ocean or a single bird on the beach."

Harper patted my thigh. "We'll figure it out. Or we'll move inland."

"I don't even think Kansas would be safe. Even if the stupid green monster is the same color as the Emerald City."

She laughed and rested her head on my shoulder.

When the bus began a long ascent, I knew we were close. Regina lived on the cliffs above the ocean in La Jolla. No one else got off the bus with Harper and I in the expensive neighborhood. In the dark, I scanned left and right, trying to get my bearings, then gestured to a road winding around the clifftop. "Five minutes that way."

"No wonder she's looked the other way," Harper said, taking in the manicured lawns and boxed hedges. "If big business makes this much money."

"All the money in the world wouldn't make me turn my back on the environment."

The driveways were lined with expensive stones and marble, and many were large enough for an army of cars.

Sprinklers spluttered on green lawns and ostentatious statues guarded wide double doors. I stared for a moment, trying to determine if I could detect any green tinges in the revolving water, but to my eyes, everything looked green. I was starting to detest the color. Outside one house, a large anchor took up most of the space on the porch, polished to a sheen.

On my right, the ocean churned a good forty feet below the cliffs. The green color wasn't as bright here and the trash wasn't as thick, but it would work its way up the coast, destroying anything in its way. Maybe it would even break off into smaller monsters, going off in different directions, infiltrating all the world's oceans. I couldn't let that happen. We needed to stop it here before it evolved further.

"Which one is it?" Harper asked as the end of the road came into view. It curled into a large turning circle that over-looked the ocean.

I pointed to an enormous house at the end of the narrow peninsula. Large windows faced the cliff-top view and tumbling ocean below. I could hear the waves crashing on the rocks. I wondered if there were any green amorphous limbs attempting to climb up here. "This last one, right here."

"How do you know?"

"I may have rifled through the paperwork of the court case looking for it. I may have even driven by a couple times."

"You are so bad!" Harper giggled.

"Gotta keep tabs on the local crime."

I chuckled, the laugh pushing away some of the nerves building in my stomach. We tiptoed closer to the house. A winding path, flanked with red roses, led to an imposing wooden and glass door guarded by two EnRG reps. Several windows were lit, as if trying to burn away the darkness. Or The Great Green.

The security light above the porch flicked on. We ducked behind a prickly hedge, waiting for the beam to stop scoping the front yard. The reps looked bored, as if this happened all the time. After a minute, the light switched off. I clamped down on a shriek as a lizard crawled across my foot. Harper covered my mouth with her hand.

I held my breath until I felt dizzy. Harper pressed herself deeper into the bush. A crunch of gravel sounded under her feet. I bit down on my lip until the lizard crawled away.

"So, how do we get past the reps?" Harper whispered.

"We're going to have to find another way in," I replied, scanning the front of the house. Many of the windows were wide open. I hoped the back of the house was the same.

On my stomach, I crawled out of the bush and snaked my way through the hedges, trying desperately not to rustle a single leaf. I thanked the heavens for the tail of the gusty Santa Ana winds that should hide the noise of our advance. As we army-crawled away from the house, I kept my eyes on the reps. They didn't so much as glance in our direction.

One of their walkie-talkies went off and Harper yelped. We were at the corner of the house and I froze. Neither of us dared to breathe. The reps moved, causing the security lights to flash on, and stepped into the front yard. Slowly, we inched our way around the house until we couldn't see them anymore. With our backs against the wall, we dared to breathe again.

"That was close," Harper whispered.

I nodded and squeezed her knee. "Come on."

This time we crawled on hands and knees until we reached the next corner. The backyard contained a huge manicured lawn. Structured bushes created beautiful beds and at the far end of the yard was a full-sized tennis court.

"Wow," Harper muttered.

"There's no reps," I said, watching the back of the house.

We hurried to the back door. Looking through the window, I saw it led to the kitchen. I put my hand on the doorknob and glanced at Harper. She nodded. I winced and pushed. Locked. But at least an alarm didn't go off.

"Damn."

"Let's try the windows," Harper said, already retreating along the path.

All of the ground-floor windows were closed and wouldn't budge even with force.

Harper glanced at the wide-open second-story windows, curtains billowing in the breeze. "We're going to have to climb."

"Don't be ridiculous," I said.

"Veronica Mars does it all the time."

"I hate to break it to you, but we're not actually Veronica Mars."

"Look." Harper pointed. "The downstairs window has a wide ledge. Then we use part of the rose trellis to grab onto the drainpipe, which will take us right up to that open window."

I gulped, feeling all kinds of stupid. Maybe this wasn't such a good idea.

Harper faced me and put a hand on my cheek. "We're

not going to be able to stop The Great Green if we don't talk to Regina."

I nodded and attempted to breathe in some bravery. This was the kind of foolish thing Danny used to steer me away from. But then why had he risked his own life to save a crate of lobsters?

Harper went first. She stuck her sneakered foot in my hand and I boosted her up to the window ledge. When a crow cawed, I almost dropped her foot and she wobbled on the edge, gripping tight to the trellis. We both froze. My heart pounded and I strained to hear over its insistent beat. I was worried the reps might come around back.

"Let's keep going," Harper whispered.

Once she had a firm foot on the trellis and a good grip on the drainpipe, she leaned over and offered me a hand. I stepped up the wall as she pulled, her face going red, until I found a balancing point on the ledge. I'd never been afraid of heights, but I reminded myself not to look down just in case.

Slowly, we worked our way to the right-hand side of the trellis and along to the drainpipe. I sent up a quick prayer of thanks that both were well maintained and not in danger of crumbling under our weight.

Harper reached the window first, ducked her head in between the drifting drapes, and then disappeared into the dark.

"Harper!" I hissed after her. "Where did you go?"

A moment later, her head appeared, and she reached both arms out to drag me inside. We landed on soft carpet with a dull thud. She giggled. I shushed her and listened for footsteps.

I smelled old-fashioned potpourri and felt the luxury carpet under my back, but I couldn't hear anything out of the ordinary. Only the lulling sounds of the ocean.

"Come on," I said, getting to my feet. "We need to find Regina."

Her lips twisted, an uncertain expression on her face. "What if she has a gun?"

It was a real possibility, one I foolishly hadn't considered. But I couldn't turn back now.

"She doesn't strike me as a gun person," I said, forcing some confidence into my voice. "Besides, she'd have her goons do her dirty work for her."

We inched across the carpet. Beside me, Harper stuck to my side like a barnacle and tripped over my feet. We came out in the upstairs hallway. Both directions were shadowed, but some lights spilled out of open doorways. Regina could be in any one of those rooms. Harper shuffled toward a grand, galleried staircase. Made of a rich, polished wood I didn't recognize, the staircase curved around and around and disappeared into the first floor. The banister was wooden with wrought-iron detail, and cold to the touch. Air conditioners hummed in the background even though all the windows were wide open. What a waste of electricity. We trailed through the house, looking for signs of life. Irritation prickled my spine at the thought she might not be here. She had to be here. I had questions, and an ocean to save.

We tiptoed down the stairs and found ourselves in a vast kitchen, everything gleaming white and chrome in the moonlight. White tiles, white walls, white counter tops, silver appliances. Everything polished and expensive. With no lamps lit, it was difficult to determine the shapes and shadows. Creeping around, I knocked over a glass bowl of seashells sitting on the edge of the breakfast bar. Harper managed to catch it before it crashed to the floor.

"And you call me the clumsy one," she muttered.

A different color drew my attention under the counter. An entire fridge full of bright orange EnRG cans shone, the orange color seeping across the tiled floor. Tyler would have a field day.

I flicked on a light.

Harper blanched. "Should you be doing that? She'll find us."

Ignoring the mounting nerves wiggling in my stomach, I turned to my friend. "That's exactly what I want to happen."

Chapter Twenty

SOFT RUSTLING CAME from a distant hallway, followed by an approaching silhouette. Regina stepped into the light, into the kitchen. She wore a long, white negligee which was covered by a satin robe of the same color. Her red hair was loose, free of her characteristic chignon. Carrying an empty crystal tumbler, she stumbled when she moved from carpet to tiled floor.

Harper inhaled sharply.

"Jack? Is that you?"

I didn't know who Jack was. One of the security reps? I hoped not a pitbull with a taste for blood.

Her gaze landed on us and she blinked rapidly, as if trying to blink us away. I planted my feet in a broad stance, as I'd seen Frank do when he spoke to the reps. I hoped it made me look confident, someone not to be messed with.

"Good evening," Regina said, recovering her composure. She straightened her shoulders and lifted her chin, ever the commanding figure. But I refused to be intimidated by her. "If I'd known I was going to be hosting a late-night party, I would have stocked the fridge."

"I'll be sure to grab a can of EnRG on my way out," I snapped.

Unruffled, she frowned. "Who are you?"

I hadn't prepared a speech. My passion would have to speak for me.

She leaned her shoulder against the wall. "Wait, I remember you. You're that pestering nuisance on the beach. Sara, is it?"

"Yes," I said, stepping forward. "I'm here to pester you again."

"How did you get in here?" Her wary gaze flicked between Harper and me, then to the front door. "Jack? Are you out there?"

Jack didn't reply, whoever he was. Maybe he was still outside chasing mysterious noises.

"Jack let us in," Harper lied. "Told him we had important business with the CEO of EnRG."

"I don't believe that for a minute." Regina laughed, then the abrasive sound cut off abruptly. She moved forward, but stumbled again. Was she drunk?

"Do you need to sit down?" I asked.

She didn't reply, but moved to a sideboard nearby, opened the latticed door of an oak cupboard and pulled out a bottle of amber liquor. She filled her glass to the brim. "Where's Jack? What have you done with Jack?" she asked, her words slurring but her tone strong.

"I don't know where Jack is," I said, crossing my arms. "I'm not here to talk about Jack." I had bigger fish to fry. Monsters, actually.

Determination made my jaw ache, but it didn't stop my nerves. I wasn't scared of Regina calling the police or being arrested for intruding. I was afraid of not getting the information Regina held in her head. I needed it. The world did. But would she part with it?

"You've created a monster," I said.

The startled look on Regina's face proved she had no idea how much I knew. "You can't prove that."

"So, you admit it?"

"Sara, dear. Why couldn't you have stuck to beach cleaning? Haven't you ever heard about curiosity killing the cat?" She sounded terrifyingly confident, but the hand holding her glass shook. Her unfiltered look pinned me to the cold tiled floor. The righteous confidence leached out of me faster than blood from a severed artery.

"Are you threatening me?"

"Threatening you?" A hand flew to her chest. "Goodness! Of course not! I would never hurt such a valuable volunteer." Her eyes narrowed. "As long as they toe the line."

A scratchy feeling irritated the back of my neck and I lost all my good sense. I saw a red mist of rage. "One of your men attacked me!"

"Attacked?" She cocked her head, irritatingly calm, only serving to highlight how emotional I was. "What are you talking about?"

"He accosted us, in public," Harper said, inching to my side. "He tried to kidnap us."

Regina's gaze darted between us as she ran a finger around the rim of her full glass. "I don't know anything about that." Her lips twitched, and something flashed through her sap-colored eyes. Perhaps sympathy. But only for an instant before they hardened into a cold stare.

"You've done bad things," I said, finding my voice. "And you're trying to cover your tracks. And we were asking too many questions. Is there a hit out on us?"

"A *hit*? Goodness me!" Regina's lips curled into a wicked grin before she evened out her features. "I don't need to explain myself to a couple of nosy teenagers who don't know how to keep their snouts out of trouble. Jack? Where are you?"

The front door swung open and a burly rep dressed in a dark suit rushed inside. "Everything okay, Ms. Harron?"

"These girls are leaving. See they get home *safely*."

"How did you get in here?" Jack marched toward us.

I raised a palm. "Stop right there! You are aiding and abetting a murderer. *Ms. Harron* is responsible for the deaths of at least four people and many more injuries." I pointed at my burns. "If I were you, I'd stay right where you are."

He hesitated, looking between the three of us and came to a stop at the threshold.

Regina glared at me, her deadly gaze making my skin crawl. I glared right back at her, taking confidence from Harper's presence beside me. I couldn't have done this on my own. And I had Danny with me too, in my head, in my heart, in my soul, cheering me on.

"I'm not leaving until I get some answers." I stood taller, straightening my back, and shooting her my most evil scowl.

She chuckled, but the sound came out brittle, like crunching dead leaves. "Who on earth do you think I am? Some mafia boss with a hitlist as long as my arm? Don't be ridiculous, girls. I've never ordered anyone to be hurt, merely..."

"Merely what?" I asked.

She shook herself, casting a quick glance at Jack, as if realizing she'd said too much. "Well, we can't have everyone running around spouting stories of... ridiculous things. I'm trying to clean up the ocean. Quickly and quietly. We can't have every busy body and reporter poking around. I needed time to keep the more curious at bay. The curious are persistent." She rolled her eyes. "So, I needed a little help."

"Ms. Harron," Jack cut in. "I need to caution you not to say anything—"

"The chief of Almond Cove's fire department is in the hospital," I yelled, jabbing my point into the air with an unforgiving index finger. "Because he was hurt while rescuing people from the ocean."

Regina took a large gulp of her drink. "I'll send flowers."

Flowers? Her statement rendered me speechless for a moment. "Flowers aren't going to cut it! Call off your men."

"I don't have any men—"

I thrust a finger in Jack's face. "Who the hell is this then?"

"Cut the crap!" Harper yelled, her voice echoing off the stark tiles. "They tried to follow us here tonight. They tried to stop us. They tried to kidnap Sara. We *know* you have men."

Regina's face paled to match the color of her satin robe. Her lips pursed, as if considering what excuses to offer up next.

"Jack, perhaps you better leave us alone to talk."

Jack gave us one last evaluating look, then backed out the door. His gaze lingered on me. I couldn't read his thoughts, but I thought I detected a hint of sympathy. Would he help us? Or did Regina have something on her reps too? How else could she get them to follow her orders so relentlessly when the whole world was falling apart?

"I've written to the press," I said, dragging in a breath, trying to still the anger and fear in my chest. "I've instructed them to open my letter if they don't hear from me by morning. Your name is *all over* that letter. Do you really want to be held responsible if anything happens to us?"

It was a complete and utter lie. I wished I had written such a letter. All I could do now was bluff my way through it.

"Yeah," Harper said. "Me too."

Regina took a long sip of her drink. I was pleased to notice her hand still trembling. She might appear like a badass, but inside, she had to be terrified. Finally, she nodded and removed a cellphone from the pocket of her robe. Raising it to her ear, she spoke softly into the mouthpiece. Only two words. "Stand down."

I had been right all along. Regina Harron was an evil woman and she didn't care who she stepped on, threatened, or burned in the process of her ambition. With her admission, the energy drained out of me, leaving me exhausted. But we still had The Great Green to deal with.

"You created a monster," I said, calmer now I was gaining traction. "You created an algae to eat the plastic. But it didn't, it combined with it instead. Tell me, am I getting warm?"

I felt like Harper, talking a mile a minute. Regina's expression changed. Her features were no longer belittling, but quirked and pulsed with curiosity.

"Combine with it?" A laugh tumbled out of her mouth, forced and unnatural. Danger ran through her eyes. I had to tread carefully. She may have called off her men, but I had no idea what she was capable of, and we stood only inches apart, facing each other. I had to be ready for anything. "Whatever are you talking about?"

"It combined with it and became something else entirely, didn't it?" I leaned forward. "It's killed people. And animals. How could you make something like that?"

Regina took another long glug of her drink, her eyes darting between us. "I don't know what you're talking about. Honestly, where do you girls get these fanciful ideas? Teenagers today..." she trailed off when she saw I wasn't buying any of it.

"It turned into a monster. A green trash monster that burns people with a horrible acid." I held up my hand. "It burned me. And it sunk an entire Coast Guard ship. A COAST GUARD CUTTER! And yet your catamaran sits there, on top of it all, completely unharmed. What the fuck?"

Damn the swear jar. These were exceptional circumstances.

While I spoke, the skin around Regina's eyes twitched, her lips pressed together and the hand holding the tumbler shook, spilling some of the contents onto the floor.

"I was trying to do something good."

"Have you seen all those dead fish and turtles and dolphins? Killed by the algae. That's not doing something good!" I slammed my hand on the table. Regina flinched. I allowed myself a small moment of satisfaction before her eyes narrowed again. I marched forward, until I was all up in her face and could smell the alcohol on her breath. Almonds. It smelled like almonds.

"Tell me how to get rid of it."

Regina laughed. Genuinely. She threw her face to the ceiling, cradled her stomach with her free hand, and laughed. She laughed so long and hard, Harper and I couldn't do anything but stare at each other.

Finally, she settled down, smoothed her hair, and topped up her glass, even though it didn't need topping up. She slumped into a chair at the kitchen table, a white wicker thing with cream cushions.

"There's nothing you can do. There's nothing anyone can do. It's too late."

"There must be a way," I said.

The smirk formed on her lips again and I was afraid she'd launch into another hysterical laughing fit. But she managed to keep herself composed. "There isn't. No one can stop it. It's growing, constantly, and killing any researcher who tries something new." She spread her hands helplessly. "I've tried everything."

The rush of cold fear surprised me. All this time, I'd known something was wrong, that something needed to be fought, killed, dealt with. Something. Somehow. I knew EnRG was responsible and that Regina held the answers. If I could get to her. But now I was here, with a drunken CEO who had entirely given up, the situation was far worse than I'd thought. Regina was supposed to have the answers, but she was as clueless as us.

What if we couldn't stop it? What if it grew and grew and grew until there was nothing left? Is this how the human race would die?

"My brother died," I said. "Three years ago. His scuba gear got tangled in EnRG's plastic wrap."

"I remember," Regina said, a level of compassion in her voice I hadn't thought her capable of. "I'm so sorry."

My chest clenched tight. "It was an awful death. Running out of air, knowing it was coming and not being able to do anything about it."

Her gaze fell to her glass. "I've lost people too."

I looked around the kitchen. I hadn't noticed the lack of usual family photos. But her words made me reevaluate the room. There was nothing like the corkboard I had at home with all the notes and family snaps and takeout menus. Here, there were vases of fake flowers, the glass bowl of seashells, a painting of the ocean, wild and stormy, and the expensive crystal tumblers and champagne flutes displayed in the frosted glass cupboards. But nothing personal. Nothing to give away the details of her life.

With tears in my eyes, I pulled out a chair and sat opposite her.

Harper stayed standing, hovering by my elbow. "We can't do nothing."

My shoulders sagged. "You created a monster and it's going to destroy everything. But why hasn't it destroyed your catamaran?"

Her skin paled, the freckles on her cheeks darkening in contrast. "A child never attacks its mother." Her trembling hand brought the glass to her lips once more and her gaze turned to the window where we could all see the sparkling green trash. "It's so beautiful, isn't it?" she slurred.

"The end of the world isn't beautiful," I snapped, slapping my palm on the table. The sudden noise made her jump. "You can't give up. Tell me how to stop it."

"I am not a scientist." Regina wiped at her tired eyes, smudging her mascara. Her face filled with misery. "I hired scientists to do the job for me. Now most of them are dead." She choked on the last word and tears spilled down her cheeks. She didn't bother wiping them away.

"Isn't there anyone left?" Harper asked.

"One," Regina whispered. Out of the ten Operation Blue Water staff who were introduced to the world five days ago, only one was still alive. This was so much worse than I'd thought. "It's too late. It's too big. No one knows what can kill it." She took another long sip. "I tried. I was trying to do something good. I tried. And now I have to live with it."

A surprised laugh escaped my lips. "Something good? Since when do you do anything for the greater good? EnRG causes weird growths and addiction, and God knows what else. Why on earth would you care about doing something good?" I swept a hand around the room. "Look at this place. It's a palace. You could live here and make your horrible drink and never have to see the effects. Stay cocooned in your private mansion for the rest of your life and ignore all the lives you've destroyed. My father makes his living on the water! And now, because of you and your atrocious drink, he doesn't have a job!"

Regina rubbed her finger across a small puddle of spilled liquor on the table. "EnRG is my company. I created it. I birthed it. I nurtured it. I was about to be fined. I couldn't let it all go. A solution had to be found." Her eyes clouded.

"More people are going to get hurt. You've convinced everyone that toxins in the trash island are causing hallucinations. That the monster isn't real. Even the Coast Guard has fallen for your crap. People need to know the truth."

"I'd be finished."

"You're finished anyway," Harper said.

"It's too late," Regina said.

I shook my head. "It can't be. You've got to give me something."

Her fingers gripped her glass, turning white. "Burn it. It's flammable. At least, it should be, or it was, before it evolved. So burn it. Extinguish it from the ocean. From the universe."

"Burn it," I muttered. "How do you burn something that lives in water?"

"I don't know," Regina whispered.

Sensing the conversation was coming to an end, I stood. I locked my eyes on her, examining this woman. This woman who had destroyed my ocean, my beach, my life. I was furious with her. I wanted to make her pay. I wanted to feed her to the monster, not let her stay sheltered in her cliffside mansion. "You need to get off your butt and do something. Don't just sit here. Get up! Get up! Do something! Find a way to help. Before it's all gone."

She looked at me, her eyes sunken and her cheeks hollowed out. "I can't. I've tried." She lowered her gaze to her glass and sipped. Again and again and again. Maybe she'd drink herself to death.

"Come on," I said to Harper. "Let's get out of here."

At the kitchen doorway, I turned back to Regina. "Where is Simona?"

Her head moved in my direction, inch by inch. "The marine biologist? I have no idea."

For once, I believed her.

Chapter Twenty-One

I was surprised to find daylight hinting at the sky as we left the house. Jack stood stationed by the front door and he grabbed my arm on the way out. I whirled on him, ready to fight. I was not going to let another one of Regina's goons touch me ever again.

He held up his hands. "Sorry! Didn't mean to frighten you. I just want to talk."

"I don't think we have anything to talk about," I snapped.

"I heard everything you said." Jack looked over his shoulder and pulled the front door closed. "About the monster. It's not a hallucination. I've seen it too."

I studied his face. He had a prominent nose that sat on broad cheeks. His hair was closely cropped and his blue eyes sincere. Although his biceps were thicker than my thighs, I didn't think he wanted to hurt me.

Exhausted, I exhaled, not sure I could speak anymore.

"Where's the other one?" Harper demanded. "The other rep? There were two of you when he arrived."

"Shift change time. Two more will be along soon."

"Then we better get going," I said.

"Wait," Jack said, raising a hand to touch me again, then letting it drop to his side. "I want to help."

"What about Regina?" Harper asked. "Don't you have orders?"

Jack's eyes narrowed. "Screw the orders. My best buddy was burned in the ocean. All over his face." He gulped. "I want to help kill this thing. It is a *thing*, right?"

I nodded.

"So, how do we kill it? Do you have a plan?"

I shook my head. "Not yet. But we'll let you know."

I took his card which had his cellphone number on it and felt a small measure of hope. We had help. Jack had promised to talk to the other reps. Hopefully, he could turn them too. Then we wouldn't have to run all the time.

Harper and I walked down the cliff road. The sun rose and muted the vibrancy of the green water and gray light bruised the lower part of the horizon.

"Fire better damn well work." Harper kicked at loose stones. "Regina will probably report us to the cops before we can launch an attack."

"She won't report us to the cops," I said. "She'd end up getting herself in trouble. Especially if her reps are turning against her. Score one point for the home team."

"We need a lot more points."

"We'll get them, but we don't need Regina anymore."

"Say what?" Harper asked.

"You know what I realized in there?"

"What?"

"She's just a shriveled, beaten woman who's run out of

options and doesn't have a plan anymore." I shook my head. "All these years I've spent hating her from afar, blaming her for Danny, wishing she was dead in his place... I don't know. All the fates I imagined for her, it wouldn't change anything. It wouldn't bring Danny back. It wouldn't alter the circumstances of his death."

Harper turned to me on the corner of the road, reached out a hand to tug at the hem of my sweatshirt. "Are you making progress in your grief? We haven't talked about Danny in a long time. I didn't know it was still so raw for you."

Unable to speak, I waved a hand. It had been three years. I should have gotten over it by now. Well, not completely over it, but I wished I could look at a picture of him without feeling so sad.

"Don't do that," Harper said. "Don't dismiss it. You always do that. He was your big brother. You loved him. Hell, I loved him."

Smiling, I allowed the tears to form. "I miss him so much. I've dreamed of challenging her one-on-one for years. It didn't go how I had it in my head. I imagined her bowing down at my feet and all that crap and expecting the pain to magically go away. Stupid really. But even though it didn't go like that, I feel... sorry for her." It was the truth, and it wrapped around me clearer than water.

"I get it," Harper said.

"Regina is just a person. Just one human being. She did a bad thing and she's lost control. She doesn't have an out. She'll probably spend the rest of her life living with her crappy decisions. Maybe she was trying to do something good. But it backfired in the worst possible way, and she isn't strong enough to deal with the consequences. But I am. I'm going to kill The Great Green and I'm going to do it for Danny."

"I'm so proud of you." Harper hugged me, and I let her, feeling the security of her arms tightening around me.

Silence whipped between us as we headed back to the bus stop and my house. We didn't climb through the gardens this time, but walked down the road and into my driveway. With relief, I noted the black SUV was no longer there. There was nothing stopping Regina from putting on the order to watch us again once we'd turned our backs, but I had a feeling she was too worn out to bother.

Thoroughly exhausted, I trudged up the porch steps, but pulled to a halt when I spotted a figure slumped across the swing chair. With a leg in a cast and a newspaper over her face, Simona snored softly.

Gently, I shook her awake. She sat bolt upright, the newspaper falling to the ground and her plastered leg thumping after it.

She winced. "Ouch. That hurt."

"What happened to you?" I asked, handing her a pair of crutches I spotted leaning by the front door.

"We thought you'd been kidnapped," Harper said.

"Kidnapped?" Simona asked, flicking her hair over her shoulder. She leaned on the crutches and pushed herself to her feet. "Why would I have been kidnapped? I sent you an email."

"With one word!" I half shouted at her. "I needed more info."

"The nurse needed her phone back," Simona replied,

then narrowed her eyes at me. "Are you okay? What's going on?"

"We've all been burned, were nearly kidnapped, and almost killed by a monster." Shock registered on Simona's face. I raised a hand. "We're okay, we're all okay." Then I told her about The Great Green and our little midnight visit to Regina's house.

"Regina has no idea how to kill it," Harper said, her words gaining speed. "She's completely clueless. Evil and clueless. The worst combination. Even her scientists have no idea how to stop their own creation. Hell, most of them are dead. The best we can hope for is to try and burn it. She says it's flammable. And one of the reps is going to help us." She ran out of steam and slumped against the house.

"Do you have any ideas?" I asked Simona. "Have you got the test results from your lab?"

She shook her head. "I called a half hour ago. Results aren't ready yet. They're going to call me as soon as they get them." She checked her watch. "And girls, before we hatch a plan to save the world, think I can get a coffee first?"

"Of course. As long as you don't mind it sparkling." I smiled at her, then added a hug. I had given and received more hugs in the past week than I had in the last three years. Maybe the end of the world brought my guard down. "I'm so glad you're okay. What happened to you?" I led them into the house and put a pot of coffee on made with sparkling water.

"I had just gotten out of the shower." Simona slid into a chair at the kitchen table, resting her crutches against the back of another. She popped a couple of painkillers in her mouth and swallowed them dry. "The winds got pretty wild, and the deck chair broke the patio door. I went to close it, but a coconut flew in, smashed the coffee table. I was still wet from the shower and slipped and fell, knocking my head on my favorite painting and breaking my leg. A neighbor heard my scream and called an ambulance."

"We went there to find you," I said. "And assumed the worst."

Simona reached for my hand. "*Estoy bien*. I'm okay. I forgot to take my phone and I couldn't remember anyone's numbers. But then I remembered your email and thought to borrow the nurse's phone."

"I can't tell you how glad I am you're here." The Great Green was bigger than me. For the first time in my life, I wanted help. I *needed* help. Adult help. Thank God Simona was here. "And you've got your phone now." I nodded at the bulge in her back pocket.

Simona patted her pocket. "Went back to my apartment first, saw the mess and couldn't face it. So I grabbed my phone and purse and came here instead."

"I'm glad you did," I replied.

"So, how do we burn this thing anyway?" Harper asked. She poured coffee into three mugs and handed them out. No one took sugar or milk. We needed strength today. "How are you supposed to burn water?"

"Burn?" Simona smiled. "I may have an idea. It isn't just water. There's trash in there too. I happen to have a couple of cases of high-proof Mexican tequila in the trunk of my car from a recent trip back home. I reckon we Molotov cocktail its ass."

I grinned.

"You want to waste good tequila on The Great Green?"

Harper asked, then lowered her voice. "We could save a bottle for us."

Simona raised an eyebrow. "I know I'm not the most responsible of adults, but there's no way I'm letting you guys get drunk. Not on my watch."

"Gosh darn it," Harper laughed, swinging her arm in a parody of disappointment.

"We can make up the cocktails, head up to the bluffs above the cove where there's no barricades, and throw them at the monster without having to go in the water. What do you think, girls?" Simona asked.

"We'd need to get it angry," I said. "So it came up and out of the water."

"I don't think that will be a problem," Harper said.

It was a plan. A dangerous one, but still a plan. At least I would be doing something while everyone else watched with their hands tied and their phone footage mocked.

"I think we could do with some help," I said, getting to my feet, dialing Jack's number from the landline. My phone call woke him up, sleeping off last night's shift. As I explained the situation, I heard him rustling around, jangling keys.

"Be there in five," he said, hanging up.

I looked at Simona and Harper. "Jack is coming."

Harper grinned. "I'm all for girl power, but it would be nice to have a bit of brute strength along for the ride."

"*Madre mía*," Simona muttered, making the sign of the cross. "Who is this guy?"

"He's backup," I replied, refreshing our coffees. Even though I didn't sleep a wink last night, I was wired, ready to take on The Great Green. I slurped at my coffee and paced the living room while waiting for Jack to arrive.

A short time later, he screeched down the street on a motorcycle, burning rubber as he pulled into the driveway. We gathered at the window to see him dressed in black jeans and a black T-shirt. His beefy presence brought immediate reassurance. He marched up the porch with his helmet under his arm and left it on the swing chair.

"I'm ready," he said, when I opened the front door.

I introduced him to Simona. Both of their eyes went wider than necessary, and I had to restrain myself from making sarcastic comments about untimely romances. But hell, we could die in the next few minutes, why not let them have their moment?

Simona had broken her left leg, so she could still drive her car. Its trunk door kept opening with all the boxes of tequila inside. We loaded in rags and matches. Jack sat next to her in the front and held her crutches for her, while Harper and I climbed into the back.

"Promise we're not going on the water," Harper said. "It sunk the cutter..." she shook her head as fear dilated her pupils.

"We won't get anywhere near the boats, not again," I said. "We'll stay on the clifftop. If we stick to the overhang, we'll be safe. We can draw it out of the water a little and let the fire do the work."

"You think this is going to work?" Jack asked, his bulk taking up most of the small car.

No one answered. I refused to be anything but optimistic. It *had* to work. It *had* to die. The alternatives were too ugly to contemplate.

Simona pulled off the main road and took the narrow cliff track. We bumped over unpaved potholes and my teeth smacked together.

"Shit, that hurts," Simona growled, a wince crossing her face.

"Be glad we're not walking," Harper said. "Took us an hour to climb up the path the other day."

"You guys need cars," Simona said.

Harper lifted both eyebrows and thrust her phone in Simona's face. "You can call my mom anytime."

Simona laughed.

Needing air, I rolled down my window, and Simona followed suit. Her hair flew in every direction, angry and aggressive, as if sensing her mood.

I watched the green ocean as we ascended above sea level. It wasn't even an ocean anymore. The waves didn't lap and there were no foaming crests. It was all trash. A monster. An irregular shape sprinkled with brilliant green. Between the finger piers in the marina, it was hard to distinguish the trash from the boats.

My stomach sank as we got closer to the cove. There were four of us to battle an immortal monster. There was no way the four of us could take out The Great Green with a few bottles of liquor. We'd be better off drinking it and obliterating the next few days from our consciousness. If I was going to get killed by a trash monster, if it was going to infiltrate the water system, burn us all, then being drunk might help with the pain. I'd never been drunk before, I'd promised Danny I wouldn't drink after Will's cousin had died from alcohol poisoning, but I thought he would understand.

"I don't know if it's going to work," I said. "But I can't sit back and let it steal my ocean."

"I'm with you," Harper said. "Jackson & Monroe until death."

Simona flicked us a gaze in her rearview. "Please don't say *death*."

"I don't understand why people aren't doing more," I said. "FEMA, the local government, someone. There are stories all over social media, but they're being completely dismissed."

Jack turned around to look at me. "Because the EnRG reps are discrediting anyone who posts about it. Calling them crackpots, conspiracy theorists, undermining their credibility, using the hallucination line. We couldn't stop people taking photos, but EnRG could make them appear off their rockers."

"But what about Homeland Security?" I asked. "The Coast Guard? FEMA? Someone has to be aware."

Jack shook his head. "We've been feeding stories to FEMA and the media and not letting them get close enough to see the real thing."

I gaped at him. "How is that even possible?"

Jack's mouth set. "It only takes money. And a little bit of persuasion."

The human race was disappointing. How could we be duped so easily?

"And yet," Simona said. "The boardwalk is lined with press crews. Nosy civilians are straining at the barricades. People are flying here to see this green trash island, not knowing it's really a monster. They think the Coast Guard cutter was a hoax. *Idiotas*. But EnRG said they are handling it. Everyone believes they are handling it. *Their* boats are still on the water. *Their* boats haven't been eaten. People believe they're in control." She made the sign of the cross.

"So, it's up to us," I said. The tangy ocean air hung on the soft breeze, but didn't quite cover the more putrid stench rolling in from the water.

Simona nodded. Harper squeezed my hand, then glanced out the back window. "Oh, shit. We've got company."

Behind us, the black SUV trailed us up the cliff road. They were a ways off, but the SUV was built for the terrain better.

"Looks like Regina put her people back on us," I said. "We need to do this fast."

"It's okay," Jack said. "I called in reinforcements."

Our car screeched over gravel and Simona reversed, so the trunk was facing the water. We scrambled out of the car, popped the trunk, and began lining up the bottles of tequila on the ground.

Beneath us, the trash ebbed and flowed. Odd clunking and squelchy noises floated up from the cove. Several caves opened into the cove, but the mouths were crammed full of trash, like the monster was trying to suffocate it.

Jagged movements within the main body kept drawing my attention. Several of its dark, green eyes winked open and closed, open and closed, watching us. The pupils were narrow green slits, and they covered the trash as far as I could see, taking information back to its... brain? Did it even have a brain? Or did it rely on pure instinct, the need to survive, to procreate, to protect itself? There was so much we didn't know. But maybe we didn't need to know it. It was obvious The Great Green was trying to claim the ocean for itself. Saving the water was the only thing that mattered. Perhaps in doing that, I could honor Danny's memory and put his death behind me.

The black SUV was halfway up the road. I sincerely hoped Jack was right.

"Let's hurry." Simona leaned on one crutch to help her balance on her good leg, uncapping the bottles and stuffing them with rags. "You two light, and Jack and I will throw. Glad my college softball skills are going to come in handy." She grinned at us, then eyed Jack's muscular body. "Jack looks like he has a good arm."

He gave a brief nod. "Played quarterback in college."

Simona whistled her approval. I tried to smile back, but I felt sick. A thick coil of fear squirmed in my stomach as I looked at Simona and Harper. I loved them both dearly, and they were here because of me. For the first time, the extent of the danger of what we were doing hit me. It was us against the monster. Left unchecked, The Great Green would take many lives. But if I hadn't stuck my nose in and uncovered the truth behind Regina's plans, we'd still be in the same situation. And perhaps we'd act ignorantly like everyone else and wait for EnRG to solve the problem. Then it would be too late.

Pushing my nerves aside, and with the sound of the SUV's huge tires crunching over the gravel road, I knelt and lit the first couple of bottles.

Simona raised one of the bottles over her head, took a second to focus on her target, and hurled it into the cove. Jack followed and lobbed a second. I held my breath as the bottles whizzed into the sky and sailed a good distance into the green trash. With the rags burning brightly, the bottles settled on top of the water a good four hundred feet below us. Two seconds passed, then the bottles exploded, hot glass hurtling in all directions. A fireball erupted. It burned brightly for a moment, licking the surface of the water with its fiery tongue. Two elements, perfectly balanced. Like an arm-wrestle between two pro boxers. But then the flames winked out. With a hissing green steam, the water swallowed the fireball, claiming its victory.

"Mother fucker," Simona muttered, standing on her good leg and waving her crutch in the air.

I didn't mention the swear jar. Simona would fill it up on a daily basis. It was one of the things I liked about her.

"Try again," Harper said. "We'll have more success if it comes out of the water."

This time Jack and Simona took two bottles each. Simona planted her crutch in the ground and leaned against it to free her hands. They held one in each hand and hurled them farther than the first.

"Burn! Burn and die, you bitch!"

The bottles met in mid-flight, crashing against each other. Before they landed in the water, they exploded. Heat rushed toward us, arcing over the cliff and toward the water. A tattoo of flames scorched my retinas. And then they too, went out.

"I don't understand," Simona said. "Why isn't it burning? Regina said it should burn."

"We need to make it angry," Harper said.

"We need to make it come to us," I added.

The SUV parked behind us. I registered four doors

opening and closing, and the subsequent skidding of several pairs of feet as they raced over the gravel toward us.

"What can we do to help?"

I recognized Ryan Phillips' voice. None of us turned around. We remained focused on the pulsing green trash. Throb, throb, throb, like a heartbeat.

"Let's hit it with everything we've got." Harper lit another bottle and passed it to Simona.

She threw that one as well. "Come on, baby."

The reps rushed forward and began lighting more bottles and throwing them with us. I noted one of them had a blow torch, but it would do little from this distance. Phillips stood next to me. There were a lot of things I wanted to say to him, but finally I settled with, "Thanks for your help."

Simona let out a string of Spanish curse words, but kept her eyes on the bottles' progress. Five of them flew in formation.

A trickle of unease crept down my spine.

The bottles arced through the sky. As they were about to hit the water, a green mouth rose from the surface. A gaping green mouth with three lines of jagged teeth. A snout came next. And two brilliant emerald eyes which nearly blinded me. The shape emerged from the water, morphing as it moved. Changing and growing and glowing shamrock green all the time. It transformed into unrecognizable shapes, nothing discernable, but it continued to move and alter its appearance and mass. It rose from the water, like some perverse lady of the lake, growing taller with each passing second, reaching level with the cliff line. An enormous *thing* that belied all comprehension. It swallowed the flaming bottles. A faint boom reached us from its closed mouth. Then it set those green eyes on us.

"I think it's angry now," Harper said.

"Holy shit!" one of the reps said. I heard the click of a loaded magazine. The four of them stepped up to the ridge with us, their gazes moving from us to the green monster. The water started to churn, hissing and angry. I no longer trusted our position on the top of the cliffs.

The older man with the graying hair held his gun prone, shaking his head at the scene beneath us. Then he looked at me. "I'm sorry I frightened you last night."

His words brought back the memory of his hand squeezing my arm. But it was insignificant to what we were facing now. "Thanks," I muttered.

"Holy..." Phillips yelled. "It's bigger than I thought."

I pivoted toward him. "You knew about it and still you did nothing?"

"Of course, we knew about it." He blinked rapidly, as if unable to focus on the scene. "I thought... I thought... Operation Blue Water was handling it. I didn't think it would... I didn't realize... I'm sorry."

"I'm not sure that's good enough."

"I'm here now. I'll do what I can." He turned back to face the burbling monster. The waves were whisked higher and higher by an invisible hand. The water near the rocks below us thickened, increasing its viscosity, ready to sprout new creatures of terror.

"What do we do?" I asked, not daring to move. *Danny, please help.*

Chapter Twenty-Two

THE ENORMOUS GREEN SHAPE ADVANCED, growing taller, slithering over the rocks, dragging its trash mass closer. Just what we wanted. But also... not.

Behind it, green trash spilled out of the cove and into the ocean, like a giant green train of a dress. It hissed and seethed, bunching into the cove, pulling its parts from the deeper ocean, making itself bigger and bigger. All the time, everything sparkled a brilliant green. I was so sick of green.

I stared into its terrifying eyes. Blinking. Winking. So close.

"Use them all!" Harper yelled.

Tearing my gaze away from The Great Green, I lit one bottle after the other. Simona and the reps threw. Again and again. Each time, The Great Green snatched the flaming weapon in its jaws and swallowed it whole. Small fires appeared on its body, but it wasn't enough. Then, with one elongating appendage, it flicked a tendril over our heads. The tip of it, covered in broken food containers and bottlecaps and plastic shards, and I think a fish's skeleton, hovered in the air, as if sniffing us out.

Below, flames erupted like shrapnel, shooting in all directions. The fireballs were picked up by thickening shoots of green trash, bringing the burning flames higher, higher, toward us.

Jack pressed forward with a volley of gunfire, aiming at the waving appendage. "Die, you son of a bitch!"

The man with the blow torch let rip, blasting fire from the end of the weapon, scorching holes in The Great Green, causing it to emit the most inhuman sound I'd ever heard. The tendril was cut in half. The severed end oozed green liquid, then slithered its way back over the edge of the cliff.

A new tendril appeared, its eyes winking open and closed, its tip dancing over the edge of the cliff, like a charmed cobra. Phillips edged forward, his gun booming in my ears each time he pulled the trigger. A tendril wrapped around the ankle of the rep with the blow torch and yanked him off the cliff. Simona reached for him, but it was too late; he was already falling. He let loose with the blow torch as he yelled, but it wasn't enough. The rep was gone.

I stood rooted, mesmerized by the gleaming appendage. Nobody moved. Nobody dared breathe. Without warning, the tendril shunted closer, flicked over one of the reps' shoes, upending him. It was the man with the gray hair. He, too, fell off the cliff, screaming, and landed in the churning trash below. His scream cut off and I watched the space where he disappeared.

"Oh my God! Oh my God! Oh my God! We're all going to die!" Harper backed away from the edge.

"We are *not* going to die!" I yelled, as I lit the last Molotov cocktail.

Simona hurled it high and far.

Phillips aimed his gun and released a full clip. Quickly reloaded.

The monster's jaws crunched and sliced, then formed into something resembling a wicked smile. With its glowing green eyes locked on us, it opened its mouth, pushing itself higher and higher. Between the three lines of shining green teeth, a fire burned. Hot and powerful, set within its jaws.

Bubbles raged across the tumultuous surface as the battle advanced. The monster threw back the fire at us. A fireball flew high and hit like a bomb, tearing chunks of rock and grass and dirt out of the cliff, turning shrapnel into speeding missiles, searing us, slicing us. The SUV, parked too close to a rogue fireball, wilted and melted and became a mess of green ash. Harper screamed, but I could barely hear her over the roaring fires and hissing ocean. Flames licked closer and green... things... flew through the air. Green things with wings and flaming mouths. Hundreds of them. Like a swarm of insects carrying a fiery plague.

"Let's get out of here!" Simona yelled, grabbing Harper and me and shoving us toward her car. She limped along on her good leg and one crutch. Jack ran with us, firing his gun at The Great Green as we retreated.

This was such a stupid idea. Why did I think attempting to blow it up would work? But I didn't have time to dwell on my poor decision making skills as the green insects swarmed in, biting at my arms and legs, burning through my skin. Judging by the curse words spewing from Simona and Harper, they were enduring the same barrage. But once the green things landed, they soaked through the dry earth and disappeared. Probably trying to find a way back to its central mass. Slapping at the fiery burns on my legs, I stumbled toward the car.

A snaking green vine emerged from the water. A substantial twisting thing with claws longer than my arm. It waved over the clifftop, shaking drops of virulent green I knew would dissolve me in an instant.

"Go!" Phillips yelled. "Run!" He faced the hovering appendage. Green drops covered his skin, which hissed and steamed. Blisters swarmed over his flesh.

The appendage slammed down on him, puncturing the cliff, breaking boulders, and causing the ground to shudder under my feet. Simona screamed. Seconds later, she was lifted into the air, her plastered leg skewered by one of the claws, her crutch flying over the cliff.

One of the insects flew close to Harper's ear. Her hair caught fire. Patting it out, I tugged her toward Simona's car, ducking under other flaming green projectiles. The thick shoot released Simona and she fell to the ground with an agonized scream. Jack picked her up and ran with her while I tried not to look at the blood saturating her cast. The four of us stumbled toward the car. Flames licked at our heels. Fiberglass twisted and melted into ugly murals. Glass shattered and popped, creating dangerous missiles. Gunshots echoed in the air. With one last look at each other, we ran.

The remaining two reps stood together at the cliff's edge, shooting at the monster. A huge trash wave formed from nowhere, starting at the edge of the cove and shunting toward the rocks, and us. I dove into Simona's car as the crest of the wave appeared above the ridge line.

"Shit! Shit! Shit!" Harper yelled, struggling with her seat belt.

"*Madre de dios!*" Simona started the engine.

Behind us, the wave crested over the edge of the cliff, splashing the two men, who immediately cried out.

"It burns!" one screamed, dropping his weapon. He collapsed to the ground, his hands covering his blistering face, his mirrored sunglasses broken by his feet. I caught a glimpse of his tongue through his cheek.

"Don't look!" Jack said, as he slammed Simona's door closed.

As she revved the engine, screaming about the pain in her broken leg, Jack ran around to the other side of the car. With his hand on the door handle, a green appendage wrenched him into the sky.

His eyes flew wide, and he roared, then brought his gun round to fire at the monster.

"Go!" he shouted at us as he fired bullet after bullet.

"We can't leave him!" Harper yelled.

Simona stamped her unbroken foot on the accelerator and the car fishtailed.

Another green appendage wrapped around Jack's body, stifling his screams, melting his skin.

"He's not going to make it," I said, unable to turn away from the macabre scene. I had to see. I had to know how evil this thing really was.

One of the men rolled off the cliff. Phillips hissed and steamed as green vapor evaporated from his pores. His skin melted off and I caught sight of large chunks of visible bone. Nausea flooded my stomach, rose into my mouth. Jack fell silent and his body was taken over the edge of the cliff, his gun no longer firing. Phillips was the last one left. He rolled away from the cliff and crawled toward his misshapen car.

"We have to help him!" I said, as we sped down the bumpy road.

"We are not going back there," Simona said. Harper whimpered next to me. "Nope. No way. *Buena suerte a él.*" Good luck to him.

As we sped around the corner, another burst of green rose over the cliff. This was the part of the road closest to the cliff edge. Simona slammed her foot on the accelerator as Harper and I screamed at her to go faster.

Green objects hurtled toward the car. A milk container, straws, plastic scraps. Many other things too numerous and misshapen to name. They landed on the car, gripping to the surface, refusing to be shaken off. Behind it, another wave amassed, cresting over the road, sending the car skidding down the cliff road. We skirted dangerously close to the edge, all of us screaming, and then spun around the other way. Green water slapped at Simona's open window. She screamed as the acid burned her skin. The car coasted down the hilly road and slammed to a stop against a concrete traffic divider.

Dazed, I couldn't think straight. I stared out the window at the glinting green marina. We had arrived at the bottom of the cliff. The engine steamed, and Simona whimpered in the front seat, cradling her broken leg. Harper yelled a slew of curse words at the sky.

"We need to get out of here," I said, unbuckling my seatbelt. I shoved the door open and crawled out. On the ground, my knees cut up by the rough surface, I hurled my guts up. Harper crawled after me and wrapped her arms around my waist. I hugged her back. She smelled of salt and fear and coffee and tequila.

"We need to help Simona." I struggled to my feet. As I approached the car, the debris which had been stuck to the windows and metal frame fell to the ground. A plastic cup, a coffee container, the circuit board for a computer, a dozen plastic food wrappers. Along with an abundance of brown muck. But the green was gone. Seeped into the soil or crawled away. I didn't care, I was relieved it was gone.

Harper and I dragged Simona out of her car. Her eyes were closed, and I worried she was unconscious. Blood oozed out of her white cast, but it looked as though it was slowing. She whimpered when I laced her arm around my shoulder. We half carried and half dragged her and her one remaining crutch the two blocks to my house. On the left, the green ocean brightened with new menace. The marina was calm, and so was the cove, as if a battle hadn't just been fought high above its cliffs. I hoped Ryan Phillips made it out okay.

"How the hell are we supposed to kill something like that?" I muttered.

"I don't know," Harper said, her face tight. "I just don't know."

Chapter Twenty-Three

WHEN WE GOT BACK to my house, we lay Simona on the couch. I cleaned her wounds as best I could and rummaged through the house for bottles of EnRG. There were a couple left over from the case Regina had delivered. I poured it over Simona's face and her skin hissed and cooled. The blisters calmed and the redness of her burns faded. But she didn't wake up. I expected the amount of trauma she'd been through in the last couple of days was enough to keep anyone comatose for a while. I called an ambulance, but was told it would be hours before they could get to me if it wasn't life-threatening. They had received dozens of calls of acid attacks. They made it sound like people were responsible.

I used a few drops of the remaining EnRG to dab at the stings on mine and Harper's skin. Those angry green flying things had stung us all over our arms and legs. Eventually, the pain started to fade with the relief of the fizzy drink. Then I cleaned up the wound on my calf, which was bleeding again.

I almost lost it, then. I had a moment when everything seemed so big. Bigger than me. How could we win this?

Blinking back a prickle of tears, I pushed the worries away. I would take one step at a time, one minute at a time, and try my best not to get killed.

There were messages from Tyler on my phone, giving us updates about Frank. Asking us questions. But I didn't have the energy to go into it.

Harper and I drank water from a glass bottle in the fridge. We cleaned ourselves up with my mom's facial pads, the ones I was always giving her a hard time about because they weren't biodegradable and were single-use. But there was no way in hell I was turning on a tap.

"Where did those things go?" Harper whispered at me when we were a bit calmer.

"What things?"

"The tiny flying green burning things. Did they die off when they left the main body of The Great Green? Or are they able to exist on their own? What if they find their way onto land? Into the water system?"

"I don't want to think about it," I replied.

"I know, but Sara—"

"I know. I know. Let's just... keep moving forward."

Simona's phone and mine bleeped at the same time. Mine was a message from Dad checking in, reminding me they'd be back tomorrow. My heart sank. I wished they were here now. At least they were safe in Paris, and I was pretty sure they wouldn't have any better ideas on defeating an evil green trash monster. Mom sent another email of a picture of her and dad having dinner at a swanky restaurant in the Centre Pompidou. I touched a finger to her smiling face, asking her to give me courage.

When Simona's phone kept chirping to *La Bamba*, I pulled it out of her back pocket. It was a message from Scripps with a whole bunch of attachments. I stared at them for an hour but couldn't make any sense out of the data. Something about an enzyme was important. Was The Great Green made from an enzyme, or could it be killed by one? An idea prickled. I scolded myself for not thinking of it earlier. It was outlandish, absurd—naturally—but no worse than the Molotov cocktails. It would never work. Unless, maybe it could. But there were so many moving parts.

Simona stirred, her eyelids fluttered. She rolled onto her side, then yelped herself awake. "*Madre mía*, that hurts." Her hands went to her plastered leg. Well, half of the cast was missing. I gave her some water and painkillers, which she gulped down. Then I showed her the messages.

Her lips parted as she read through the documents, and she played with a gold chain around her neck. "I'm not sure I'm taking this in right. Too foggy from the pain. But—"

"What is it?" I asked, placing my elbows on the table and leaning into a cupped palm.

Simona's gaze darted over her small screen. Her features twisted constantly, punctuated with the occasional "Of course!" and "No wonder!" She looked at us, excitement dashing through her eyes, along with a little chemical haze. "The acid is a defense mechanism. It secretes it when it feels threatened. Which explains why not everyone who's come into contact with it has been injured."

"Like when it first arrived," Harper said. "Tons of people were swimming in it before they closed the beach."

"Exactly," Simona said. "Before it started to feel threatened... or..."

"Or?" I questioned.

"It's evolving," Simona said. "It's evolved from reacting when threatened to going on the offensive."

"Simona, none of that tells us how to kill it." I resisted the urge to tap her leg. "What is it? How do we kill it? Because, I don't know if you realize, that little experience we had on the clifftop? That was a fucking nightmare. It was playing with us. Toying with us. It knows we don't stand a chance." Unless I told them about my idea. Would they think I'd gone off the deep end?

Wordlessly, Harper pointed at the swear jar on the mantle above my head. I laughed and said, "Fuck, fuck, fuck," and almost felt better for it.

"You were right about everything, Sara," Simona said, smiling proudly. For the first time ever, I didn't revel in the metaphorical pat on the back. Too much was at stake.

"She's always right," Harper said. "Except when she's not."

"Ha, ha!" I said to Harper, nudging her side.

"I've got a genetic report here," Simona continued. "It confirms the algae can grow exponentially, that it can merge with other substances, and it can alter its own DNA. I'm no geneticist, but it looks like we've got some strange... symbiosis, maybe. I think. If I'm reading this right."

"Sounds about right," I said, flicking on Mom's favorite lamp; a tacky tourist thing with a stem covered in shells. The cone of light illuminated the glass heart box I'd given her last Mother's Day and the framed picture of my parents at their wedding. *Stay safe.*

"So, what do we do?" Harper asked. She lay on the opposite couch with her legs stretched out and her hands folded across her stomach. "I'm all for hibernating until everything is over. Let's liquidate Jackson & Monroe, monster hunters extraordinaire, and, you know, retire."

I hugged her.

"It's never going to be over unless someone does something," Simona muttered, still scrolling through her messages.

Harper frowned. "Then we need a new plan. Something better. Something bigger. Something so wild it's bound to work. Any ideas?"

Simona sighed, put her phone down, and began picking at the loose chunks of plaster on her leg. "I'm not sure I'm in any condition to do much. If we talk to Regina again, we can convince her to try something else."

"Regina is useless," I said. "But her drink is not."

Two sets of eyes swiveled in my direction.

"Whadd'ya mean?" Harper asked.

"When I burned my hand, the first time, Tyler had a can of EnRG on him. It was the only thing that took the burning away. It calmed the white blisters, the heat, everything."

"Yeah," Harper said. "And we used it on Frank too."

"And Simona just now. And on our stings." I looked at them both. "Regina's own EnRG drink is the answer to killing the monster."

Harper swung her legs to the floor. "We can't throw a bunch of EnRG cans into the ocean. The monster will use it to grow even bigger. It already consists of, like, thirty percent EnRG cans and bottles as it is."

"Not cans," I said. "*EnRG.*"

Simona smiled. "I like where this is going. There must be an inhibitor in the drink that can neutralize the enzyme produced by the trash monster."

"Speak English," Harper said to her.

Simona chuckled. "Don't worry. I'll figure out the science stuff, give you the green light once I do the research. It won't take me long." She picked up her phone and scrolled through the reports.

Harper raised a finger and glared at me. "I am *not* going anywhere near the ocean again."

"I don't think we'll have to, but we need Tyler."

"Where are we going to get a shit ton of EnRG?" Simona asked. "*Not* in cans."

"There's a warehouse off I5, heading toward LA," I said. "We can get it there."

"What, like, walk in and take it?" Harper asked. "Are you insane?"

I grinned. "All we need are the trucks. Tyler once told me about the distribution of EnRG. The liquid sits in giant vats in the trucks, ready to be taken to the canning site. We need to get to those trucks."

"And then what?" Harper goggled at me. "Drive them off the cliff all Thelma and Louise style?"

"No," I said. "This is where we need Tyler. And Frank. We fill the fire planes, fly over the ocean, and dump it on the mother fucker."

Simona chuckled and clapped. "I like this plan. You are one ballsy chick." This time, the praise flowed through me and heated my cheeks. "But I don't think I can help. I can barely drive a car with this mangled leg, let alone a tanker. I need to get my leg re-cast. And I need to make some calls into the office to test your theory."

"Thanks, Simona," I said.

"How are we going to get the trucks here?" Harper asked.

I punched a fist into the opposite palm. "Regina is going to organize it."

Simona let out a whistle.

"Maybe she's not so useless after all," Harper said. "Let's try your crazy plan. Which I kind of wish was my crazy plan."

"Girls," Simona said. "You need someone to go with you. You need an adult. I don't like the idea of you manhandling Regina on your own."

"I've done it before," I said. "I'm not scared of her. Frank will help us with the planes."

"Frank is in the hospital," Harper said.

"He can still make phone calls," I replied.

Simona nodded and leaned back on the couch, her eyelids drooping.

Harper stood, tied up her hair and smoothed her clothes.

I threw an arm around her shoulder. "Think of the medal we'll get when it's all over."

She laughed. I laughed. It released some of the tension. But it didn't do anything to dissipate the fear swimming in my stomach. It crawled up my throat, a hard mass I couldn't swallow down. This was our last chance. It was crazy. It was wild. It was daredevil. But it was our last hope. If this failed...

I looked out the window, wincing against the consistent

green light. Always there. Growing brighter. Never going away.

I called for a cab, and we were on our way to Regina's house ten minutes later. This time I remembered to bring both my phone and my wallet. We dropped Simona at the hospital, making sure she was handed over to a triage nurse. Then the cab wound up the steep roads to the mansion properties perched on the cliffs of La Jolla.

I clutched at the leather seats, ignoring the slickness of my hands and the slight tremble in my calf muscles. But we couldn't go back. There were no other solutions. Regina had the EnRG we needed to defeat The Great Green.

"This is going to work, right?" Harper said, swallowing audibly.

I gave her a curt nod and went over my speech in my head.

Harper fidgeted in her seat, which made me more nervous. The cab driver let out a low whistle when we pulled into Regina's drive. I didn't intend to break in this time, but I wasn't sure announcing our presence was a good idea either.

We got out of the car and walked between the manicured rose bushes to the imposing front door. Two security reps flanked the entrance, hands clasped in front, earpieces trailing into their collars.

"We're here to see Regina," I said, looking between the two of them.

"Sure." One of the reps replied and rang the bell for me.

The four of us stood there and waited. The ocean crashed behind us and the sun pressed down on my shoulders. A wall of awkwardness grew. The reps didn't look at us and we didn't look at them.

After another minute, I pressed the button again. And again. Leaving my finger on the buzzer until the door flew open.

Regina Harron stood on the threshold dressed in a linen pantsuit. Her hair was back in a chignon and her makeup firmly secured. The weaknesses she'd showed last night were hidden away.

"You're back," she said.

"We're back," I replied, stepping into the house.

Harper shut the door behind us.

"I told you, there's nothing else I can do." Regina splayed her hands. Although she appeared to be the same ambitious and determined CEO she'd always been, the authority in her voice had disappeared.

"That's not strictly true," I said. "We need your help with something."

Regina looked between the two of us, then gestured for us to follow her into the kitchen. She grabbed a coffee pot from the counter and moved to the sink.

I dashed over to her and put a hand on the tap before she could turn it. "No. It's in the water system too."

She shrank back, her eyes wide, and placed the coffee pot on the counter again. "Are you sure?"

"Positive."

A deep frown flickered across her forehead, and she put a hand to her temple. "I'm sorry."

"We don't have time for coffee, anyway," Harper said.

"We know what can defeat the algae monster," I said.

Regina inhaled sharply. "You do?"

I stared at the fridge of EnRG cans. How much would be enough? "Your very own drink. EnRG. The enzyme you use to jack everyone up—"

"Not the time." Harper pulled on my T-shirt.

"The enzyme you put in it, it kills the algae."

"It does?" Regina put a hand on the counter and the skin under her freckles turned whiter than the kitchen tiles. "All this time, it's been under my nose."

My anger burbled. "Under your nose? Seriously? I'm in high school and I figured it out. You claim to have the world's best scientists and they haven't come anywhere close."

"We were looking in a different direction—"

"Then you try another one until you get it right."

Regina inhaled slowly. "What is it you want me to do?"

I resisted the urge to yell at her. We had a way out of this. It wasn't too late.

"We need access to a lot of EnRG," Harper said.

"You have a factory up the freeway in LA. We need it brought down here."

Regina frowned. "And then what? We drive it off the cliffs into the ocean? I can't afford to lose so much stock. I'm preparing for a class action. One tanker alone would cost me thousands."

I narrowed my eyes at her. "Next time you turn on your tap and fill your coffee pot with water... it might not be water. You might not notice at first. The Great Green can be sneaky, flow into your pot without any fanfare. But then you'll brew your coffee, and you'll drink it, and the algae will burn you from the inside out. If that's how you want to go out, have at it."

Regina stared at the coffee pot, then the sink, then shifted her gaze back to me. "How much do you need?"

"As much as you've got," I said.

"And then what?" Regina asked.

"Have the tankers drive to the wildfire department headquarters. We'll take care of the rest."

Regina shook her head. "I don't have any drivers. They're on a weekend strike. Wage issues."

"Why does that not surprise me?" Harper muttered.

"You don't have *any* drivers?" An anxious flush heated my skin. It was all going to fall apart at the last moment.

"Not in California," Regina replied. "Other states, but by the time they got here..." She checked her watch. "It could be late this evening. More likely tomorrow morning."

"I don't want to wait that long."

I paced the shiny tiles, chewing on my lower lip, my thoughts cycling. Harper slumped into a chair at the kitchen table while Regina handed out bottles of water. If she'd offered me a can of EnRG, I would have thrown it in her face.

Regina remained standing, her hands pressed into the countertop, watching me think.

"I've got an idea," I said, finally. "Regina, you make sure the warehouse is prepared for our arrival. We'll bring our own drivers."

Nodding, Regina picked up her phone.

"And we'll need one of your reps to drive us to the hospital," I said.

Regina walked us to the front door, all the time barking instructions into her phone. She handed car keys to one of the reps and told him to take us wherever we wanted.

I turned back to her. "While I'm sorting out your mess, you need to tell the world there's a problem. No more lies."

She covered her mouth with a hand and mumbled, "I don't know if I can do that."

"You have to," I said. "Or more people are going to get hurt."

We got into one of the black Range Rovers with tinted windows. For the first time, I was on the inside of the vehicle, and I hadn't been kidnapped. The thought raised a small smile.

Harper buckled her seatbelt next to me. "Where are we going to find drivers?"

I pulled out my phone and scrolled through my contact list until I found Will's name. Danny's best friend. My hand shook. I hadn't spoken to him in three years.

Chapter Twenty-Four

I PRESSED Will's number and brought the phone to my ear. I wished I was alone for the phone call, but we were running out of time, and I couldn't afford to be emotional about it.

Will picked up. "Hello?"

Memories rushed back at me. Emotions churned in my stomach and chest and my throat thickened.

"Hello?"

"Sorry! I'm here. Will?" I knew it was him. I'd recognized his voice instantly, but I needed a moment.

"This is Will."

"Hi, Will. This is... This is... Sara... Sara Monroe. Danny's sister?"

A booming silence came across the airwaves.

"Will?"

"I'm here. Sorry. You caught me by surprise. Sara. Jeez. How are you?"

Harper squeezed my hand. The rep looked at me in the rearview mirror. Outside the window, the green ocean broke on the empty beach.

"Will, I need your help."

"Of course, anything for you, Sara."

"This is bigger than a lobster cage," I said.

Will inhaled. "What do you need?"

"Can you drive a truck?"

It took us a half hour to get near the hospital, so we got out and walked the last couple of blocks. The place was crowded. Car horns blared and a long line of people snaked out of the entrance. The triage nurses ran in and out, giving people ticket numbers.

"Jeez, what the hell happened here?" Harper asked as we wound our way through the clumps of people. Many of them revealed white blisters and burned skin. Others wore shell-shocked looks in their eyes. There were whispers of something in the water.

"The monster happened," I replied. I told as many people as I could that EnRG would soothe their burns.

News crews were stationed outside the main entrance accosting anyone who looked a tiny bit bedraggled. I marched up to a reporter. "It's not just the acid. There's a monster in the water. EnRG is keeping the whole thing quiet and it's burning so many people." I indicated the trailing clumps of people trying to get through the hospital doors.

The reporter smirked at me. "The toxins cause hallucinations. We've heard it before."

"No." I shook my head. "They are not hallucinations. The Great Green is real."

"The Great Green?" he laughed. "That'll make a killer headline."

I wanted to tell him to go for a swim, find out for himself, but I didn't want anyone else to get hurt.

"Leave it," Harper said. "We have a plan anyway."

As Harper ushered me through the main doors, an ambulance screamed by in front of us, pulling to a screeching stop. The first responder leaped out of the vehicle and wheeled the patient through the front doors. The patient was unconscious, but white blisters ran the length of his face and arms. A handful of reporters trailed him as far as they could.

Harper and I cut around the edge of the press cameras and snuck through the hospital. Not bothering to join the long line at the reception desk to find out what room Frank was in, I messaged Tyler. A few seconds later, my phone pinged, and we headed to the elevators. The ride to the seventh floor was accompanied by a lone saxophone playing demurely over the speakers, and about fifteen other people sandwiched in with us. Most were quiet, but one spoke of burns and pain and blisters. She didn't mention the word "monster."

I burst into Frank's room, the news of our plan hovering on my lips, then stopped myself. Maybe they wouldn't want to help. Maybe they'd think my plan was ridiculous.

"It's about time," Tyler said, his burning gaze centered on me.

"We have a plan. We know how to kill The Great Green," Harper said.

Tyler held up a hand. Frank pressed a button on his bed and raised himself into a sitting position. Tubes snaked from a machine and into his arm. A heart monitor beeped softly in the corner and a dismal bunch of carnations faded in the sunlight by the open window. It didn't mask the smells of bleach or latex. A flicker of guilt prickled as I realized I should have brought flowers, or chocolate, or a beer. Something.

"I would have come earlier if I could..." I trailed off.

Tyler dragged me into the hallway. Doctors and nurses rushed between rooms and a couple of patients were wheeled past us in their mobile beds. The walls were painted in a nondescript cream, but I noted the prints of the ocean hanging on the walls were of better quality than I expected. A blue ocean. A color I desperately missed.

"It's nice to see you too," Tyler said.

I pulled my thoughts away from the ocean and faced him, surprised by the tone of his voice. "I've been busy—"

He raised his eyebrows. "Busy? *Busy?* Did it not occur to you, just once, that I could use your support? My dad was almost killed. *Killed.* My mom is out of town and I can't reach her. I needed you, Sara." He splayed his hands and his eyebrows formed one angry line.

"Why didn't you say something?" I asked.

"Seriously?" His glare scorched my face. "I didn't think I had to."

"I'm sorry," I said, dipping my head as my cheeks flamed. "You were giving us regular updates and I thought you were both okay."

Tyler's eyes closed briefly as he shook his head slowly. "I am *not* okay. How would you feel if your dad was almost killed?"

"Devastated, but Tyler—"

He raised a hand, not wanting to hear more, and pivoted away from me.

"Tyler! This situation is bigger than us. And if you needed me here, why didn't you ask? I'm not a mind-reader, you know."

He swiveled back to face me, the hurt mounting in his eyes, the thunder exploding. "I didn't think I needed to."

"The Great Green—"

"Is not your problem."

I gaped at him. "How can you say that? *I lost my brother.*" I sucked in a breath, trying to calm the burbling emotions and the needle of loss that followed me everywhere. "Because of trash. Because of EnRG."

"I know that."

"I live with his death every day. I miss him. I love him. I hear his voice in my head. I imagine him sucking in his first mouthful of seawater. I wonder what he thought about when he knew he was going to die. It's been *three years*. It's a long time. I know. But I think about him *every day*. Don't you see? I can't let more people die like Danny. I can't let a monster destroy our town, our people. I can't, Tyler."

Tyler leaned against the wall and rubbed at the short hairs on his neck. He searched my face, but I couldn't tell what he was thinking. "I get it, Sara, I do. It hurt my dad too. But you can't fight a monster on your own."

"I'm not on my own." I placed my hand on his chest, hoping my touch would help him understand. I needed him. I wanted his help. I didn't want to be alone anymore. He stepped away from me. "Everyone thinks EnRG is handling it. They're not. Regina has no idea. I went to her house and —"

"You went to her house?"

"Broke in, actually." I smiled, then let the expression fall when I took in Tyler's flat gaze. "Tyler. She doesn't know how to stop it. Neither do her scientists. They keep telling everyone they're on it, but they have no idea." I reached for him, but he held himself distant.

"What is it you think *we* can do?" Tyler asked. "Aren't FEMA here? Homeland Security? Someone more... capable than you..."

"Thanks a lot." I pressed a palm against the cool wall, seeking reassurance.

Tyler's hand moved between us, gesturing rapidly. "My dad was hurt. I do not want to tangle with a green algae... whatever it is, nor do I want to face off against EnRG's security detail."

"That's exactly why we need to act. Together. So no one else gets hurt, like your dad. Like Danny," I said quietly.

He pointed at the TV in Frank's room. There was a breaking story on the news channel. There was a shot of Regina outside her home, admitting there was something in the water. That The Great Green was real and she had a plan to kill it.

"Jesus Christ," Tyler said. "I can't believe she's come clean." He turned to me. "There's a plan, Sara. It's not your problem anymore."

"You don't understand, Tyler. Her plan is my plan. It's all up to me. To us."

"Are you kidding me?"

I shook my head. "I need your help."

He held my gaze. A medley of emotions passed through his eyes. His jaw tightened and I could feel him wavering.

He glanced at the TV, where Regina was her controlled self, not letting on she didn't have a clue about the plan to defeat The Great Green. But if she wanted to feel she was doing her bit by making a few phone calls, then she could have at it.

Tyler's shoulders sagged. "If you think we're the only ones who can take down this monster, then of course I'm going to help you, Sara. *Of course* I'm going to help. But I don't like it. I don't like the way you treated me, and we have a lot to talk about when this is all over."

I nodded and followed him back into Frank's room.

Frank arched an eyebrow. "Everything okay?"

With emotion clogging my voice, I dipped my chin at him.

"Anyone care to fill me in on what's going on?" Frank asked.

"Sara and Harper have devised a plan to take down The Great Green. And I'm going to help them," Tyler replied.

Harper collapsed into a free chair and poured herself a glass of water from Frank's water jug.

Frank eyeballed us all. "Care to explain?"

I took a second to organize my thoughts. I needed Tyler. And Frank. I needed them both. Will and his friends were already onboard. I knew this plan would work if they gave me the chance to prove it. I couldn't mess this up. "Do you remember how I was burned at the marina, that first time before we realized the algae was what it was?"

Tyler nodded.

"And it didn't stop with water, did it? The pain wouldn't stop until you poured your EnRG drink on me."

"Yeah, I remember," Tyler said.

I glanced at Frank. It was odd to see the big bear of a man all tucked up in white sheets with his arm in a cast and several painful blisters decorating his skin. Bruises and scrapes covered his face, but his blue eyes were alert.

"EnRG kills it," I said. "The same enzyme that causes all those side effects—"

"Are you serious? EnRG?" Tyler said. "*My* EnRG?"

I smiled. Frank laughed.

"Think what it's doing to your insides," Harper muttered, flicking absently through a magazine.

"Simona is waiting on some test results," I said. "But we're pretty sure it's going to tell us that the same enzyme inside EnRG is what can kill The Great Green."

"An enzyme inhibitor," Harper piped up. "I remember that much."

I chucked her a smile, then looked at Frank and Tyler. "We can still fight this thing."

I wanted to punch my fist in the air. I wanted everyone to rally around me with big grins and high fives. I wanted Frank to crawl out of bed, even though he couldn't, and tell me it was the best plan ever. I wanted the look in Tyler's eyes to be softer.

"Wahoo!" Frank swung his plastered arm, then grimaced. "No freaky-ass green monster is going to take over our town. You've got a couple of ass-kicking friends here. This is a fantastic thing to be part of, son. And I don't want no sorry excuse for a side-kick either."

Tyler stared out the wide window for a moment. His gaze rested on Harper, then his dad, then back to me. He shook his head. "You guys are nuts."

"Aye," Frank agreed. "But my kind of nuts."

"So, what do you need me for?" Tyler asked.

"I need you to fly a plane."

He laughed.

"I'm serious." I looked at Frank. "We need you too."

Frank smiled, already pulling at tubes and wires. "Oh, I'm not going to miss this."

"Don't get out of bed!" I held up a hand. "I only need you to call your fire department. The wildfire department. I want to fill those planes up with EnRG and fly them over the ocean."

All the wrinkles on Frank's forehead shot high.

"I don't even have my license yet..." Tyler trailed off, his voice small and shaky. "Is that going to be a problem?"

Frank pushed himself straighter. "I'll call ahead. Everything will be ready for you. You *can* do this. We've got the planes, but not the pilots. I think Almond Cove needs you."

Tyler gave a curt nod. "That thing needs to die. I'm going to kill it. For you, Dad."

"I'll come with you," I said. "I'll sit right next to you and do whatever you tell me."

He nudged me. A small gesture, but it filled me with hope. Maybe he could forgive me. "That'll be the day."

"And I won't ever give you a hard time about flying again."

Frank laughed, then groaned, clutching his side. "Please don't make me laugh."

Together, we hatched a plan. While the others got ready and Frank made phone calls, I found Simona's room. She lay in bed with her leg in a new cast.

"Hey," I said, walking to her bedside.

She was scrolling through her phone, her eyes darting

over the screen. She barely looked up at my entry. "You're good to go."

My heart pounded. "The results came in?"

She chucked the phone on the bed, then grinned. "Yep, got my colleagues to run some quick experiments at the lab. They were rudimentary, but they've given us the information we need. EnRG will kill The Great Green."

I threw myself into her arms.

"*Madre mía*, watch the leg!"

"Thanks, Simona," I said, as I walked to the door. "We couldn't have done this without you."

"Sara?" I turned back to look at her. "Be careful."

I gave her a salute and went to find the others.

Half an hour later, Will picked us up from the hospital. He'd parked down a side street in a battered old SUV. When Harper, Tyler and I approached, he was standing on the sidewalk, throwing his keys in the air, and chatting to his two friends. He hadn't changed. I mean, he'd gotten older, but the shaggy brown hair and kind eyes were exactly the same.

He spotted me. "Sara."

"Will." I didn't try to hide the tears.

He wrapped me in a hug and lifted me off my feet. "It's so good to see you."

"You too," I replied, swiping at my cheeks. Then I noticed his Coast Guard uniform. "You work for the Coast Guard?"

Will dipped his chin. "Ever since I graduated high school. I enrolled in San Diego's Coast Guard Academy and asked to be stationed here."

"Because of Danny?"

He nodded. "Because of Danny. I still want to go the officer route, but I have to wait until I'm twenty-one."

"You'll get there."

He smiled. "Working on it."

I'd never blamed Will. He had tried his best to free Danny from the trash. But he had been so thickly entangled that Will's air ran out before he could cut through it all with his dive knife. It wasn't his fault. It was the trash. A horrible accident.

"I don't think John's my biggest fan at the moment. Am I going to get you in trouble?"

Will smiled. "The story has broken. More reports are coming in about the... what did you call it? The Great Green? People are starting to believe."

"Those same people think Regina is handling it." I rolled my eyes.

"I figured it was a ruse," Will said. "And all it's done is attract more people to the beach trying to see the monster."

"Shit," Harper muttered.

I climbed into the SUV. "We better get going. We need to stop this thing before it's too late."

Will drove north. I sat in the passenger seat and stared at him, comparing the images of him in my memory to his new, older man. He'd become a man. This is what Danny would look like now.

Chapter Twenty-Five

WILL SCREECHED into the entrance road leading to the EnRG lot and pulled up to the barrier by the security hut. The sun was setting over the ocean. This much further north, it still looked blue, and I couldn't spot any signs of the trash. But it wouldn't be long until it was here.

The guard came out of the hut, a bewildered look on his face, and handed Will three sets of keys for the trucks. "The tankers are all full."

Relieved Regina had been true to her word, we parked in the corner and approached the three trucks at our disposal. We watched as the employees trailed out of the factory for the night. The building consisted of one giant warehouse, a massive parking lot filled with employee cars and the tankers parked in a line. Smaller sales vans gleamed orange in the fading light, the bolts of lightning painted on their sides appearing like an omen of war, from God or Thor maybe. A chain link fence topped by barbed wire surrounded the entire lot.

"You sure you know how to drive this?" I asked Will, taking in the size of the mammoth vehicle.

"Yep. Sam, Miguel and I spent a summer driving to make some cash for our Coast Guard academy fees."

"Nah, man," Miguel tapped his arm. "We spent the summer singing songs over the CB radio."

Will chuckled. "We did that too."

Sam, a muscular guy with surfer blonde hair, stepped up to one of the trucks. "You sure this stuff is going to kill a monster? I mean, I got a look at it when I was surfing last week, got myself a chest full of blisters, it was huge."

I approached one of the cabs. "I'll go with Will."

"Of course you will," Tyler muttered.

I turned back to him, took in the pain flashing through his eyes. Was he still mad at me?

Or course he was. I hadn't once called him since his dad was taken to the hospital. I figured once we'd received word Frank was okay and out of the woods, I could get on with battling the monster of the millennium. It never occurred to me Tyler wouldn't understand. He wasn't as passionate about the environment as me, but he still cared. He could see with his own eyes the effects plastic waste was having on our waters. And not just our waters, but all over the world. And now this. The Great Green. I hated it.

But none of this was my fault. Frank's accident was nothing to do with me. The Great Green was out there whether we liked it or not. Nothing would stop me from wanting to save my beach, my ocean, Almond Cove. For everyone. For Danny.

I'd spent the entire drive talking to Will. Not trying to

make things better with Tyler. But I hadn't seen Will for three years, and now that we were thrown together in this, we had a lot to catch up on. Tyler would understand. Wouldn't he?

"I'm sorry," I said to Tyler, although I didn't know what I was apologizing for. I felt he was expecting one, and I didn't know what else to say.

"I know you are," he said, a sad half smile propped on his lips. "Me too."

I wasn't sure what he was sorry for either. Giving me such a hard time? Or Danny?

Will climbed into the cab of our truck. Harper went with Miguel and Tyler went with Sam.

"I'll see you on the other side," I said to Harper and Tyler.

Tyler nodded at me, while Harper stuck an orange EnRG cap on her head.

"Let's go, and let's go fast," I said to Will as I buckled my seatbelt.

He offered me his knuckles. "For Danny."

I tapped his knuckles with my fist. "For Danny."

The engine roared to life.

You can do it. Danny's voice in my head. *One step at a time.*

I took a moment to remember the quality of his voice, the deep tones which reminded me of tree bark and fertile soil. The lilt at the end of his questions that always contained a teasing note, and the warmth of his laugh which brought the sun closer. I leaned into his voice, his image, his memory, and asked him to give me strength.

Will rolled forward, advancing on the security hut and road that would lead us back to the freeway. We fell in behind Harper and Miguel, with Sam and Tyler at our rear.

The engine stalled as we passed through the exit barrier. Will offered me a chagrined smile and said he'd do better. My stomach churned. Not at the prospect of Will's driving, but at the fact we were so much closer to our goal. A short trip back down the freeway, a quick fueling of the fire planes, and we'd be in the air, killing The Great Green. Or not.

Not bothering to wait for the traffic light to turn green, Harper's truck turned the corner to a squeal of angry horns. I braced myself as Will followed, yanking the massive steering wheel. He took the corner too quickly, taking out a concrete curb and a couple bushes. It felt like we were up on two wheels. I winced, thinking the truck might overturn, and I'd end up in the middle of road in a puddle of bright orange EnRG. Then the wheels caught and we bumped over the curb.

I was coming. We were all coming. The Great Green was about to be annihilated.

"Well done, everyone." Tyler's voice came from the CB radio on the central console. "We can do this. I actually think we can do this."

"I hope so," I said. Any minute now, I was expecting a battalion of police cars to appear on the road, sirens wailing, bright lights flashing, chasing us down for speeding. But I'd rather be chased by police than The Great Green.

Harper's truck let out a long toot of its horn. The deep, throaty noise buoyed my spirits. Will picked up the CB radio and started talking to his friends. There was a bunch of "you remember that time" and "I can't believe we didn't get arrested when we" and "you sure you remember how to drive this thing?" I wanted to enjoy the banter, but I was too tense.

Will snapped on the radio and a breathless reporter's voice filled the cab.

"...hospitals overrun..."

"...can't cope with the burns..."

"...death toll is rising..."

"...monster in the water..."

"We need to hurry," I said to Will.

He floored the accelerator and told the other two to do the same. Within seconds we were speeding along the fast lane of the freeway. Going way too fast. But not fast enough. I gripped the door handle with one hand and my seat with the other, clenching my teeth and praying we'd make it to the fire station in one piece.

I gave agitated glances to Tyler in my side mirror. I bit down on the inside of my cheek, drawing blood, hoping against hope my plan would work. I couldn't let Harper and Tyler down. I couldn't let myself down. I wanted to save my beach, my town, my ocean. And Danny. That's what it all came down to. I still wanted to save him.

Halfway through the drive, flashing lights appeared in the rearview mirror. The police had found us.

"What do we do?" Tyler asked across the radio waves. Panic lined his tone and I knew he'd be rubbing the back of his neck.

"What's going on?" Harper said.

"Police have arrived," I replied.

"Shit." Her muted voice came back. "But we gotta keep going, right? I mean, we're fulfilling a civic duty. We're taking EnRG down. We're going to kill The Great Green. They're just gonna have to get on board. Right?"

"We don't have time to stop and explain it all," Tyler said.

"We keep going," Will said, eyes narrowed on the road ahead.

"We keep going," I repeated. "Tyler? Sam? You okay with that?"

"Go big or go home," Tyler replied.

I smiled; it was one of his dad's favorite expressions.

The police flanked us on both sides. I counted three cars. Then two more. By the time we reached the outskirts of San Diego, we had an entourage of eight police cars, all sirens blazing, all lights flashing. Ahead, the freeway had been cleared. Which meant we could go faster. But we'd have to get off soon, and then we could get stuck in a maze of traffic.

The police spoke to us over a bullhorn, then found the frequency of our radio channels.

"You are speeding. Pull over. No one here has to get hurt."

Hurt? HURT? My legs went to jelly and my hand slipped off the door handle. I chucked Will a nervous glance.

"It's going to be okay, Sara," Will said. With one hand on the wheel, he touched my hand with the other "Really. We're going to be okay. I promise."

I shook my head. "You can't promise that."

"Yes, I can," he risked a glance at me. "I feel it in my bones."

"I wish I had your bones."

He chuckled and shifted his gaze back to the road. "One step at a time."

Danny's mantra.

"Pull over." The order went on a loop. Eventually, I was able to tune it out, along with the sirens.

We couldn't use the radios to talk to each other anymore without being overheard. When Harper's truck indicated to leave the freeway a few minutes later, I sighed with relief. Frank's station was only a couple miles away.

Miguel kept his hand on the horn, or maybe it was Harper, blaring pedestrians and smaller vehicles out the way. We didn't stop for stop signs or traffic lights, but warned people with our horns. The fire station came into view. Harper and Miguel took the long corner, slowing their speed.

Will kept close on their heels. A quick glance in the rearview showed Tyler's truck slowing down too.

Frank, dressed in fire department fatigues, bandages still wrapped around his ribs, stood there, waving his good arm and pointing us toward the hangar.

Tyler and Harper drove in ahead of us. Will and I came to a shuddering stop.

A swarm of police cars screeched to a halt behind us. "Come out with your hands up!"

"We made it," Will said.

Unable to find my voice, I nodded.

"Come out with your hands up!" The command repeated over a bullhorn.

"Sit tight. I'm going to go help clear the air." Will opened the door and jumped from the cab.

I sat there, heart thundering, pulse pounding in my ears, amazed I was still alive.

My legs shook. I didn't think I could move. The sirens weren't blaring anymore, but the red and blue lights whirred faster and faster, making me dizzy. I rested a hand on the door handle of the truck, preparing to face the music.

In front of my truck, the door on Tyler's cab inched open a fraction. Behind me, Frank and Will appeared between the end of my truck and the line of police cars. An animated conversation ensued, which I watched in the side mirror. Lots of hand gesturing, finger-pointing, and stern looks. I decided to stay put.

While the police were busy talking to Frank and the three drivers, Tyler crept out of his cab, tiptoed to me, and opened the driver's door of my truck.

He slid inside, leaving the door ajar. "Hi."

"Hi," I said, unable to utter anything more complex.

"That was some ride, huh?"

I cried. Right there in the cab. Didn't even feel it coming. Tyler wrapped his arms around me and we hugged. Despite the weirdness between us, it felt natural.

"What's your dad doing here?" I asked once I'd calmed down a bit. "I thought he couldn't leave the hospital."

"When the police turned up on our tail, I called him and gave a Code Red. Said we were going to need some help on arrival." He reached between his legs and removed a single can of EnRG that had been rolling around the footwell.

"Thank God for your dad."

Tyler popped the tab on the can and took a long sip. "Ahhh! That's better." He wiped his lips on his sleeve.

"You seriously going to drink that? Something powerful

enough to kill a trash monster and you want to put it inside you?"

He gave me a considered smile. "See, here's the way I figure it. I'm going to have to go fly one of those fire planes over this damn trash monster. And if the monster has any ideas about taking my plane out of the sky, well, it's going to get a nasty surprise when it tries to eat me."

I reached for the can. "Give me some."

He faced me and swept some hair out of my eyes. "You don't have to come with me, you know." He moved his hand to my cheek and brushed it with his thumb, tracing the tracks of dried tears. "I think you've been through enough."

"We've all been through a lot." I took a sip of the can. It wasn't as bad as I thought it was going to be. It tasted like bubbles. Orange bubbles that fizzed on my tongue. I could use the extra energy. I hadn't slept in two nights. Suddenly, I was exhausted. "I'm coming. We're going to do this together. I'd never let you face off against something so evil alone. This is me supporting you."

He tapped a nervous rhythm on the dash, then someone opened the driver's door of the cab. Frank stood on the ground, a smiling Harper beside him.

"Hey," he said. "You guys okay?"

We both nodded.

"You can get out now," Frank said. "I've explained the situation to the police."

"Phew," I said. "Thanks, Frank."

"But no one is going anywhere tonight. It's not a good idea to fight something you can't see."

"It's bright green," I said. "And glows. It's hard to miss."

"Aye," Frank said, wavering.

"We might not have time to wait until tomorrow," Tyler said. "We need to do this now."

"While I still have the nerve," I muttered.

Tight-lipped, Frank nodded.

I climbed out of the cab. Once on the ground, I became aware of the bustling activity of the hangar. The policemen rushed around, taking orders from a reduced fire crew, attaching fuel lines from the tankards to Frank's three wild-fire planes.

I was surprised to find John in conversation with Frank. The Coast Guard officer offered a wave in greeting as I approached, then a sheepish smile.

"I owe you an apology," John said.

I stared at him. A string of white blisters decorated his bald scalp. He must have had his own up close and personal with The Great Green. Been forced to believe.

"It doesn't matter," I said. "You're here now, right? To help?"

"I am," he replied. "Frank explained the plan to me. I've called in a crew to cover your back. Will is one of the best. His crew is going to be up there with you. And I'll put the boats out."

I shook my head. "Not the boats. It will eat the boats."

"All I've got is the one helicopter," John said.

Frank put a hand on his shoulder. "It'll do, John. Thank you."

"Thank you," I echoed.

John stuck out his hand. "No, Sara, thank *you*. I'm sorry it took me so long to listen to reason. There was a lot of pressure from the government, from EnRG, to keep the panic to a minimum. So many people around here depend on the water for their livelihood. And with tourist season in full swing..." he looked at his feet. "Well, I can't apologize enough. I'll find a way to make it up to you."

"Just cover my back," I said.

I turned to Frank and Tyler. "We need to get moving."

Frank rubbed at the back of his neck. Perhaps that's where Tyler got the gesture from. "We've got enough EnRG here to fuel the planes twice over."

"Perfect," Tyler said.

"I only have two pilots. I called around, hoping you wouldn't have to fly, Tyler, but the rest of them are inland fighting the wildfires."

Tyler's gaze flicked between us. "Sara asked me to fly, and I'm going to fly."

I stuck to his side. "And I'm going with him."

Frank's lips puckered. One of his arms was in a cast and the other hand rested on his waist. His blue eyes danced, coming to a decision. "Okay. Okay. We need to kill this thing, and we need to hit it fast and hard. We need you up there, son. If you're sure you can manage it."

"I can manage it," Tyler replied.

They hugged. I smiled. Harper jumped on me and the aches and pains I'd accrued over the last few days sprung to the surface, the burns on my skin hurting the most. But I couldn't fault her exuberance. Despite how exhausted I was, a new wave of energy sang through my veins. Or maybe it was the EnRG.

"I wish I knew how to fly," Harper said. "You guys get to have all the fun."

One of Frank's crew jogged up to us. "We're ready."

Tyler gulped and I gave him my best reassuring smile. After we had a brief meeting involving strategy and a few instructions for Tyler, Frank and his crewman led us over to the three Bombardier 415 planes. Bright yellow, with huge tails and wide wings, they symbolized hope. Yellow. Bright yellow. Like lemons or corn or the sun. So much better than green.

Tyler and I were handed headsets and life jackets. The life jackets were also yellow, uninflated. We were to wear them in case of a crash. I slipped it over my head and prayed we wouldn't need it. A mobile staircase was parked against each plane.

Will came by as we were getting ready, holding dive gear and wetsuits. My stomach churned.

"I've got your back," he said. "Not going to let anything happen to either of you."

I believed him. "Thanks, Will."

Tyler placed his foot on the first step and turned to me. "You ready?"

I nodded and ignored my dry mouth and heaving stomach. This was our last stand. Our last weapon. Our last everything. If this didn't work... well, I tried really hard not to think about that.

"See you out there," Will said.

I wanted to hug him, but we were out of time.

Before we reached the cockpit, the pilots of the other two planes stopped by. They offered fist bumps and wishes of good luck. The one with fiery red hair and a thick red mustache introduced himself as Dan. His eyes twinkled with excitement, like this was a walk in the park for him. "Let's take this thing down."

The second pilot's blue eyes reminded me of the color I preferred my ocean to be. "Good luck." He saluted us, then jogged away to his own plane.

Tyler and I climbed into our seats. The plane smelled of fire. Probably from all the wildfires it had fought. Underneath the smoky scent was a trace of lingering sweat and fear. And pine. I spotted the tree-shaped air freshener hanging near Tyler's knee.

Harper hovered on the forecourt, a hand shielding her eyes from the floodlights, which looked oddly green. Of course they did. The Great Green tainted everything. She waved and gave us a thumbs up. Part of me wished I was standing on the ground next to her, but I needed to show Tyler I had his back. And I wanted to see the monster die.

A couple of press vans screamed into the fire station. One of them barely came to a stop before four men leaped out of the van and aimed cameras and microphones in our directions. The police and Frank didn't let them get close. The monster story had broken, and now perhaps our involvement was too.

We put on our headsets. The older pilot's voice, Jeff, spoke in our ears. He told us not to worry about the press and instructed us to buckle up, then walked Tyler through the controls again.

"It's not much different from the Cessna," Tyler muttered. "Apart from this extra big lever here."

"That's for dumping the EnRG," Jeff laughed.

After a few minutes, Tyler pressed the ignition and the engines roared to life. Under my butt, the seat shuddered as

Tyler revved the engines, waking them up and preparing them for a quick takeoff. My teeth jammed together, and I sucked in short, shallow breaths between my lips. With trembling fingers, I made sure my seatbelt was secure. I wondered how Tyler was feeling. I wasn't even flying and I could barely keep myself together.

"Sara?" Tyler said over the headset.

"Yeah?"

"Let's do this." Confidence oozed around his words. He'd flown a plane countless times before. It was probably like me getting on my bike, which I couldn't remember where I'd left.

I relaxed a bit and decided to trust him. I wasn't alone. I didn't have to do this by myself. And not everything was about Danny. Relinquishing control didn't feel as frustrating as I thought it might. We were a team. Tyler and I. Frank and the firemen. John and Will. The other two pilots. Harper and Simona. We were all part of the same team to take down The Great Green. I was about to face the most terrifying moment of my life. It felt good not to be alone.

I whooped and punched a fist into the air, only to slam it into the roof of the plane. Wincing, I cradled my hand and encouraged Tyler to take off. He pointed the nose of the plane down the runway. Excitement thundered in my stomach, pounded in my ears, streaked through my veins, along with my nerves.

As we rumbled down the runway, the police cars flanked us on both sides, sirens blaring, lights flashing; a procession to the sky. This time, I wasn't scared. Well, not of the cops, anyway. I grinned and waved at them. We zipped down the runway, heading away from the hangar, moving inland.

Tyler whooped as the wheels lifted off and sang himself a song of triumph.

"Don't get too cocky," I warned, but with a smile on my face. "We still have to face The Great Green."

As we gained altitude, he turned, banking toward the ocean. Within minutes the coastline came into view. The boardwalk, still barricaded, heaved with people trying to get closer to the beach and water. Cameras whirred, but I doubted most of them were of sufficient quality to record anything during the night. The red Coast Guard helicopter lifted into the sky, Will hanging out the open side. His presence brought me more reassurance than I'd expected. Until I looked down.

The trash monster sat there, hugging the coast, surrounding the EnRG catamaran and other vessels. Everything was green. The color stretched so far and wide. And it had grown out of the ocean too, piling itself higher and higher, up the sides of the catamaran. Under the light of the moon, it was the only thing visible, and muted the lights in the boardwalk and the rest of Almond Cove. It pulsed with life, glistened with menace, and undulated with nefarious intent.

I hated it.

The trash, the putrid green of alien blood, lapped at the beach. My beach. Gleaming. But this was no beautiful night sky on a summer's evening. This was the goddamn water. Within the glowing green, shadows swam. Dark shadows and impossible shapes. Gaping jaws and wickedly sharp appendages. Whipping tentacles and throbbing suckers bigger than dinner plates. Staring eyes that didn't blink, all made of glowing green light and trash.

The sand sparkled, like after a heavy rain when the beach glimmers with new crystalline properties. But the beach was as green as the ocean. Some of the dark shadows washed up on shore and crept their way up the beach toward the deserted boardwalk.

The pulsing green light lit the dark sky in one repulsive color, and I wondered if we were on Earth at all.

"It's... it's... it's..." I trailed off, unable to put into words what I was seeing.

"It's a goner." Jeff's voice came over the headset. "That's what it is."

"You sure this is going to work?" Dan asked, as the three planes circled The Great Green.

My stomach swam with uncertainty. I had no idea if this was going to work. I could only hope.

"We're going to release our loads at the same time," Jeff said. "Tyler, remember where the release lever is?"

"Affirmative," Tyler replied.

"Let's get into formation, then we'll release our loads on the count of three. Then speed back to the station and refuel. Got it?"

"Got it," Tyler replied, lowering his altitude.

It took a couple of minutes for the planes to form a loose circle and surround the trash monster. It was so big, I lost sight of the other two planes, but I could hear their reassuring voices over the radio. I could no longer pick out individual items of trash. It was all one green shape. A single solid mass. No longer trash, but a giant sleeping behemoth.

"Three, two, one!" Jeff called.

Tyler pulled the lever. A rushing gush of noise exploded from the plane as the bright orange EnRG rained down on the glowing green. Suddenly lighter, we bobbed in the air currents. Without waiting to see what happened, Tyler banked toward the station.

I turned in my seat to watch the effect. Behind us, the ocean churned and foamed. It bubbled and hissed. Green steam rose from the trash monster. Angry eyes appeared in the middle of the mass, searching, searching, fixing on us. My throat tightened as it locked its alien gaze on our small plane. At the edges of the mass where the EnRG hadn't yet infiltrated, vines and tendrils whipped the air, seeking a target.

They splashed the catamaran and rocked the smaller boats. The tendrils searched through the air and slapped at the water, shaking the ocean, pushing unruly waves onto the beach in an angry death dance. But the center of it foamed and churned and burbled with a desperate ferocity. Trash broke off from the green mass, becoming individual items once more. Will's helicopter rose in the sky to avoid the furious green tendrils. Then the ocean was out of view.

Tyler landed a moment later. We sat in the plane and waited for Frank's crew and the police to refuel us. Harper did star jumps on the asphalt, a huge grin on her face. Frank nodded at us, a proud smile on his lips. John came by and shook Tyler's hand, telling him he'd make a mighty fine fire pilot one day. Or a Coast Guard.

Half an hour later, we were back in the air. This was the last load of EnRG for each of the planes. Nervous energy sent a burning, stinging sensation through my limbs. This was it.

The beach loomed. The lights of Will's helicopter flashed in the dark sky. The Great Green was there. The center of it continued to hiss and burble, to swell and scream, while the edges produced its shooting tendrils of burning vines. But they were smaller and thinner and slapped back to the water with increasing frequency. The EnRG was working, but the monster wasn't dead yet. Before we could all get into formation, one of the thready vines wrapped around the tail of Jeff's plane.

He swore through the headset, wrestling the controls, trying to get to the lever.

"Do something, Tyler!" I yelled.

"There's nothing I *can* do!"

I looked on in horror as the tendril yanked the plane down, down, down, into the water. The ocean bubbled, the trash burped, fizzing and dissolving under the effects of the concentrated EnRG in Jeff's plane. A murderous eye followed us. Jeff's plane never came back up.

Two of the divers from the helicopter dove into the churning mess. My heart froze, until I spotted Will still sitting in the open side of the craft. With my gaze back on the ocean, I lost sight of the two divers.

"Shit, Tyler."

"I know. I know."

Dan released his load too early, only hitting the edge of the monster, and narrowly avoiding another waving arm. But the immediate area quickly hissed and foamed and several more appendages dissolved back into the water. Trash bobbed, freed from the monster, crashing in the tumultuous waves.

"Dump it and go!" Dan yelled into the headset. "Don't let it get you!" And then he was gone.

Beneath us, the ocean turned a murky brown. Steam

rose from the water. The last few remaining appendages appeared out of the burning mist and slapped against the windows, throwing us off course. It was The Great Green's final effort.

"Got to get closer!" Tyler called.

"How can you see anything?" I screamed.

"Just a minute! Just a minute!" Tyler's eyes were fixed on his controls, on all the bleeping lights and screens.

The EnRG catamaran sat in the middle of it all, completely unaffected. An insectile shape the monster called Mother. I couldn't spot any movement on board and prayed Regina had stayed at her oceanside mansion. As much as I had enjoyed imagining an ill fate for her in the past, I didn't want her to die.

Frothing and churning, the water burbled like a volcano bubbling to the surface. Orange fought green. The water belched, spewing steam and trash and feelers into the sky. Only a handful of appendages left. They broke free of the main body, slapping against the water, writhing in an absurd death dance. Everywhere I looked, the green hissed and foamed. The monster was dying.

Will's voice came across the radio. "We've got your back. Do what you need to do."

I shook my head at his words. Why had I put him in this situation? What if a tendril ripped his helicopter out of the sky? I couldn't bear to be the death of Danny's best friend.

Tyler circled closer. Eyes winked at the edges of The Great Green, as if it had poured all its energy into its outer limits. A few weak tendrils shot to the sky, but they steamed and hissed and fell back to the water before causing harm. I lost sight of most of the Operation Blue Water boats in the steam, but caught a glimpse of one sinking. Was the monster trying to refuel itself? We needed to release our last load before it could recover.

"Hurry!" I called.

Cutting around the frothing center, we flew low. Tyler steered away from another shrinking, but insistent vine.

In muted silence, we kept our eyes trained on the main mass. Green waves whipped into the air and slammed over the small vessels, dragging them down, feeding on their parts. All but the catamaran, which sat there dominating everything.

Without warning, something from below shunted into a boat and sent it rocketing out of the ocean and sailing into the sky. It was weird. Seeing a boat arc so high above the water, pretending to be a plane. Like a broomstick over the moon. It made a beeline for Will's helicopter. Until green hands and arms reached out of the water, plucking the boat from its course. More hands than before. Hungry mouths appeared. Perfect circles with hundreds of teeth chomping at the air. It was growing again.

"Whatever you're going to do, do it now!" Will yelled across the radio.

I clutched Tyler's shoulder. "We need to hurry!"

The ocean filled with noise. The water hissed and steam thickened around us, blocking our view out the windows. It seeped inside the plane, causing my eyes to sting and lungs to burn. It brought with it the most vile, toxic smell I'd ever had to endure. I gagged, gasping for breath, like I'd inhaled a lungful of razors. Tyler coughed.

"I can barely breathe!" Tyler gulped.

Never having piloted a plane before, I had nothing to do

but struggle for breath as I stared at the green mist and angry tentacles. One slammed us sideways, and suddenly we were falling.

"Now, Tyler! Now!"

Tyler yanked on the lever, but it didn't budge. "It won't move! It's stuck!"

The plane spun out of control. I banged my head against the window, horrified to see several glowing shapes adhered to the outside of the plane. All of them hissing, burbling, dissolving. Did we have enough EnRG to take this thing out?

With my stomach in my mouth, I unclicked my seatbelt to reach for the lever with Tyler. We stared at each other, amidst the spinning and the hissing and the burbling and the trash trying to kill us, we shared a look. Then we both pulled.

The skin under my neck tightened with the effort and I bit down on my lip. I pulled. Tyler pulled, and finally, the EnRG was released.

A second later we hit the water, causing a great splash to spray the windows. I was thrown upward, my back slamming against the ceiling and sending a new flare of pain through my body. Tyler lurched forward. But we were alive. Miraculously. Wondrously. We were alive.

"How do we get out of here?" I yelled, only to realize Tyler's eyes were drooping and blood dripped down his forehead. "Nooooo!"

I searched for a release button. Outside, the water level rose and angry shapes butted against the plane. Finally, after an agonizing minute of searching, I found the emergency release and yanked on the bright red cord. The roof flew open. I tugged off Tyler's seatbelt and pulled on the cord of his life jacket.

Beyond the sinking plane, The Great Green roared. One last sweeping appendage brushed close to the plane, searching for us. But it never made contact and dissolved into the water.

The helicopter thundered overhead. Will perched on the edge, preparing to jump.

With no other choice open to us, I eased into the water and pulled Tyler after me. It burned, then went cold. I stifled a scream as something wrapped around my legs and arms. I screamed until the hissing liquid filled my throat, always burning. But in my stomach, the burning stopped. The EnRG I'd drunk.

I held tight to an unconscious Tyler as The Great Green dissolved. The hissing and frothing became a foaming and fizzing. My legs and arms were released and the circle of green water I treaded in shrank, shrank, until only a pinprick of green light was left.

"Sara!" Will's voice across the waves.

The water started to calm and the smell of wrongness was replaced with salt. Not realizing I had closed my eyes, I opened them to see a wonderous sight. Blue. The water was blue. Blessed blue. And filled with trash. But there wasn't a speck of green.

Tyler and I bobbed in the water, knocking against netting and plastic cups and containers and milk bottle lids and toothbrushes and six-pack rings and all the other things I'd been picking up from the ocean for the last six years. I was almost pleased to see it, because it was just trash, no longer a monster.

A fish swam by my leg, tickling my shin, and I laughed with the joy of it.

"Tyler! We did it!" I yelled as another Coastie dove from the helicopter.

Beside me, he groaned and his eyelids fluttered, but remained closed. He was going to be okay. And so was my ocean.

Chapter Twenty-Six

Tyler and I sat in the helicopter, watching the ocean. It was past midnight and the only lights I could see were from the shops along the boardwalk and nearby homes. The ocean was black. Beautifully black, like the freckle at the corner of Tyler's mouth. With little white caps shining in the moonlight. I couldn't spot a trace of green. There was still a huge section of the Eastern Garbage Patch to deal with, but I could save that problem for another day.

Tyler and I held hands. Will put oxygen masks over our faces. Finally, I could breathe again. My lungs still ached.

"Thank you," I said.

He brushed his ear, signaling he couldn't hear me. There was no point in conversation while the rotors roared above our heads. So I stared at him. And he smiled at me. And Tyler coughed up a lung.

When we landed on the roof of the Coast Guard's office a few minutes later, Will helped us out and covered our shoulders with blankets.

"You saved us," I said to Will, my voice gruff after all the burning steam I'd inhaled.

"No." He smiled at me, the movement shrinking his crow's feet and turning his nose askew. "You saved us all."

Will placed an arm carefully around my waist, escorting me through the main doors. "Danny would be so proud of you."

My heart lurched painfully. Was that what I'd been waiting to hear? That he wasn't angry, that it wasn't my fault?

Something clicked inside, some fundamental truth that eased the grief surrounding my heart. Impulsively, I threw my arms around Will and hugged him tight.

Will ushered us into the medical center, and while we were examined, Harper handed us both a can of EnRG. Tyler and I popped the tabs without hesitation. The burning in my throat ceased immediately. Just as I was starting to feel vaguely normal and lucky to have escaped death, my parents rushed through the door.

They stood inside the threshold. Mom's hands covered her lips and Dad searched my face.

"Tell me that wasn't you in the fire plane fighting that... that *thing*?" Mom asked. She looked tired and worried and rumpled.

"What was it?" Dad asked. "On the news, they said it was a... monster... since when do we have monsters in Almond Cove?"

"It's a long story," I replied.

"I thought the stories on Instagram were a hoax," Mom said.

Frank approached. "It's all real. Regina finally admitted the truth."

My chest lifted. The whole world knew what had tried to destroy my town. No more crackpot conspiracy theorists. No more laughing and pointing fingers. But it didn't matter anymore. It was dead. We had killed it.

"By the way," Harper said. "Jack and Ryan Phillips are both alive. They made it. In hospital, severe burns and in intensive care, but they made it."

"How?" I asked, remembering the awful moments when they both went tumbling over the cliff. Then I remembered how calm the ocean had turned only minutes after we sped away. Perhaps The Great Green had stopped attacking, left them alone, and they were able to get to shore.

My conscience eased. I was glad they were okay, that I hadn't left them on top of the cliff to die.

I hugged my parents, pressing my body tightly into our huddle. I wanted to hug them forever and never let them go.

"We saw the whole thing as we landed," Dad said. "I mean, I don't know what I saw, but I recognized Frank's planes."

We were given sweet tea and cookies. Mom kept touching my hair and kissing my cheek, then she got angry. She gave me a look that could wither skeletons. "I cannot believe you took such risks. Why didn't you call us?"

I hung my head. "I don't know... I thought... I thought I could handle it. I didn't want you here... getting hurt."

She wrapped her arms around me again. "You don't need to take on the world by yourself. And it's *us* who are supposed to look after *you*."

I nodded into her chest. "I know."

Dad looked at me, admiration in his eyes. "You were very brave. I saw some hairy stuff in my SEAL days, but nothing like that. That was incredible, Sara."

I blushed. "I did it for Danny."

He loved the ocean. I wanted to picture him in the water, the ocean as his final resting place, not the cold starkness of the polished coffin. That shell had never been Danny. Not the real one.

Now that I had killed The Great Green, he could get back to swimming out his afterlife. "And for you, Mom, and Dad's business, and Tyler and Frank and Simona's work and me. I did it for myself too. I love the ocean. I can't let anything destroy my ocean."

It was my ocean. Mine. Danny would always be there, but I needed to establish a new relationship with it.

"I wanted Danny to be proud of me."

Frowning, Mom sat next to me. "That's why you put yourself in danger?"

"Danny was always so brave," I said. "He always put other people first. He showed me a rare horned tail lizard. And introduced me to my first seal. He showed me how to hold a crab, and not be scared. And how to dive. He gave his life for a cage of lobsters. He was perfect."

Dad sat on the other side of me. "Danny wasn't perfect."

"I mean, I know he wasn't *perfect*. No one is perfect, but I..." I trailed off. Did I think Danny was perfect? Is that the yardstick I'd been holding myself accountable to all this time?

Will, back in the room in a clean set of Coast Guard

fatigues, was in earshot. "Danny got drunk at my cousin's funeral. *So* not cool."

My eyebrows rose. "You mean your cousin who died of alcohol poisoning?"

"The very same," Will replied. "My parents were furious."

"And so were we," Dad said. "He was grounded for a month."

"He told me he was never going to drink again," I said, thinking back.

"He was a risk taker," Will said. "Yeah, he did a lot of good for Green Clean and the environment, but he took it too far. He put his life in danger more than once. And I let him do it."

"It's not your fault," I said.

"It's not your fault either," Will replied.

"I was so mad at him when he biked you over to Mission Bay on his handlebars. Across the main roads! And no helmets!" Mom said.

The day we went to catch more plankton. I'd never seen Danny in this light.

His death wasn't my fault. And it wasn't Will's or my parents', or Danny's either. It was an accident.

Tears glistened in Mom's eyes.

Dad held me tight. "I love you so much, Sara."

"Me too."

Mom put her hands on my shoulders. "Don't let Danny's death shape your future."

"I won't," I replied automatically. In truth, I didn't know if I could prevent it. I'd been so young when he died.

Impressionable. I wanted to put the unhealthy attitudes behind me, but I didn't know if I could.

John brought us a round of hot chocolates and more cookies. It was all they had in stock. We sat in the medical center waiting for FEMA to arrive and take statements. Simona had a new cast on her leg and Frank's bandages were changed. He promised he'd go back to the hospital in the morning. Tyler and I both had mild concussions and were treated accordingly.

I noticed with relief there was no hint of a vile green in the night sky outside the windows, but a beautiful midnight blue with a few stars thrown in for good measure. Stars. I'd forgotten how much I loved the stars. A shooting one winked by the window. I called it Danny-5799 and didn't make a wish. I had nothing left to wish for.

When most people had fallen quiet and my eyelids were drooping, Frank sat down next to me. "Regina's been arrested."

I lifted my head to look at him. "For real?"

He nodded.

I didn't know how I felt about that. She had been my nemesis for so long. EnRG trash had held Danny down, but blaming her wasn't going to bring him back and it didn't do anything for the anger I'd been carrying. I couldn't blame EnRG for all the ocean's problems. Ocean trash was a global issue, one that needed solving by more than me alone.

Regina might have created The Great Green, but it was over, and I never needed to think about her again. It was up to me to decide how I wanted to live the rest of my life.

It was time to let go.

"About fucking time," Simona piped up from her bed, clicking her seaweed gum with unhealthy vigor. Harper sat next to her, doodling on her white cast with a black sharpie. One of the images was The Great Green, getting its ass kicked by Tyler's plane, with the hashtag #Operation-Kickass written at the bottom. "And there's mention of EnRG being recalled."

"Aw, man," Tyler muttered. Everyone laughed.

"You okay?" Frank asked me.

I wiped at a rogue tear running down my cheek. "I think so."

"They might need you to testify."

My stomach rolled.

Mom touched my hand. "You don't have to think about it now, sweetheart."

Frank hugged me. Frank had never hugged me before. "Justice for Danny."

I smiled. "Closure for me."

We spent hours answering FEMA's questions, then ventured outside for some air. The press was waiting, and we received a volley of impressed looks and arched eyebrows along with their quick-fire questions.

Ignoring them, we strolled to the beach. I blinked against the sunlight and then plopped onto a chair at the only open diner on the boardwalk. We feasted and stared at the ocean. The blue ocean. Blue. Blue. Blue. It was the best color in the world.

"You did it, Sara," Dad said, cupping my face. "You did it."

"There's still the trash." I couldn't ignore the problem, the realms of plastic items bobbing in the shallows, stretching to the horizon. The Eastern Garbage Patch was still here, but I didn't have to single-handedly pick up every piece of it. I had friends, and a family to help. And Green Clean.

"There is," Mom said. "But it has purpose. With it so close to shore, people can't ignore the problem." She pointed along the beach where people stood in a scattered line, plucking trash from the sand and stuffing it into net bags. They weren't wearing the Green Clean T-shirts. These were civilians, come to help.

"We did it," I said to everyone, my gaze sweeping the group. "We *all* did it."

"I'm considering a change in career," Simona said, sticking a fresh piece of seaweed gum between her lips. "Something on land. Not sure I'm in a hurry to get back in the water."

Tyler laughed. "One monster isn't going to keep a ballsy woman like you down. Not for long."

"Nor me," I said, blowing across the top of my mug of tea.

"The Coast Guard is getting involved too," Will said. "A couple more units flying in to help organize the cleanup."

Mom filled Will's coffee cup. "Will, please don't be a stranger. Come around to the house anytime you want."

"I'd like that." Will cradled his cup. "If it's okay with you, Sara?"

I smiled.

Chapter Twenty-Seven

A FEW DAYS LATER, Dad and I sat on the back porch late one night with the telescope trained on the cloudless sky. The back gate squeaked open and Tyler bounded around the corner in a pair of flip-flops. I'd finally convinced him to ditch the sneakers. He jumped up the porch steps and leaned against the handrail next to me, pecking me on the cheek.

"Hey, Tyler," Dad said as he adjusted the magnification. "How's your dad?"

"Better," Tyler replied. "Moving around again, although it's going to take a few weeks for those ribs to heal. But you know what he's like."

"Stubborn as an ox," Dad replied, sipping from a beer bottle.

I stared at him and gestured for him to shoo.

He grinned and made smooching faces behind Tyler's back. I blushed all the way to my roots. "Dad!"

Tyler turned, catching him in the act, and laughed.

"Teenagers," Dad muttered. "So much harder than I thought it was going to be."

"Hey, I saved the world, remember?"

"That you did." Dad smiled. He took a quick glimpse through the telescope, then went inside to give us some privacy.

When the door slid shut, I dared to look at Tyler. Although we'd messaged each other constantly, this was the first time we'd seen each other since killing The Great Green.

Tentatively, I leaned against the handrail while Tyler fiddled with the telescope settings.

"How's your head?" I asked.

Tyler wrapped his knuckles against his temple. "Takes more than a little concussion to keep me down. How about you?"

"A few headaches," I replied. "But mostly okay."

Silence wound between us. Crickets chirped in the hedges, and I scuffed a foot along the deck. "Do you want a drink?"

"I'm good," he said.

"Tyler—"

"Sara—"

We both spoke at the same time, then smiled.

"You go first," he said.

"I couldn't have done it without you. I mean, I don't know how to thank you. You were amazing. You killed it."

"Me and two other pilots. And you. We all did."

"It was mostly you."

He brushed the compliment aside.

"I wanted to help. I always did." He stepped to the handrail, his eyes searching my face. "But I was worried about my dad. I needed to be there. And I didn't understand why you didn't get that."

"I did get it." I touched his arm, but it felt weird, so I let my hand drop to my side. "In my head, you were looking after your dad and I was looking after the ocean."

"And Danny."

I nodded.

He made a noise. Half sympathy and half amusement. "Who was taking care of you?"

I shrugged. I thought back to all the times I felt close to losing it. When we thought Simona had been kidnapped, my parents on the other side of the world, Frank in the hospital. I had doubted every decision. But I couldn't wait around for something else to happen either. "I know I can be a bit of a bulldozer when it comes to the things I'm passionate about."

Tyler chuckled. "You don't say."

"But I've learned a lot about myself. I've been too wrapped up in Danny, how he died, wanting to make people pay. It's taken all this to make me realize I can't live in the past. Not in Danny's shadow. I have to be true to myself. Whatever that ends up being..."

This time, Tyler touched my hand. His touch was warm and comforting. "You don't owe me any explanations."

"I feel like I do."

"Sara, you're just you, and I wouldn't change any of it..." he trailed off as his gaze turned to the backyard.

"Really?"

"Nope. Dancing with death makes you appreciate people more. I like you just the way you are." He smiled.

I blushed.

He lowered himself to one of the deck chairs. "You still planning on working at Scripps with Simona?"

I nodded. "For a whole month. When are you heading off to Yosemite?"

"After my flight test next week," Tyler replied.

"For the rest of the summer, right?"

Tyler tilted his head. "Parents think I could use a break from the ocean."

I looked at him, sweeping my gaze over his handsome face, down his jawline to the slope of his muscular shoulders. Down his chest, his tanned legs. It felt like I'd known him forever. We'd been dating for two years. I wasn't entirely sure I remembered a time without Tyler in my life, considering how our dads were best friends.

He frowned. "What is it?"

I toyed with the hem of my T-shirt. "I think the time apart might do us some good."

His face wrinkled as he scratched at the back of his neck. "What are you saying?"

What *was* I saying? This wasn't something I had planned, but seeing Tyler again, in my gut, I knew it was the right thing.

"I think I need some time on my own—"

"You don't care about me anymore?" His face fell.

"Of course I care about you." I looked at my feet, scuffed my toes along the wooden deck, earning myself a new splinter. Finally, I looked at Tyler again. I had to do this. For me, for him. For both of us. "I love you. I can't imagine you not being in my life, it's just... it's just that... I've spent so long living in Danny's shadow. Then dating you. Relying on you. I think in some ways, I relied on you to protect me like Danny always used to do—"

He half rose. "You've never—"

I raised a palm. "Let me finish."

"Sorry." He sank back into the chair.

I chewed on my lip. "I think I need to discover who I am. I need to deal with my baggage. You suggested I go back to therapy. I think it's a good idea, among other things. I need some time to figure out who I am before I can be of any use to anyone else. Does that make sense?"

"Unfortunately," he replied with a long sigh. He leaned back in the chair and rubbed at his forehead. "I want you to be happy, Sara, I do, and if you think a break is what we need, then okay. But I'm going to miss the hell out of you."

I leaned over, cupped his jaw and pecked his lips. "I'm going to miss you too."

His fingers twitched, pulling at the bottom of his shorts. "Will you still come watch me get my pilot's license?"

"Of course, wouldn't miss it." Above all else, Tyler was my friend. I'd always support his big moments.

"I suppose you're going to spend your summer cleaning up the Eastern Garbage Patch, huh?"

I cocked a shoulder. "Well, I was thinking of *not* helping."

"Say *what?*"

"I'm taking a break from environmental cleanup duties. Thought I'd volunteer in the rescue aquarium for a while, let other people handle the trash for a bit. I could use a pause."

"Good for you." Tyler stood and smoothed his shorts. "By the way, I saw Simona sitting on your front porch." Simona had been living with us while her apartment was repaired, and so we could help her while her leg was in a cast. When she wasn't resting, she visited Jack in the hospital. They'd started a romance after all. "She said the water results came through."

I socked his shoulder when he dragged out a dramatic pause. "And?"

"The Land and Water Quality Division have been involved, testing samples all over the state. No trace of the algae in the drinking system. Nothing strange at all."

"So, whatever we did to it in the ocean, we did to all of it."

"Seems that way," Tyler said. "I don't care to think about the hows and whys. I'm just glad it's all over."

"I never found the Tupperware container," I said, casting a glance at the yard.

Simona came out on her crutches. "Thought I heard my name being used in vain."

I smiled. "Never in vain."

"I don't think you need to worry about the parts of the algae which came on land, or took your container. The studies in the lab show that when separated, smaller bits try to get back to the main body. If it makes it."

I raised an eyebrow. "If it makes it?"

"It can't survive without water."

I let out a sigh of relief, thinking of all those biting insect things which had attacked us on the clifftop, and the missing container. It was dead, all of it, finally.

Simona patted my shoulder, then headed back inside.

"The ocean is safe again." I closed my eyes and leaned into the gentle breeze. I smelled the salt of the ocean, food cooking on barbecues, the herbs in Mom's planter, Tyler's sun lotion, and the fainter odor of stale beer from Dad's favorite chair. They were all the smells I loved about home, about Almond Cove. "In other news, Regina was released on bail yesterday. Under house arrest. Her trial is scheduled for November."

Tyler raised both eyebrows. "How do you feel about that?"

I shrugged. "I thought I'd feel happy. But I feel... exhausted." I picked up a medal from the porch table. I'd left it out here, not knowing what to do with it. The government had bestowed one on Tyler, Harper and me for our bravery. The ribbon was green, Danny's favorite color. I'd always wanted to be recognized for my contributions to the environment, but holding this medal in my hands, I didn't want anything to do with it. Why did it take a freaky trash monster to show everyone how important the planet was? The Eastern Garbage Patch was still out there, and more people were helping than ever before. That's all I ever wanted.

Tyler glanced at the sky. "Why don't you show me this new star you found?"

I walked to the telescope and pressed my eye to the lens. There it was, so small and distant, hardly more than a speck. Dad and I hadn't been able to find it on any astrology maps or websites.

"That's amazing," Tyler said, his warm breath brushing my ear. "What are you going to call it? Nothing boring like something-or-other-minor-3.2, I hope."

"I'm not sure yet. It needs to be good, whatever Dad and I decide."

"It's beautiful," he said.

"Thank you," I replied, glad the awkwardness between us had melted away.

Tyler turned to leave, but I pulled him back. "I'll miss you." I took his hand, then pressed my lips against his. A goodbye kiss. It was bittersweet and tears prickled.

"I'll miss you too." He hugged me, then walked away without looking back.

The summer would be long without Tyler, but I knew I was doing the right thing. Even though it hurt, I had to make a healthy decision.

With the moon high, I sank into Dad's sagging porch chair and watched the sky, thinking about the last week. I had saved the world. More importantly, I had put Danny's death behind me. Not that I had forgotten him, or it wasn't still hard, or I didn't feel sad when I thought of him. But something had shifted. In battling the monster, I had to make room for other things. I couldn't let myself be dragged down by grief. Danny would want me to be happy. So that's what I was going to try and do. The brittle thing inside me softened, allowing me to smile more often.

I was Sara Monroe, of Jackson & Monroe Associates.

I was Sara Monroe, protector of the oceans.

I was Sara Monroe, with the wispy blonde hair.

I was Sara Monroe, who would learn to become her own person.

I was Sara Monroe, afraid of failing. But that was okay, I wasn't the only one.

I wasn't perfect. Neither was Danny. I had a lot to learn. But I was looking forward to it.

Dad came out and let me have a sip of his fresh beer. "I just got off the phone with the conservatory."

I leaned forward. "And?"

"And, it's an uncharted star, all right." He grinned. "We can name it whatever we want."

"I don't know what to call it," I said.

Dad smiled. "I was thinking *Danny*."

I stood. Happy tears filled my eyes. "That's a lovely idea." I hugged my dad. On that warm evening in June, I hugged him tight and didn't let go.

The next morning, I rode my bike to Mission Bay, the same spot where Danny and I had captured glowing plankton. My cellphone was stuffed in one pocket, Danny's skimming pebble in the other. The water was flat and smooth and sailboats stood erect on a breezeless day. There was no trash here and the blue water welcomed me.

I walked to the water's edge, removed the pebble from my pocket and felt the weight of it in my hand. It was a flat gray thing, like so many other pebbles, and I'd been carrying it around for too long, weighed down by the memories it contained.

Kicking off my flip-flops, I stepped into the water. The frigid greeting made me smile. Its soothing coolness trickled over my feet, kissed at my ankles, whispered at my toes. The ocean was part of me, always had been, always would be.

Closing my eyes, I kissed the pebble, then balanced it in my palm. Eyeing the water, I exhaled, then flicked the pebble out of my hand. It skimmed across the water perfectly, bouncing a record six times. Somewhere out there, Danny was watching and smiling.

"Goodbye, bro. I'll see you around."

The End

Read on for a sneak peek of **The Shadow Keepers**, a YA dark fantasy horror…

Freebie!

The ocean has always felt like a second home to me. I'm kind of disappointed I wasn't born a mermaid. But I do like to immerse myself in water as much as possible, and I care about all its inhabitants deeply, from the smallest of ponds to the largest of oceans!

Thank you so much for making it all the way to the end of Sara's story. I hope you enjoyed reading it as much as I loved writing it. If you did, leaving a review is the best possible present for an author!

You can do it here: https://geni.us/Plastic

If you're interested in my other books, you can read the first chapter of all of them on my website at **www.marisa-noelle.com**, or buy from any bookshop. Please sign up to my mailing list to get the latest news, free stories, novellas, as well as gain the opportunity to win some fantastic prizes.

You will receive all the Unadjusteds prequel novellas COMPLETELY FREE!!!

Read on for a sneak peek of *The Shadow Keepers…*

Facebook Readers Group

If you want to experience more of my books, do join my Facebook readers group where you can chat with other readers and discuss my books, as well as anything else you're reading. I am very active in this group, and you can expect book jokes, puzzles, riddles, quizzes, giveaways, the opportunity to name characters, as well as secret information about what I'm working on, cover reveals and so much more!

Just click here: https://www.facebook.com/groups/840324970233576

Read on for a sneak peek of ***The Shadow Keepers...***

Acknowledgments

Writing a book takes a village, and I am endlessly grateful for mine. I want to give a big shout-out all my support peeps who have kept me going through thick and thin!

Team Swag—the ones who held my hand while I navigated the wild world of publishing. We've tackled every twist and turn together, sharing laughs, support, and wisdom. You're an amazing bunch of writers and even better friends.

Anna, Emma & Sally—you guys are some of the best people I know. Friends online, friends in real life, and you keep me smiling through the blood, sweat, and tears. Couldn't do it without you!

To Fay—the cover is nothing short of gorgeous! I couldn't have asked for anything better.

Neil, my rock and my "Steady Eddie"—you stole my heart in one night and still keep it safe every day. Love you endlessly.

Riley, Lucas, and Quinn—my biggest supporters, as long as I don't embarrass you at school fairs with my book stacks! You're my go-to brainstormers whenever I'm stuck, and you always help me find my way.

To my parents, Larry and Rita—your unwavering support means everything to me. And Mom, you're my super-sharp proofreader… unless there's a typo—then it's totally on you!

To my early supporters—Sasha Newell, Michelle Oliver, Nikki, Adrian, Darcy & Hetty Kane, Louise Chambers—thank you for your invaluable advice and feedback. You've each been a vital part of this journey.

BookTok! You've been an absolute blast! From making me buy crowns (yes, multiple) to supporting my books with enthusiasm, you've given me so much. I've found the best beta and ARC readers here, and I know I've found my people.

To Michael Fox, my A-level English teacher, thank you for teaching me to think for myself and defend my ideas. That lesson has carried me far.

To the charity 4Ocean who do so much wonderful work ridding our oceans and lakes and rivers of all the terrible plastic and trash. You helped to inspire this story!

And last but not least, to my readers—thank you from the bottom of my heart. You make every word worth it. I hope you stick around for more adventures to come!

Oh, and if you fancy learning more about my books and want to be in with the chance to win exclusive giveaways, sign up to my website below!

www.marisanoelle.com

Read on for a sneak peek of ***The Shadow Keepers…***

About the Author

Marisa Noelle is the author behind a treasure trove of young adult and adult novels across multiple genres, but they all have running themes of mental health or the ocean (And usually with romance too!). She tends to gravitate toward the speculative arena and loves to write science-fiction, fantasy, horror, dystopian, romance, romantasy, or a combination of them all.

Marisa's books include:

The Shadow Keepers—a spine-tingling tale to keep you up all night and semi-finalist of the BBNYA book awards.

The Unraveling of Luna Forester—a novel impossible to talk about because of its huge twist, but it snagged several awards, including: First Place Incipere Award, Write-Blend Finalist, BBYNA Semi-Finalist, Bookshelf Finalist.

Plastic—a powerful eco-thriller exploring grief, corporate corruption, and the fight to save our oceans. This contemporary YA novel blends activism with heartbreak as Sara Monroe battles her brother's death, a plastic-choked ocean, and the secrets of a billion-dollar beverage empire.

The Unadjusteds Trilogy delves into one of her

favourite genres—dystopian. *The Unadjusteds, the Rise of the Altereds, and The Reckoning* make up the trilogy, but there are eleven further companion novellas that follow the secondary characters (**FREE** to subscribers). *The Unadjusteds* also placed as a semi-finalist in the BBNYA awards.

The Mermaid Chronicles is a seven book romantasy series that includes: *Secrets of the Deep, Quest for Atlantis, Fight for Freedom, Ghost Pirates, Vendetta, Denizens of Darkness, Vorago Returns*, as well as its own companion guide. The entire series is coming to audio with Tantor Media soon!

Marisa also writes steamy romance under the pen name Savannah Wilde.

When Marisa's not weaving literary spells, she's helping mold the future of MG and YA authors as a mentor for the Write Mentor program.

When not writing, Marisa likes to imagine herself as a mermaid, and can often be found in the local pool...or lake...or ocean. Despite her undeniable bookworm credentials since she was knee-high to a grasshopper, the author gig took Marisa by surprise. You see, she had a secret past as a bit of a science geek during her school days. But hey, science and storytelling make a surprisingly magical concoction! Currently, Marisa calls Woking, UK, her home sweet home, where she resides with her trusty squad, including her husband, three amazing kids, and a furry four-legged friend named Copper.

Marisa loves to hear from her readers. You can find and connect with her at the links below.

Twitter, Instagram & Threads: **@MarisaNoelle77**
Tiktok: **@MarisaNoelle12**
Website: **www.MarisaNoelle.com**

Turn the page for a sneak peek of ***The Shadow Keepers…***

The Shadow Keepers

Whatever you do, don't look in the mirror...

Sixteen year-old Georgia Boone knows the shadows are going to kill her. It's only a matter of time. They live in mirrors and look like humanoid crows. And stare at her with hungry red eyes. The insidious monsters have hunted her all her life, forcing her to drop out of school and driving her to the brink of insanity. But how can she prove their existence when no one else sees them? She is alone.

When Georgia is sent to the UK's most prestigious mental health centre, Brookwood Hospital, she is forced to face her fears and answer the question...

Are the shadows real, or is it all in her head?

THE SHADOW KEEPERS

Marisa Noelle

Chapter One

I STARE at the imposing front door of what is to be my prison for the foreseeable future. Solid wood. Oversized ornate door knocker of a lion with the ring through its mouth. How appropriate. The surrounding building is made from yellow bricks and the roof is grey slate. It matches my mood. Ivy crawls over the hospital, maybe a suggestion of cheerfulness. To me it looks like it's strangling my new home.

"Shall we go inside?" Bart shakes raindrops out of his hair as the smell of last night's vodka oozes out of him.

Something in my chest skitters. I don't want to be here. I don't want to go inside. But I don't have a choice.

I nudge the heavy front door with a wet trainer, testing its strength, hoping it's locked so I can remain in the world of the sane for just a little longer. It remains firmly closed—a small miracle—but I know this is only prolonging the inevitable. The court ordered me here, and here I must stay. I stand there, waiting for my parents, my anger pooling in my stomach, my skin prickling with indignation.

Bart throws an arm around me. I remain stiff, inconsolable. I can no longer let my guard down. I can no longer give in to emotion. My mother and stepfather arrive, my stepfather dragging my suitcase through the puddles. Gee, thanks *Dad*.

They join me in the portico. My stepfather turns the stupid handle of the door. We go through the wide front doors and drip rainwater onto the wood floor of the yawning entrance foyer. I immediately lock my gaze on a large bird statue standing at the foot of the sweeping staircase.

It's a crow.

Not a crow.

My mouth goes dry.

The statue is taller than me. It wears its chip marks and dents with pride, as if to say nothing could ever destroy it, not even time. At some point in its life, it was kept outside; old bird stains mottle its surface. Its stone eyes keep vigil over the foyer. Its wings are half-erect, as if preparing to take flight. My heart picks up tempo, and my tongue becomes this weird, heavy object that doesn't fit in my mouth. The panic attack is coming, building. It will be here soon.

I scan the room for reflective surfaces. I find only the windows, but as it's morning, they are translucent. For now.

Grabbing my mother's sleeve, I plead with her silently. Tears form in her eyes.

"It's going to be okay, Georgia." She pats my hand.

I shake my head and grit my teeth. "I don't belong here."

"We don't have a choice. It's what the court decided," my mother replies. "It's only ninety days."

Three months. A quarter of a year. I'll miss Halloween. Out in time for Christmas, if I prove I have recovered.

"Why don't you believe me?" I shake her arm. If Mum, or the damn court, or anyone of my non-existent friends actually tried to believe me . . . they'd know the court order was bullshit. "I'm not crazy!"

My mother and stepfather exchange a look. It's one I've seen a hundred times in the last few months. They've been here before. We've had this conversation before, but they've made up their minds.

"No one is saying that," Mum says softly. "But after the incident . . ."

Bart steps between us. "Give her a break, Mum. I'm sure she remembers."

I reach for his hand, and he squeezes it back. I can't bear to look at him. The pity in his eyes would break me. Who am I kidding? I'm broken already.

My mother takes a long yoga breath, then sets her face into an emotionless mask; guarded eyes, flat smile. "You're here to get better, and put this…bird stuff behind you once and for all."

"I won't make it," I mumble too quietly for anyone to hear. They'll make me look in the mirrors here. Mirrors I've avoided all my life. And then they'll come for me. The shadows.

"Georgia," Mum says with that flat smile again. "This place isn't what it used to be. They don't do electric shock therapy or hose patients with water. It's not like that anymore. There's no shame in it. The doctors and nurses here are the best suited to understanding and helping you."

I look around the foyer again. Brookwood Hospital. Or

Lunacy Asylum for the Insane and Unreachable. It's the place people with money put their loved ones when they don't know what else to do with them.

"Why can't you help me?" I stare at Mum.

"We've tried, sweetheart. And we haven't been able to. Now it's time to let others in. You heard what the judge said; it's here, or it's the NHS hospital. We no longer have a choice. And to be quite honest, Georgia, there's nothing else I can do for you."

Bart nudges my arm, and his wobbling smile crushes my resolve not to cry.

"Your father never got the help he needed," Mum says. "I don't want that for you. I watched him struggle every day until he died. He joined the army because he felt he had something to prove, that he was tough and could look after us all. He went off to Afghanistan and he died trying to prove it. You're so like him, Georgia, in many ways. You need to be here. You need to get better."

Two nurses and a doctor emerge from an office door I hadn't noticed. They stand in a line like teeth in a monster's mouth. Their Stepford smiles have me taking a step backward and looking over my shoulder.

"Georgia Boone?" One of the nurses asks, distracting me from my quickening pulse.

I turn towards the voice. According to her label, she is the head psychiatric nurse, and her name is Marion.

"Yes," Mum answers for me. "Yes, this is Georgia."

"We've been waiting for you," Marion says, looking down a puffy nose at me.

My heart thuds painfully in my chest again. It picks up

speed, as if trying to gallop out of my body completely. I clutch my mother's sleeve again.

"I'm Nurse Marion," she says. "And this is Nurse Willow." She points to the other woman.

Deputy Psychiatric Nurse Willow, according to her name badge, is tall and skinny. Her eyes are blue, and I detect a flash of some intrinsic warning in them when she looks at me.

"Hello, sweetheart," Willow says, a warm smile propped on her lips.

"I'm Paul. I'm a psychologist here," the man says, stepping forward to offer his hand. My stepfather shakes it, and my mother smiles sadly at him. "Don't be alarmed. We'll take good care of Georgia. That's what we're here for after all."

"Yes, of course," Mum replies.

"We need you to sign some paperwork," Marion says to my parents. "Paul will show Georgia and her brother to a pot of tea."

She gestures to the office door. My parents follow the two nurses into the room and leave Bart and me standing in the large foyer with Paul under the penetrating gaze of an antique grandfather clock. It leans Pisa-like on the thick carpet, its gentle ticking the only audible noise in the hushed expectancy of the room. It strikes the hour, and I jump, grabbing onto Bart's arm.

"This way." Paul leads us around a corner to a small niche with a couple of floral sofas and polished coffee tables. A pot of steaming tea sits on a tray with a couple of cracked mugs and a plate of biscuits.

Paul pours two cups of tea and excuses himself to take

my luggage to my room. I sip at the tea, but it scalds my throat.

"Easy," Bart says.

I point to the other cup. "You could do with some sobering up."

He gives me his sideways grin.

"Was it a big night?" I ask.

He winks. "It's always a big night."

I sigh as a tremble shoots through my legs. Bart notices and rests a heavy hand on my knee. "I wish I could go with you. I wish you could stay. I wish . . ." I close my eyes against the threatening tears.

Bart brings me in close and hugs me, smoothing the back of my head. "I wish all that too. But we can't get out of it. I've tried."

Bart is a junior lawyer for a swanky outfit in London. During my case, he was allowed to liaise with my defence attorney. But there's nothing to be done. I hurt another individual. The last straw in a string of offences.

I stare into the swirling tea. "I was with you when I first saw them, you know."

Bart pulls away. "Saw what?"

"The shadows."

Bart nods. Everyone knows about the creatures I see in mirrors. We just don't talk about it anymore.

If you'd like to carry on reading, click here:
https://geni.us/ShadowKeepers